Praise for Kendra Elliot

"Elliot's best work to date. The author's talent is evident in the character's wit and smart dialogue... One wouldn't necessarily think a psychological thriller and romance would mesh together well, but Elliot knows what she's doing when she turns readers' minds inside out and then softens the blow with an unforgettable love story."

—*Romantic Times Book Reviews* on *Vanished*, 4½ stars, Top Pick

"Kendra Elliot does it again! Filled with twists, turns, and spine-tingling details, *Alone* is an impressive addition to the Bone Secrets series."

—Laura Griffin, *New York Times* bestselling author, on *Alone*

"Elliot once again proves to be a genius in the genre with her third heart-pounding novel in the Bone Secrets collection. The author knows romance and suspense, reeling readers in instantaneously and wowing them with an extremely surprising finish . . . Elliot's best by a mile!"

—*Romantic Times Book Reviews* on *Buried*, 4½ stars, Top Pick (HOT)

"Make room on your keeper shelf! *Hidden* has it all: intricate plotting, engaging characters, a truly twisted villain. I can't wait to see what Kendra Elliot dishes up next!"

—Karen Rose, *New York Times* bestselling author

SPIRALED

Also by Kendra Elliot

Bone Secrets Novels
Hidden
Chilled
Buried
Alone

Callahan & McLane
Part of the Bone Secrets World
Vanished
Bridged

SPIRALED

KENDRA ELLIOT

Montlake
Romance

This is a work of fiction. Names, characters, organizations, places, events, and incidents are either products of the author's imagination or are used fictitiously.

Published by Montlake Romance, Seattle

www.apub.com
Amazon, the Amazon logo, and Montlake Romance are trademarks of Amazon.com, Inc., or its affiliates.

ISBN-13: 9781477830321
ISBN-10: 1477830324

Cover design by Marc J. Cohen

Library of Congress Control Number: 2014959437

Printed in the United States of America

For Dan

1

Blood exploded out of Misty's thigh and splattered across Ava's legs. A fraction of a second later, Ava heard the shots.

She yanked Misty down to the concrete floor of the mall, assisted by the teenager's near collapse. Her screams didn't block the blasts of more rifle fire. Ava scanned for the shooter as people sprinted past the two women huddled on the ground. Terrified people made eye contact, but no one stopped.

"I've been shot?" the teen gasped. "Am I going to die?"

"No!"

Blood pulsed out of the girl's thigh.

Artery. Tourniquet. NOW.

She grabbed Misty's tiny purse with the long narrow strap. She unhooked the strap, tightly wrapped it around Misty's upper thigh, and knotted it. The blood slowed to an inconsistent ooze.

Find cover.

She slid an arm under the girl's shoulders. "Can you get up?" Misty shifted her leg and screamed as tears covered her face.

More shots.

The crowd of morning walkers and shoppers at the open-air mall had vanished, and Ava didn't see anyone with a gun. The closest two stores hadn't opened yet for the day, but Ava scooted away from Misty and tried the doors anyway. Still locked. She looked for a store that was open. No luck.

Can I get Misty back to the yoga studio?

"Ava?" A smear of blood across Misty's cheek stood out against her pale skin, and she suddenly seemed much younger than her eighteen years. "Don't leave me!"

Bending over, Ava dashed back to the teen. "I won't. But we've got to find cover."

"Why are they shooting?" The girl grabbed Ava's wrist, determined not to let her leave.

"I don't know. But we can't stay here in the wide-open aisle." Her gaze stopped on a closed sunglasses kiosk twenty feet away in the intersection of two of the wide mall walkways. It wasn't great cover, but she had no choice. "I'm gonna drag you a little ways, okay?"

Misty nodded and pressed her lips together. Ava squatted behind her head and lifted the girl's shoulders. She was heavy. Ava slowly scooted backward, biting her cheek as the girl cried out in pain and her leg was jostled along the sidewalk.

Two more shots. Closer.

Ava got Misty as close to the kiosk as possible. They weren't hidden. Anyone walking past would see them, but at least there was something between them and the gun. Ava pulled her cell out of her bag and called 911, her heart pounding in her ears.

"Come on!" She pressed her cell against her ear. *They're not picking up immediately because they're deluged with calls from this mall.*

"Nine-one-one. What is the nature of your emergency?"

"This is Special Agent Ava McLane of the Portland FBI office. I'm in the Rivertown Mall at the Sunglasses Hut. There is an active shooter in the mall, and I have a woman who's been shot and needs medical assistance ASAP."

"Yes, Special Agent. We're getting calls. Please find a place to hide until the police arrive and we'll get medical to you at the first opportunity. Have you seen the shooter?"

"No, but people are running away from the mall's center toward the—oh, shit!"

Ava caught her breath as a man ran by, clasping his bleeding hand to his chest. "An injured person just ran toward the garage. The shooter is not in the garage. All of the people I've seen are running toward it."

She peered around the corner of the kiosk and saw the shooter.

"I see him," she said into the phone tucked against her shoulder. "He's wearing all black with a full mask that covers his hair and face. He's tall, probably over six feet, and lean. He's carrying a rifle and jogging past Sur La Table, moving in the direction of the garage."

His head moved in a rhythm, scanning from the right to left. Even without the rifle and mask he would have stood out in his black outfit on the hot August morning. Three women dashed out of one of the intersecting corridors and immediately reversed direction at the sight of the shooter.

He couldn't be more than thirty yards from the sunglasses kiosk. Ava watched him stop, plant his feet, and aim his rifle at the backs of the running women. Ava started to rise out of her hiding space, sweat swelling under her arms, knowing she was powerless. "I can't stop him," she breathed to the operator. Her weapon was locked in the trunk of her car. She hadn't known she'd have a use for it after yoga.

"Get down," Misty hissed. "What are you doing?"

The shooter lowered his gun, gazing after the group of women, and then glanced at his watch. He walked over to the kitchen goods store and yanked on the door. Locked.

"Please find a safe location and wait, Special Agent," the operator stated. "Police are on the scene, and I've relayed your information.

I'm going to end this call if you are okay with that. We're being over-loaded with calls."

Ava agreed as the shooter turned down another artery of the mall and vanished.

She slid back down behind the kiosk. She'd been walking through the mall and chatting with Misty, one of the younger women in her morning yoga class. They had just left the small exercise studio in the suburban high-end outdoor mall. The mall was the type with manicured flower planters lining the walkways, honor system umbrellas in stands outside every shop, and live weekend music. The blazing-hot August morning had early walkers roaming the aisles with iced coffees, pretending that fall, cold temperatures, and rain weren't a month away.

Now it was a crime scene.

"Are they coming to get us?" Misty gasped. The blond girl was extremely pale and wheezed as she talked. Ava smoothed the hair out of the teen's face and tried to smile.

"They will. As soon as they can."

Ava knew they had to wait. The police's first priority would be to stop the shooter before he caused more harm. Medical assistance came second. The city of Cedar Edge had a small police department, so Ava knew they'd request a mutual aid assist from the Washington County Sheriff's Department.

"Is there just one shooter?" Misty asked.

"I don't know. I only saw one."

That would be one of the police's main questions. As much as she'd wanted to stay on the line with the 911 operator, Ava knew she had no additional information to give. She had to leave the line open for other witnesses who might have important information for the police.

She strained to hear footsteps. Instead she heard shots and more screams.

Misty shuddered, but didn't cry. Ava gripped her hand and they both scooted a half inch closer to the kiosk. Her mind constantly ran through escape options. But she saw no option . . . unless she left Misty behind.

She couldn't do it.

What will Mason say?

Her fingers trembled slightly as she tapped out a text to him.

AT RIVERTOWN MALL. ACTIVE SHOOTER. I'M OK. CAN'T TALK.

There's a text no cop wants to receive.

LOVE YOU.

She switched her phone to silent and dug Misty's phone out of her purse and turned off the sound.

"What's going to happen?" The teen's voice shook. "What's taking them so long?"

"The police will be entering soon." Ava spoke in a slow, low voice, trying to calm the girl. "They'll probably be in small groups and have shields and helmets. The first teams are to find the shooter and stop him. The second wave of police will get us out."

The teen lifted her head and touched the blood on her leg with a shaking hand. "Is it bad?"

"The bleeding has nearly stopped," Ava reassured her. "I know that strap is uncomfortable, but it has to stay there."

"It was spurting," Misty whispered. "I know that's a bad sign." Blue eyes pleaded with Ava for reassurance.

"It means it hit an artery, but we've got it under control."

"What if he finds us?" she whispered. "He's going to kill us." Fresh tears leaked down the side of her face.

"I won't let that happen."

Running footsteps came closer.

2

Ava held her breath. Misty heard the steps and bit her lower lip, her hand squeezing Ava's in a death grip. The steps stopped, and the teen closed her eyes.

The steps started again, jogging, the pounding of heavy boots, not the flip-flops that everyone wore in August. Ava knew it wasn't the police; there would have been multiple pairs of feet.

Something moved far down the branch off the main aisle to her left, and she spotted a gray-haired man step cautiously out of one of the storefronts. He saw her and Misty and moved in their direction. Ava waved him back into the safety of his store.

Get in and lock the door!

Active shooter protocol for public places: lock doors, hide inside, wait for police.

The man stuck close to the walls of the mall as if he could blend in with the paint. He froze, looking beyond Ava's hiding spot, and abruptly raised his arms in front of his face.

He collapsed in a volley of shots, blood splattering the wall behind him. Unaware of the gray-haired man's presence, Misty cried out at the sounds while Ava stared in horror at his still form on the concrete next to a planter of petunias.

The shooter is close behind us.

Boots sounded and shifted direction behind her. He moved into Ava's line of sight, his back toward her as he paced past the wounded man, his rifle trained before him. Ava put her finger to her lips, holding Misty's teary gaze. The teen was flat on her back, unable to see the shooter or his victim. The shooter ignored the wounded man, and Ava watched his rifle track to the right and left as he moved down the short aisle.

Don't turn around.

It was a dead-end branch of the mall with bathrooms and a few silent storefronts. He stopped and moved his arm, making Ava believe he was checking his watch again.

Is he counting minutes?

Her heart did a double beat as the thought of explosives entered her brain. *Is he expecting something to go off?* The shooter shook the handles of the doors of the last two storefronts and then turned around.

Ava met his gaze.

He was too far away for Ava to see his eye color, but she had an impression of deep-set dark eyes.

It's just the mask.

He raised his rifle in her direction, paused, and looked at his watch. He looked at Ava again and then spun around, jogging toward the men's bathroom. He yanked open the door and disappeared.

Ava exhaled noisily, her limbs limp, wanting to lie down beside Misty. *Why didn't he shoot?*

Shouts and shots sounded from the bathroom.

A man carrying a boy raced out of the restroom. He sprinted in Ava's direction, slowing as he spotted the bloody man on the ground. The father turned the boy's face from the still man as they raced past. His steps slowed near the sunglasses kiosk as he spotted Ava and Misty. "Do you need help?"

Ava took in the size of the large child. The man couldn't carry him and help her get Misty out. "Get your son out of here. Tell the police where we're at."

Inner turmoil flashed on his face. He hesitated.

"Go," Ava ordered. "Don't risk your boy. Are there more people in the bathroom?"

"Yes," he panted.

"Tell the police. *Now!*"

He ran, his hand over the boy's head in a protective gesture.

Ava pulled out her phone to dial 911 again and froze as she saw three missed calls from Mason.

Later. She hit the three digits.

The wait to get an operator felt like forever. She relayed the shooter's location and that more people were still in the restroom. The operator questioned her safety, asking if she could move to a better location. Ava studied the girl beside her.

She couldn't move Misty. And she wasn't leaving her behind.

She ended the call.

"Are they coming?" Misty whispered. Her eyes didn't seem to focus.

"Soon," Ava promised. "Very soon."

• • •

"Back off!" the Washington County deputy barked at Mason from behind the yellow tape. "This area is for staging only."

"My wife's in there!" Mason Callahan shot back, flashing his Oregon State Police badge. Ava wasn't his wife, but she was the closest damned thing he had to one.

"Everyone knows someone in there! Let us focus on getting them out!"

Mason turned away. He knew he was wasting his and the deputy's time. He needed to speak to someone with more authority. He scanned the growing crowd of law enforcement and firefighters inside the staging area in the north parking lot of the mall. All responding law enforcement were to report to staging to be logged and assigned a role. He knew Cedar Edge's small police force had responded first, sent in contact teams to locate the shooter, and cordoned off the mall. Then Washington County had swooped in with reinforcements and its tactical negotiations team. More teams would be sent in to help the injured and sweep every square inch of the mall, reporting back to the incident commander. Shoppers were being methodically evacuated store by store and the injured were being triaged. Mason had heard that three people had died from gunshots inside the mall.

No one could tell him the sex of the victims.

Ava hadn't answered her phone.

Hot anxiety washed over him, making him dizzy in the sun's heat. *Déjà vu.* He'd been in this same helpless position last spring when Ava had vanished, grabbed by a serial killer on a crazed mission. He bit his lip, welcoming the distracting pain.

Who can get me some answers?

The Oregon State Police patrol units in the area had responded and were assisting with rescue and recovery. The mall's perimeter swarmed with a mix of different uniforms. He took off his cowboy hat and fanned his face. As a Major Crimes detective for OSP, he didn't wear a uniform, and he was thankful he'd put on a cool short-sleeved shirt with his jeans that morning. The cops in the navy blue uniforms were sweating like marathon runners in the direct sun.

Mason spotted a familiar face and jogged to intercept Sergeant Shawn Shaver, head of Washington County's Violent Crimes Unit, as he headed toward the staging area.

"Hey, Callahan," Shaver acknowledged him, his hand over the speaker on his cell phone. "Hang on." He wrapped up his call. "Holy shit. What a nightmare." The tall man had a bushy mustache and sounded like the actor Sam Elliott. Once he'd had a few beers, he'd voice Dodge Ram truck commercials to whoever would listen.

"What's going on, Shaver?" Mason tried to keep the panic out of his voice.

Shaver glanced around and leaned close, lowering his tone. "So far we're getting reports of a single shooter. And the last report had him in a restroom in a dead end of the mall."

"Any word on the sex of the victims?" He held his breath.

Brown eyes scrutinized him. "Someone in there?"

"Ava's in there. She's not returning my texts or calls."

"Ah." Shaver's brows lowered. "I heard one of the victims was a woman. The other two were men. Don't know ages or descriptions. And there could be more victims that we haven't come across yet. Sorry, I don't know more."

Mason wanted to vomit. He glanced at his cell phone screen again. Nothing. *Dammit, Ava, where are you?*

"Wait, Ava's FBI, right?"

Mason nodded.

"Some of the intel coming through 911 is from a female witness inside who identified herself as an FBI agent."

Relief and anger swept through him. *Why didn't she get out?*

"The agent is with a wounded woman and won't leave. How much you want to bet that's Ava?"

Oxygen flowed into Mason's lungs. His knees vibrated oddly, and he wondered if he should sit down. He bent over and rested his hands on his thighs as a large chunk of his stress evaporated. "Why am I not surprised? God damn," he muttered, breathing deep through his nose. He was close to losing his breakfast.

"I heard about her close call last spring. She's got guts," said Shaver.

"Damn right she does. But I don't know if I have enough."

Shaver's mustache twitched. "Love's a bitch, isn't she? And she's definitely got your pair in her grip."

"You try dating someone in our line of work."

"Hell no. I like to sleep at night. My wife works in a nice safe office from eight to five."

Mason glanced at the mall in front of them. "No such thing as a safe place anymore."

"Ain't that the truth. I need to get back at it. You might as well stick around. We've asked OSP for investigative assistance. We're stretched too thin, so I wouldn't be surprised if you got a call from your boss within the hour."

"I'm not leaving until Ava comes out."

"I'm sure she's fine. She knows how to look out for herself." Shaver hustled back to work as Mason scanned the groups of shoppers being methodically escorted out by the Cedar Edge police and divided into small groups to give their information and statements. If Ava was a witness, she'd have a debriefing. But when? There were hundreds of eyewitnesses to interview.

What if the female agent isn't Ava?

Anxiety started to crawl under his skin again.

Deep breaths.

His phone rang. Ray Lusco. "Callahan."

"Hear about the shooter at Rivertown Mall?" his partner asked.

"Yep. I'm standing outside the staging area."

"Good. Because Washington County has reached out for investigative support and Schefte assigned it to us," said his partner. "What are you doing there?"

"Got a text from Ava. She was inside when it started."

"Holy shit! She okay?"

"I don't know. I'm waiting to hear from her. She's not answering my calls, but I was just told a female agent who's sticking with an injured victim has been relaying intel."

Ray was silent for a full five seconds. "Seriously? Think that's her?"

"Who else could it be?"

Ray ended the call, promising to be there in half an hour. Mason rubbed his neck, knowing they had a long day ahead of them. He checked in with the staging coordinator and headed toward the biggest hub of cops, knowing he'd find the incident commander. Now he had an official assignment to be on the inside, but every cell in his body wanted to dash through the mall and find her instead of interviewing witnesses.

Eight months.

Ava McLane had radically changed his life since they'd met eight months ago. In that time he'd realized he was the luckiest bastard in the world.

Now she was trapped with a shooter, and his world was spiraling out of control.

3

Looking in the direction of the parking garage, Ava saw two groups of police steadily moving in her direction. Two teams of four, wearing helmets and carrying shields, progressed simultaneously along the edges of the mall's main aisle. The front man carried his rifle up and forward; the three men directly in line behind him kept theirs down. The men looked in all directions, scanning for anything. Up, from side to side, in the windows. The last man in each group constantly checked their six o'clock.

The contact teams.

Their goal was to find and stop the shooter. Medical assistance would be in the second wave of teams.

"The police are here," she whispered to the girl. "They'll move past us to corner the shooter. The next round of police behind them will get us out."

The girl nodded, her eyes closed.

Hang on, Misty.

Ava figured the perimeter of the mall was nearly established. No one was getting in or out without being spotted by the police officers forming the perimeter. The steadily advancing teams ordered people inside the stores to stay put.

The teams edged closer to Ava and Misty. Ava raised her hands and identified herself. "I watched the shooter enter the men's room at the end of this branch of the mall. I heard shots. A man who left after the shots said there're more people in there. He carried an AR-15, is dressed head to toe in black, and is wearing a mask. I don't know what other weapons he could have."

One of the team leaders nodded as he eyed Misty. "Medical will be in soon. Sit tight." Determination and anger covered their faces; they had an objective. They'd looked at Misty with sympathy, but Ava understood their primary mission was to stop the shooter before he hurt more people. The two teams turned into the dead-end artery of the mall and continued their thorough progression. One team paused at the shot man lying on the right side of the aisle. A member rapidly checked for a pulse as a team member covered him. The man shook his head and they moved on.

Oh, no.

Ava blew out a breath, her fears confirmed. The man hadn't moved since being shot.

The team leader spoke into his shoulder-mic, but Ava couldn't make out his words. They passed the last storefront and stopped, sticking tight to the walls of the aisle. Their weapons trained on the door to the men's room thirty feet away.

"This is the Cedar Edge Police Department," the leader shouted toward the restrooms. "Put down your weapon and exit backwards out of the bathrooms with your hands above your head."

Shots sounded inside the restroom and an older man stumbled out the door with his hands raised. The teams shouted for him to stop and get down. Ava recognized the man from her yoga class. He froze and slowly lowered himself to the ground in the awkward way Ava had noticed in class. Arthritis had claimed many of his joints.

"He's still in there!" he yelled to the teams.

He was rapidly frisked by two of the team members as others covered them and the rest kept their attention on the bathrooms.

"Are there any other people in there?" Ava heard a team member ask.

"Yes. At least one other guy! Maybe more!"

The older man was deemed unarmed. The leader asked him questions about the layout of the bathroom and then instructed him to leave the area but to keep his hands on top of his head as he moved toward the perimeter. He stopped as he reached Ava and Misty, recognition in his eyes. "Do you need a hand?"

Ava recalled his pain-ridden movements. "No, but thanks. Her bleeding has nearly stopped. Someone will be here soon." She shooed him away. "We'll be okay." He reluctantly moved on, limping.

"That was kind," Misty murmured sleepily.

Ava shook her. "Stay awake!" Her blood pounded in her ears. She checked the ligature around Misty's thigh and pulled it tighter, making the teen sob. Red and swollen flesh bulged above the purse strap. Ava caught her breath at the sight of the large dark puddle beneath the leg.

When did that get so big?

"This is the Cedar Edge police! Please send out the rest of—"

A single shot interrupted his request.

A man in a cap dashed out of the bathroom a moment later. "He's down! He shot himself!"

The team put him through the same on-the-ground search routine as the previous man. "Is there anyone else in there?" someone asked.

"No." The man hesitated. "Unless someone is in the stalls—I don't know."

They sent him on his way with the same orders to keep his hands on his head.

Ava saw his face was wet with tears as he approached the two of them.

"He shot himself?" she asked.

He wiped at his face and studied Misty. "Yes. Do you need help?"

Is it over? Cautious relief swept over Ava. "No. Unless you're a doctor."

He shook his head, regret in his eyes. "I can help you carry her out."

Her immediate impulse was to accept his help. They could probably get Misty upright between them. She glanced at Misty's leg, hoping her latest tightening of the strap had stopped the bleeding. "If the shooter is down, the medical teams should be here soon. Hopefully with a board of some sort. I'm afraid we'll make the bleeding start up again if we try to move her."

She regretfully waved him on, tired of passing up the offers of help. *Where's the REAL help?*

She leaned back against the kiosk, keeping her fingertips on Misty's pulse, calmed by its steady rhythm, and kept an eye on the teams, knowing they wouldn't rush the bathroom. The hostage had said the shooter was down, but even injured, someone could still pull a trigger as the police entered. A team leader made two more announcements, asking the shooter to exit the bathrooms. Time ticked by, and she started to worry that she'd made the wrong decision about turning down the last man's help. She checked the bleeding for the umpteenth time; it still appeared in control. The leaders had updated the police outside the perimeter through their walkie-talkies but Ava hadn't been able to hear the words. They put their heads together for a discussion. Ava imagined the options they were considering for entering the bathroom. *Flash-bang? Canine unit? Tear gas?* She put her money on the tear gas. She saw the men occasionally glance her way and knew they'd requested help for Misty.

But how many others are injured in different parts of the mall?

Looking down the main artery of the mall, she saw a team with a stretcher cautiously headed in her direction. Relief swept through her.

Thank you, Lord.

"They're coming for you now, Misty."

"Good," muttered the teen. "Leg fucking hurts."

The leader announced they were launching tear gas into the bathroom, gave a final command to exit, and waited.

No reply.

He gave a signal and three of the team smoothly opened the door, covered each other, tossed the canister, and moved away from the door as if they'd practiced it a hundred times. They probably had.

The bathroom was silent.

"Hey, ladies, how's it going?" A four-member team in protective gear knelt next to Misty. With economy of movement, they assessed her condition and moved her onto the stretcher. An impossibly young-looking EMT with red hair studied the blood spray and messy trail where Ava had dragged the girl. "You got her out of sight?" he asked. She nodded, suddenly exhausted. "Her blood loss isn't as bad as it looks," he reassured Ava. "You probably saved her life by putting the tourniquet on her leg."

Shouts sounded near the bathroom, and Ava turned in time to see the teams rush in. Shouts of *Clear, clear, clear* reached her ears.

No shots.

One officer stepped back outside and hollered at the medical team. "We're gonna need medical!"

"He can wait," muttered the red-haired medic.

Ava agreed.

4

Mason watched as Ava was escorted out of the danger zone and toward the staging area. She'd finally texted him fifteen minutes earlier, stating that she was fine and the shooter was down.

Recent reports had the shooter dead with his own bullet in his brain.

The staging area had settled into an organized arena of police, EMS, and fire departments working as a team to address the needs of the exiting shoppers. Five ambulances had left with victims. Two still breathing, three not.

Her gaze instantly found him, as if she heard his thoughts across the crowd.

Relief flowed out of him again. He'd known she was safe, but tension had woven its ugly fingers through his spine as he waited. She said something to the officer escorting her, who eyed Mason and then replied. The officer pointed to the coffee shop, and Ava gave an answering nod. Mason had watched some victims being led to the coffee shop to be interviewed.

She pushed through the crowd of uniforms.

She's all right.

A smile curled her lips as she drew closer, and for the hundredth time he was struck dumb by how lucky he was to go home to her every night.

Mine. She strode with the poise of a woman with confidence. Strands of her dark hair had come loose from her ponytail, and she had blood splattered across her legs, but he focused on her dark-blue eyes. She was never glamorous; she had girl-next-door looks that were enhanced by a sharp brain and dry sense of humor. The perfect woman for him.

She moved into his arms and clutched him tight, her face in his neck. He felt her chest expand and slowly deflate with a long, slow exhalation. The smell of sunshine on her hair and skin wafted across his nose, and he gripped her tighter. His eyes started to burn, and he rubbed a knuckle across one, blinking rapidly. "Dammit."

Her torso vibrated with a low laugh.

"Not funny," he said. "I didn't know what was going on in there."

She pulled back to meet his gaze, her dark eyes calm. "I know. It wasn't easy to put what I *knew* you were thinking out of my head."

"What happened?"

His toes curled in his boots as he listened to her story. "You could have left."

She lifted a brow at him.

"Or not."

He got it. He needed to let her do what was right. Didn't mean he couldn't worry.

"I have another debriefing. And I'm starving. What are you sup-posed to be doing?" she asked.

"They're pulling together a task force to review statements, video, and every scrap of evidence to figure out why this happened. Ray and I have been assigned to it, but they're still figuring out the best place to set it up. For now, I'm helping taking statements until they find a location. Ray's already taking some in there." He nodded at the coffee bar.

"That's my destination."

He took her hand and led her across the parking lot. It no longer mattered how late he worked today; she was safe.

• • •

Ava sat at a table in the mall's coffee bar. The employees were gone except for two managers who'd asked to stay and brew free coffee. Plastic cups holding iced coffee and thick green straws sat on every table. The staging coordinator had designated the shop as a temporary interview station, and rattled shoppers waited in nervous groups to give statements.

At the next table, Mason interviewed the older man from her yoga class who'd been in the bathroom with the shooter. He was focused on the witness, listening closely as he made careful notes in his perfect printing. He glanced her way, and she understood his need to have her in his line of sight for a few hours.

She'd felt horrible when she spotted the missed texts and calls from Mason on her cell phone, fully aware of his terror and anger last spring when a serial killer had kidnapped her, believing Ava belonged to him. She still jerked awake out of nightmares to confirm she wasn't sinking to the bottom of a river in the killer's van.

Now Ava didn't know when either she or Mason would get to leave the scene. Every time she turned around, one of the incident commanders had "just a few more questions." Ava had downed a grande iced coffee and a scone and tried not to talk with her mouth full. She looked patiently at the Washington County sergeant across from her. His mustache triggered 1970s porn music in her head, but his voice made her want to watch a Western.

"I think we're done," Sergeant Shaver finally said. "This incident could have ended a lot worse."

Ava nodded. Four people had died, one having just succumbed to injuries in the hospital. *Will there be more?* She tried not to think about the man she'd seen shot.

"My understanding is that people who carry out these types of shootings start them with the assumption they'll end up dead," she said. "I don't know what the shooter's story is, but something pushed him over the edge. Still no identification yet?"

Shaver shook his head. "Male in his early twenties. He'll be identified soon enough."

"This is the second mass shooting this summer in Oregon," Ava added. "The other shooter in Eugene was about the same age." In June a young man had opened fire at a small park and killed four people. He'd also taken his life in the restroom.

"Young men," commented Shaver. "I was one once. There's a hell of a lot of crap going on in our heads at that age."

"No excuses," stated Ava. "There's no reason to take out anger on innocent victims."

Shaver held up his hands. "Not making any. But I hope this is the last mass shooting. Next thing you know they'll be installing metal detectors at shopping malls and baseball games. I've been avoiding the media all day. I can just imagine the spin they're putting on both of these incidents."

"You'd think they'd give us time to get the facts out."

"Someone told me he's heard three different stories from the media about who the shooter is," said the sergeant. "*We* don't even know who the shooter is. The important part is that he's not going to hurt anyone else. Right now we're still trying to manage the aftermath of the scene. We got the word out that the mall will be closed for a few days and the Cedar Edge police will be in charge of getting belongings to shoppers and releasing cars from the parking garage. Hopefully people will be patient."

"How many people were wounded?" Ava asked.

"Fortunately not many. Two were wounded by gunfire, one of them your friend, and there were several skinned knees plus one broken arm from someone who tripped while trying to get away."

"Apparently he knew how to take his shots," Ava said softly. "He shot to kill. Not to randomly shoot into a crowd." She paused, remembering seeing the shooter aim at the backs of a group of women. "I told you that at one point I thought he was going to do exactly that, but he stopped. He seemed to have something important to do right at that moment."

"He may have been looking for the bathroom to end it. I'd like to see the statistics on why shooters do that in bathrooms; it seems to happen a lot. It's like they don't want any witnesses to their final act. Which is odd, considering they've just done the most publicly destructive act possible. I guess shooting others is glorious; shooting yourself still needs to be hidden away."

"Wish they were available for interviews," she said, twisting her mouth.

Shaver snorted. "Answers would be nice. Instead we'll have to pick apart every minute of his last few days and see what we can find."

"Ava? You okay?" Zander Wells asked behind her.

She turned in her chair, knowing her FBI colleague's voice instantly. "Zander, what are you doing here?" She performed quick introductions. The men were shaking hands when Zander said, "The FBI is now involved. One of the murdered victims was under our surveillance because he's the brother-in-law of a suspected international jewelry fence who's vanished."

"Suspected?" asked Shaver.

Zander met his gaze and gave a half smile. One brow lifted slightly.

Ava knew Zander had been loaned to Jewelry and Gem Theft. She'd been on vacation for nearly two weeks, using the time to get a jump start on the kitchen remodel of the home she and Mason had purchased two months ago. She hadn't realized how out of touch with her office she'd felt until she saw Zander in his subdued suit and tie.

"Think he was our shooter's target?" Ava asked. "Which victim was he?"

"Dick Olsen. He was the second death. He was shot in front of the movie theater."

Ava nodded. "More people were shot after that. If that man was the target, why shoot so many more?"

"You're reading my mind," said Zander. "But I don't like the coincidence. The bureau was closing in on this fence a month ago when he disappeared with three million dollars' worth of gems. The brother-in-law and he were close. It was a good lead, but now it's suddenly been snuffed out."

"Definitely something to look at as we analyze the shooter," Shaver added.

"That's why I'm here," Zander said with a casual smile, and he headed toward the incident commander.

Ava bit her lip. It was easy to underestimate Zander Wells. Nearly everyone did upon first meeting the low-key agent, but she'd noticed the sergeant was reserving judgment. *Smart man.* Zander's talents became crystal-clear after one briefing. He had the memory of a supercomputer and the spry brain of a hacker.

Mason claimed the agent had a thing for her, but Ava didn't see it. Zander was a good friend. Nothing more.

Suddenly she was exhausted. The sugary scone and caffeine hit were making her gut churn in a sour way.

Shaver was staring at her.

She blinked. "I'm sorry, what'd you ask me?"

How much longer will this take?

5

"I attend the yoga class three times a week," stated Walter Borrego.

Mason lifted a brow at the man sitting across from him in the coffee shop. "You must like it."

"I do. It's easy on my joints, and I can do as little or as much of the positions as I'm capable of. My flexibility has improved drastically in the last year." Walter had a bit of an Einstein aura. His white hair was rather wild and his eyebrows continued the theme. "I stay in the back of the class." He leaned forward and whispered, "It gives the best view."

Mason bit his cheek. "So you have several motivations to attend classes."

Walter nodded conspiratorially. "Several," he said solemnly.

Mason scratched at his temple and studied his notes. *So what if the guy likes checking out the women in his class?* "You'd stopped in the bathroom after class and were in one of the stalls when you heard some noise outside, correct?"

"Yes. My first thought was fireworks. Even though the Fourth was long ago. Gunfire didn't even enter my thoughts."

"Until someone fired a gun in the restroom."

The bushy hair waved as Walter nodded. "The sound was deafening. I knew that wasn't fireworks."

"What did you see when you first went in?"

"There was one guy at the urinals when I went in. He had a youngster with him. The boy was playing in the water at the sink and singing at the top of his lungs as I walked by."

Mason slid a rough sketch of the layout of the bathroom across the table. Four sinks were directly to the right of the door as a person entered. Past them on the same wall were four urinals. Four stalls faced the sinks from the opposite wall and another four stalls, sinks, and urinals mirrored the pattern behind the first row of stalls. He didn't like that second area. Anyone in the first area was blind to who or what was in the second. "Remember where you were?"

Walter put a stiff finger on the first stall and added, "The father was at the urinal closest to the wall."

"Did you see anyone else? Hear anyone else?"

He grimaced. "My hearing's not the best. I mainly heard the boy." He lifted a finger near the hearing aid Mason had spotted at the beginning of the interview. "And once he'd shot the gun inside, my ears were ringing like crazy. But I had the impression there were others in there . . . back around in this area." He pointed at the second set of stalls. "I can't say I heard anything specifically."

"What did you do after the first shots?"

"Pulled up my shorts," he answered promptly. "The boy started crying and the father said something like 'Jesus Christ!' The shooter yelled at them to get out, and I heard the door open and close again. That's when he kicked at my stall door and shouted for me to come out."

Mason nodded, encouraging the man to continue. He'd let Walter get everything out and then they'd go back through and pick the story apart, looking for things he'd forgotten to mention. Immediate interviews with the eyewitnesses were vital. Witnesses couldn't go home and rest and come back. Stories change. Memories change. People overthink and wonder if they imagined certain aspects and revise their memories to be more logical or to be what they think the police want to hear.

"Sliding that latch on the stall door was one of the damned hardest things I've ever done. I didn't know what was waiting on the other side. I only knew it'd terrified the boy and his father. But he'd let them go. And I hoped I'd get to do the same."

"What's the first thing you saw when you opened the door? Did it open in or out?" Mason already knew the answer but wanted to judge Walter's memory.

"In. I opened it a bit, keeping my body behind the door. The first thing I saw was the barrel of a rifle and a masked man pointing it at my face. He ordered me to come out."

"What was he wearing?"

Walter frowned. "You said he shot himself in the bathroom after I left. I'm pretty sure you guys know what he was wearing better than I remember."

"Humor me."

The witness's eyes closed and his forehead crinkled. "Black athletic pants. A lightweight jacket out of the same type of material. Black ski mask. I remember thinking he looked straight out of a movie. Why do people feel they have to dress the part of the bad guy?" He opened his eyes. They were a very pale blue set in tired, bloodshot whites. His eyelashes were nearly nonexistent and the corners of his eyes were reddened, as if he'd been reading for several hours.

"Then what?"

Walter's chest expanded as he took a deep breath. "He told me to put up my hands and come out."

"Could you see any facial features? Was he taller than you?"

"Everybody's taller than me these days. I swear I've shrunk three inches in the last ten years."

Mason straightened his hunched shoulders.

"Eyes were dark. I want to say brown, but I can't say I actually saw the color. Could have been the mask making them seem dark."

"What'd you do next?"

"He told me to go face the wall. The one at the far end of the stalls. It put the urinals on my right." Walter wiped at his brow. "I thought he was going to shoot me in the back. I don't know how long I stood there. Felt like forever."

"What was he doing?"

"I heard him walk back to the other area of the bathroom and yell at someone else to get on the floor and not move. I could hear him going back and forth, keeping an eye on me and checking on whoever else was back there."

"Did you hear other voices?"

"At first. I couldn't make out the words. He told them to shut up and that stopped any talking."

"You didn't talk to him?"

"No. I looked over my shoulder at one point, and he immediately had the gun aimed my way and shouted at me to turn around. I didn't look again."

"How did you get out?"

Walter snorted. "He let me go. He said, 'Guess what, old man, it's your lucky day.' I held still. I didn't know if that meant he was going to shoot me or release me. Then he screamed at me to get the fuck out of the bathroom. I glanced back at him. He had the gun at his side and was pointing at the door. 'Get out! Get out!' he screamed. I couldn't move. He yelled again, and I took a few steps, not believing he was letting me go, but he nodded and shouted some more. I'd taken two steps when he started shooting into the ceiling. I stopped but he waved the rifle at me to keep going. I decided to go."

He held Mason's gaze. "At that point I figured I was dead if I ran or dead if I stayed. I decided to die trying."

"That took guts."

"No, I was scared out of my mind. The only guts involved were the ones I nearly threw up. When I came out of the bathroom the first thing I saw was more guns pointed at me. They told me to get on the ground, but I was terrified the guy in the bathroom was going to follow me out and shoot me in the back. What drove me to the ground was the thought that I needed to be out of the police's way so they could shoot him." Another deep breath. "They searched me and told me to head toward the parking garage and keep my hands on my head." He turned his head and nodded at Ava at the next table. "I saw Ava. She was hiding with Misty from our yoga class. I wanted to help them get out, but Misty had been shot in the leg and couldn't walk. Did she make it?"

"She's at the hospital. I think she's going to be fine." Ava had called for an update and been told Misty was on her way to surgery, but the doctors were optimistic.

"Good. Misty's a sharp kid. Hope the experience doesn't mess her up too bad." He looked at Ava again. "She's cool as a cucumber. Barely seemed rattled back there."

Mason looked over and recognized the signs of exhaustion on Ava. She hid it pretty well. But he knew the slight downturn to her mouth and curve to her back meant she was wearing down. Months of living together had taught him her tells. They were all small. She knew how to hide her feelings, but most people didn't have his fascination with every aspect of her face and habits. He could watch her forever at home. Whether she was doing laundry, gardening, or cooking. He paid attention. Her focus on Shaver was still sharp; she'd never let the sergeant see how tired she was. But to Mason she was waving a white flag.

He turned back to find Walter studying him.

"So you're Ava's guy. I heard in class that she'd been seeing a cop."

"Is it that obvious?"

"All over your face. You must have been worried shitless knowing she was in there."

Mason cleared his throat. "That's one way of putting it. Let's get back to you. When he started shooting at the end, did he point the gun back toward the other stalls? Or was he focused solely on you?" Walter scrunched up his face and thought. Mason sneaked a look at his watch and decided he'd offer to run Ava home after he was done with Walter Borrego. He'd seen Zander Wells stop by and chat with Ava for a moment, and he wondered what'd brought the agent into the hub. Was he just checking on Ava? Or was the Bureau involved already?

He spent ten more minutes fine-tuning Walter's story, and the man seemed to run out of details. Mason wrapped up the interview and handed him off to an officer. He moved over to Ava's table. "You guys about done? I can run Ava home and be back in less than an hour."

She shot a grateful look at him, and her heavy eyelids told him she was more tired than he'd realized. Shaver cleared them to go but told Mason to hurry back.

"I just want to go to bed," Ava whispered as they left the shop. Her steps were slow, and she leaned heavily on him as he wrapped an arm around her.

"Soon as we get home," Mason promised. "You can crash and sleep the rest of the day away."

And I'll come back and help figure out who shot up the mall. And why.

6

Zander followed the small group of senior officers. The Washington County sheriff, Bernie North, had hand-selected a few men from each responding division to walk the scene. It was nearly eight P.M. and the mall felt empty and quiet, and the sun was well hidden behind the tall firs to the west. Nighttime was closing in rapidly. The forensic evidence collection had been turned over to the state and the teams worked silently or with low murmurs. Mason Callahan and Ray Lusco represented the Oregon State Police Department's Major Crimes division. The police chief from Cedar Edge, one of his detectives, and three men from the Washington County Sheriff's Office made up the rest of the group.

They'd started at the edge of the mall where the first sightings of a man with a gun had been called in. They hadn't located video footage showing where the shooter had actually entered the mall. Yet. "Calls say the shooter aimed down the main aisle and Misty Helm was the first person hit. He was then seen moving to the aisle in front of the movie theater. He stopped and shot a woman who'd been using the mall for her morning exercise," North stated, referring to a clipboard.

Zander had encountered mall walkers several times. The indoor malls were popular during the rainy and cold months, and most of them opened their main buildings early to let exercisers walk their daily miles. By the time the retail stores opened, the walkers were done and enjoying coffee at one of the shops. During the summer months, the outdoor malls like Rivertown were popular in the same way. He assumed it was the same routine across the nation.

"Reports say he shot multiple times but only Gabrielle Gower was hit."

Lousy shot or lucky?

"How many camera angles are there?" asked the Cedar Edge detective.

"Lots," North said dryly. "We have hundreds of hours of footage to look through. Even though the shooting only lasted about ten minutes, we want to look at the hours before and after. That includes the parking garage and any views from the outside. I want to see every movement of this guy starting the moment he got up this morning until he went down in that bathroom. Hell, maybe even earlier. There's a team assigned to sift through it all." North ran a finger along his clipboard to figure out where he had left off. He located the spot and continued. "After the first shots, people got smart and started to leave. Dick Olsen was shot moments later in front of the theater." He pointed at a team of techs working a bloody area in front of the ticket window, and then he looked straight at Zander, knowing Olsen's death had pulled the FBI into the case.

"Why was Olsen at the mall this early?" asked Ray.

"We don't know yet," said North. "He's retired, lives alone, and we haven't reached any family members that have an answer." He looked at Zander again.

Zander met his gaze and gave a small shake of his head. The FBI wasn't holding anything back on Olsen. They didn't know why he'd been at the mall, either. Olsen's family was scattered across the US and UK. They'd have to find a friend or neighbor who could give some insight into Olsen's actions.

"What was Olsen wearing?" asked Mason.

North shot a questioning look at one of the Washington County investigators. "Shorts, T-shirt, tennis shoes," answered the man.

"Possibly one of the walkers?" Mason asked. "We'll need to ask some of the other mall walking witnesses. He might be a regular."

Zander eyed the Major Crimes detective. He'd seen Mason leave earlier with Ava. She'd looked ready to collapse. Mason had returned with a determined glint in his eye, and Zander was glad he was part of the joint effort to find out the who and why of the shooting.

The group moved on. "Next the shooter walked down the main artery of the mall several hundred feet. Reports say he stopped and checked some of the doors of the shops and looked in the windows. Until we get the video report, we won't know for certain if he stepped inside any stores. A few salespeople who were getting their stores ready to open said they saw him or heard him yank on their doors."

"Could have been anyone yanking on doors, looking for a place to hide," added one of the county investigators.

"Yes," agreed North. "Video will tell us if it was him."

Or terrified bystanders searching for cover.

The men moved in silence, and Zander noticed that the group was exclusively male. *How did that happen?* He worked with a large number of female agents every day. This group almost felt like the good ol' boys' club. Was it simply coincidence? He noticed the forensics teams were pretty evenly split.

They paused at a children's play area in the center of the walkway. Zander nearly stumbled as he stepped onto the brightly colored flooring around the jungle gym and slide. It was spongy under his feet. He watched one of the county investigators step on it and bounce to test the cushion of the flooring. It made sense. The mall couldn't have kids toppling off the bars and cracking their skulls on the concrete. No doubt the mall didn't want shooters, either, but they couldn't protect against that.

Who can?

No one said a word at the play area. Zander avoided looking at the turquoise-and-red equipment, choosing to study the men's expressions and take in the anger and relief that they couldn't hide. *How many of them are fathers?* No children had been hurt—this time. The mass shooting in Eugene in June had injured two children and left four adults dead.

At a large intersection in the mall, North stopped. "This is where Misty Helm was standing when she was shot in the leg. She was the first injured." He pointed at dried brown blood sprays on the walkway's concrete. *Arterial spray.* The evidence techs had already finished with the area, but it was still cordoned off. A dark smeared path from the initial blood patterns led across the walkway to a nearby kiosk.

"The woman was talking to an FBI agent at the time she was shot. The agent got a tourniquet on her leg and dragged her to safety, where they waited until the shooter was dead."

Zander's stomach turned. *The victim was lucky Ava knew what to do.* He'd known Ava had helped someone, but hadn't realized they'd been so exposed and smack in the center of the shooting.

North looked at his clipboard. "The FBI agent said the shooter stopped in front of this kitchen store and took aim at a group of women but didn't fire. Then he turned and went down that aisle for a few moments."

The group moved forward. "Here is where the special agent and the teen hid," said North, and stopped at the pool of dried blood near the sunglasses kiosk.

Two of the men coughed. It wasn't a hiding place; it could barely be called cover. The scent of hot, baking iron hit Zander's nose and mingled with the odor of blood in the air. Their entire walk had been a hot one. The air had cooled down a few degrees, but the ground was releasing the sun's energy that it'd soaked up all day. He watched Mason out of the corner of his eye. He'd frozen as he saw the dried blood pool, and Zander wondered if he imagined it as Ava's. She could have been shot as easily as the teen.

"They were fucking lucky," muttered the Cedar Edge police chief. "They were sitting ducks."

Mason looked away, his face blank.

"The suspect shot Anthony Sweet instead of the women." North pointed at the blood on the wall and ground fifty feet down a wing of the mall. "Sweet was an employee at the card shop. The special agent believes he left the store to try to help her and the teenager."

The men shifted their feet and mumbled. Was Sweet a hero or a fool? Zander understood the drive to help someone in need. Would he have done the same as Sweet? Or followed standard operating procedure and stayed hidden?

He didn't know.

"Then the shooter entered the restroom toward the end of this wing."

They'd passed plastic evidence markers all throughout their walk. But in this section of the mall were the most markers, increasing in number as they neared the restroom. The activity in and just outside the bathrooms had been high during the investigation, and Zander knew the shooter still lay as the police had found him. There'd been nothing a medical team could do; they couldn't fix dead. The shooter had blown off part of the back of his head and had been left in place to preserve evidence. Zander noticed two guys from the morgue standing to the side, cooling their heels as they waited for their opportunity to remove the body.

"Three guys and one child made it out of the restroom before he shot himself," North continued. "They were damn lucky. He could have shot them all. We'll probably never know how he selected his victims."

He glanced at the group. "Everyone have good stomach control?"

Silence.

"All right then. Let's take a look."

• • •

Mason had felt Zander's gaze on him the whole walk. If the agent hadn't been such a nice guy it would have annoyed the hell out of him, but he knew Zander was watching out of concern. He didn't know the agent's history, but he'd heard he'd lost his wife somehow. Whether that somehow was divorce or death, Mason hadn't heard the facts, but he respected the man. Zander Wells was a sharp investigator, gave a damn about victims, and didn't create pissing contests.

Mason wished Ava were beside him. She deserved a look at the guy who'd shot her friend and kept her pinned down in a danger zone. He wanted to hear her perspective on the scene. She'd watched the crimes play out and didn't need to refer to a clipboard to keep the timeline straight.

He was glad he'd been assigned to the case. He hadn't been involved with the mass shooting case in Eugene in June, but he'd followed it closely, disturbed that it'd happened again in Oregon. Nearly two decades ago, not far from the site of the June shooting, an expelled teen had decided to take a weapon into his high school after killing his parents. Children had died, and the memory had never faded from the community. Mass shootings seemed to happen in batches, breeding like rabbits. How many would it take to finish this batch?

Mason prayed this was the final one.

He'd listened and watched closely as they'd walked the path of the shooter. The mall was silent except for the swarm of evidence technicians and police. A different atmosphere from the never-ending sirens, tears, and screams of that morning. Mason wanted immediate access to a murder scene to do his job efficiently. The best time was before the techs arrived, when nothing had been disturbed, no crime scene tape, no black dust, no evidence bags.

He always felt a subtle vibration in his bones as he walked murder scenes. As if a million microscopic voices were shouting at him, trying to lead his feet and eyes to the answers. *Is it from the souls of the departed?* He didn't know. He didn't subscribe to the woo-woo beliefs of ghosts or the supernatural. He trusted his eyes. And his gut. And he used his brain to search for answers—not for spirits.

He liked the silence of a scene that allowed his mind to process and wander through the puzzle of what the hell had happened. Everything frozen in time, waiting for him to follow the subtle clues and answer the million questions.

In a mall like this, 90 percent of the crime should be visible on video.

"Cameras in the restrooms?" he asked North.

The sheriff shook his head. "Can you imagine the outcry if people found out there were cameras in public restrooms? No mall will go for that, but the doorway is covered from that one." He pointed up at the opposite roof line. Mason had to stare for a few seconds before he spotted the discreet camera.

"Not a lot of room inside the bathroom. You three first." North pointed at Mason, Ray, and Zander. The rest of the group stood to the side as the investigators slipped on booties and gloves.

"Make it fast, ladies," one of the county investigators quipped. Mason ignored him.

Inside, a crime scene photographer spoke to the medical examiner, who was pulling off his gloves, clearly finished with his examination of the body. Dr. Seth Rutledge looked up as they entered, his face brightening as he spotted Mason and Ray. "Evening, detectives." The men had met over several corpses, but Mason preferred to meet the good-natured ME over a beer. Sadly, the corpses had outnumbered the beers.

"Hey, Doc." Ray lifted a hand in greeting. "Whatcha got?"

Mason took in the body. It was as Ava and Walter Borrego had described. Black from head to toe. Black Nike tennis shoes, black baggy athletic pants, black athletic jacket, mask. Tall. Not heavy. Someone had pulled up the mask to expose his face but left it covering most of his hair and what was left of his head. The face seemed young. Clean-shaven. Dark eyelashes and hair. Someone had closed the eyelids, but Mason wanted to see the eye color. Low murmurs told Mason that more people were in the rear of the restroom.

"Gunshot to the mouth."

"With his rifle?" Zander asked.

"Yep. It's not that hard when you've got long arms." The medical examiner pointed at the sinks. "I think he balanced the butt of the gun on one of the sinks, shoved it in his mouth, and fired. See how he fell backward?"

Mason nodded. The shooter's feet pointed at the sink and his head was nearly at one of the stall doors. A fine dark mist and small chunks of . . . something . . . covered the stall door. And the ceiling. Beneath the head, blood had pooled. The center of the pool still gleamed wetly, but the edges had thinned and dried.

"God damn it," Mason muttered. Beside him Ray nodded, spotting the dried smeared footprints in the blood on the floor that'd made Mason swear. "We've got the contact team's boots for comparisons, right? And the medical guys'?"

"Yes," said North.

"The back of his head has a big chunk of skull missing," said Dr. Rutledge. "The size I would expect for this caliber and how close the weapon was."

Mason carefully stepped as close as he dared and squatted to get a better look at the suspect's clothing. The jacket was zipped as high as it could go. Its Nike logo on the breast matched the one on the hip of the pants. He pointed at the logos and glanced back at Ray. "Looks like he supports local businesses," he said, referring to the Nike's world campus a half hour away. "And likes to color-coordinate."

"Even you can match black with black," Ray gibed.

Mason made a mental note to find out if the Nike athletic wear was from a newer line. Had the shooter recently shopped for a new outfit for his last day on earth? He stood, ignoring the quiet popping in his spine as it straightened. "Who pulled up the mask?" he asked the ME.

Dr. Rutledge frowned as he studied the corpse. "I was told the contact team. They checked his vitals and breathing."

"Young," commented Zander.

The cheeks, chin, and jawline of the shooter were angular, that look that younger men have when they burn more calories than they eat. Their energy levels keep them lean until they discover the joy of nightly beers, steaks, and burgers.

"I'll guess early twenties," said the ME.

"Eye color?" Mason asked.

"Blue," answered Dr. Rutledge.

Suddenly tired of the gore in front of him, Mason scanned the rest of the bathroom, recalling Walter Borrego's description. He turned around and walked past the row of stalls to the back portion of the restroom. The layout mirrored the area he'd just left. Stalls, urinals, sinks. Two evidence techs were huddled over a sink as one swabbed something and the other snapped a picture. Mason didn't want to know what sort of bacteria grew in a public bathroom. Granted, the Rivertown Mall's restrooms were pretty darn sparkling compared to other public restrooms. They'd been constructed with marble and high-end finishes. Glancing around, Mason figured the janitor made very regular stops to keep the rooms as pristine as possible. He stepped closer. "Find something?"

"Blood on the side of this sink," said the younger tech.

"Fresh?"

The other tech shrugged. "It's dried. Don't know if it's been there for five hours or five days."

Mason took a hard look at the clean floor. "Find blood anywhere else?" At the looks on their faces, he amended his statement. "Find blood anywhere else in *this* section of the restroom?"

Both men shook their heads.

"Anything else odd catch your interest?"

"Not yet, sir."

Mason gave them a nod and went back to the other group, where Dr. Rutledge was stating that he'd take a closer look at the body once it arrived at the morgue.

"We need something to identify him with," North was saying. "Scars, tattoos, see if there's anything we can put out there."

"I'll see what I can find and let you know immediately," promised the medical examiner.

"I interviewed Walter Borrego, the older yoga guy who was in the bathroom when the shooter entered," Mason said. "Who interviewed the father with the boy and the last guy out of the bathroom?"

"Not sure." North flipped through a few pages, shaking his head. "I don't have that here. Seems like I saw one of my guys talking to the father. Don't know about the other witness. I'll find out."

"Okay, everyone got their look?" North asked. "Then get out. I need to bring in the next group."

Mason followed Zander out of the bathroom, feeling the touch of a million tiny vibrations from the death scene scatter along his bones, and wondered what the dead were trying to tell him.

7

At eight in the morning, Ava poured her second cup of coffee as she watched her dog, Bingo, plead with a squirrel in the backyard to play with him. She was attempting not to look at her kitchen. The room was a work in progress. A big, gigantic, messy piece of work. The contractor had ripped out every shred of the previous 1970s kitchen, demolished a wall, and promised her she'd love it one day.

Six weeks, my ass.

Three weeks had passed since the demolition, and she wasn't seeing much progress. Her usable appliances were reduced to a microwave, coffeepot, and mini-fridge. A million boxes holding her kitchen's contents were piled in her formal living room. She and Mason had bought the old Tudor home in June. It perched on a corner lot in an older Portland neighborhood with a huge fenced backyard and quiet neighbors. The lot was large but the home was small and needed lots of work to restore it to the condition of its glory days of the 1920s. She'd stepped through the front door and fallen in love. Where Mason had seen money pit, she'd seen quality and strength. It just needed tender loving care. Their contractor loved it, too—maybe too much. If he had his way, their remodel would cost as much as the home. Ava reined him in except when it came to her dream kitchen. Nothing was held back there.

It'd be a while before they could afford to restore the rest of the home.

From behind her, Mason slipped a hand around her waist and pressed his lips against her neck. "You smell like coffee."

"No better perfume," she said.

"What's wrong with Bingo?" he asked, peering over her shoulder and out the window. "He's been whining for the last ten minutes."

"The squirrel refuses to play. It just sits on the fence and chatters at him. Are you leaving already?" She'd briefly awoken when he'd crawled in bed, and had noticed it was two A.M. She'd asked him if he knew how Misty was doing. He'd told her the doctors had said she'd make a full recovery. Ava had instantly relaxed at his words and gone back to sleep for a total of twelve hours.

"Yes. They spent part of the night setting up a room at the Cedar Edge Community Center to use for the investigation. Zander pulled some strings and got an amazing amount of federal technical support. Washington County had no complaints about the FBI having a foot in the case once they saw the resources he finagled."

"They shouldn't complain." Ava frowned. "The cases crossed and now we'll work together. They should be thankful we have an interest in why a shooter decided to act."

He tightened his arms around her stomach. "Last night I stood at the place where you hid with Misty." He pressed his mouth against her hair, and she felt him shudder.

She exhaled. "I saw it all night long in my dreams."

"That was no hiding place, Ava. He could have easily spotted you."

"He *did* see us. He turned around and looked right at me on his way to the bathroom."

Mason straightened, his arms stiffening. "You didn't say that last night."

"I told Shaver during my debriefing. I thought I'd mentioned it to you," she lied. She'd held back that morsel of information from Mason. There'd been no point in his worrying about something that'd already happened. He'd had enough to think about.

"I'd remember if you'd said that. What'd he do?"

"He looked at me." She shrugged, covering up the need to shiver. "He was checking the doors in that section of the mall. I met his gaze. He lifted his rifle and pointed it at us, but didn't shoot. He looked at his watch and left. I felt like he didn't have time to deal with us."

"*He aimed at you?*" Mason spun her around to face him. His eyes were wide and his hands were tight on her shoulders. "You said nothing last night. Dammit! Don't try to protect me. You held that back, didn't you?"

"What good would telling you have done?"

Emotions flitted across his face. Terror, anger, understanding. "Nothing. It would have affected nothing," he admitted.

She lifted her chin. "I knew that. It would have only thrown off your concentration."

He pulled her tight to him and kissed her on the forehead. "Don't do that again," he growled.

She slid her hands around him, guilt creeping over her at the sensation of his heart pounding in his chest. "I won't."

They stood in silence for a few seconds, forgiveness and intimacy weaving between them. She knew her boss would call about the shooting and no doubt he'd steer her toward seeing a therapist before she returned to work. That was okay with her. She wouldn't mind dumping her thoughts in a stranger's lap instead of holding back the scary parts the way she did sometimes with Mason.

"Did they get an identification yet?" Ava asked softly.

"Not yet. We obviously couldn't give a photo to the news stations, and the description of a tall man in his twenties is too vague. Early this morning the medical examiner told us he had a tattoo on his upper arm, so we've added that to the description. I'll bet twenty bucks the morning newscasts will trigger the right lead once they broadcast that information." He pulled back and glanced at the silent television. "Not going to watch?"

"No. I don't need to watch speculation about what happened yesterday." She'd dreamed about the shooter all night. Sometimes he was still alive as the police rushed the bathroom entrance, and he killed all the team members. Then he stalked up the aisle and shot her and Misty. Other times the shooter had a hostage: the small boy who'd been carried out in his father's arms. One time she'd dreamed the bathroom was empty, and it was her fault for telling the police she'd seen him go in. Several times she'd dreamed he shot her and Misty during the moment she'd finally told Mason about.

She didn't want the TV on; the silence inside the old house was soothing. The occasional sounds of the frustrated dog and the teasing of the squirrel kept her grounded after her surreal experience yesterday. She needed normal.

"I get to go watch an autopsy this morning," Mason said.

"I assumed the examiner already did it, since you mentioned the tattoo."

"He only looked at the body, trying to put together a better description to broadcast for an ID." Mason stepped to the counter, poured coffee in his *Star Trek* travel mug, and kissed her good-bye. "I love you," he said, pressing his forehead against hers. "Don't go to any malls today," he added half-seriously.

"No worries." She shuddered.

He winked as he left, but she saw the stress in his face.

It was over, and there was no point in worrying over something that had already happened. She wasn't in a hospital with a gunshot wound. *This time.*

She watched out the window as he backed his vehicle out of the driveway, feeling very domestic and June Cleaver-ish. She still had another week left on her vacation. Her goal had been to paint one of the guest rooms, but so far she'd read two books and played with Bingo at the dog park every day. She'd watched the other dog parents, wondering what they did for jobs that allowed them so much freedom during the day.

She could get used to a life of leisure.

Too bad she bored easily.

She glanced at the huge pile of boxes from her kitchen and moaned as she remembered she needed to dig through them to find more coffee filters. The sight was so overwhelming, she couldn't move. She'd tried to label them as they were packed, but her previous searches for chopped almonds and her cheese grater had proven that something had gone drastically wrong with her labeling technique.

Go buy some. She'd already made multiple trips to Target to buy supplies she *knew* she had. How many more trips would there be?

How about just finish the damned kitchen?

Last remodeling project ever. The dated master bath popped into her head. It was next on their list to tackle. Surely a bathroom wouldn't be as disruptive as a kitchen?

Her cell rang, and the sight of the number made her heart speed up. No matter how well her sister might be doing, Ava sweated when she saw Jayne's number on her phone.

"Hi, Jayne," she answered, setting down her coffee. She situated herself in an easy chair and propped up her legs. Calls with Jayne often required a comfortable place to sit. Jayne liked to talk.

She was par for the course that morning. Ava heard about Jayne's previous day at work, and her roommate's odd clothing choices. Ava smiled, enjoying her sister's talkativeness. Jayne was currently in a stable position both mentally and emotionally. Her twin had completed an extensive drug rehab program and had spent the last twelve weeks in a good halfway house. She enjoyed her job at a coffee shop, and the customers found her to be amusing. She claimed she was avoiding men and "trying to get myself fixed before taking on someone else's baggage."

Ava prayed it would last.

But part of her knew it couldn't. It never lasted. *Maybe this time it will?* She never completely gave up hope. Several times she'd washed her hands of her sister, but she'd recently watched Jayne make several good decisions in a row, so Ava had her fingers crossed. Right now Jayne was on a solid streak. *Please don't let her fall.*

Even Jayne's voice sounded in control. Her previously high-pitched, speedy, pointless chatter had been modulated into normal conversation—pleasant and polite. And right now the best Ava could do for Jayne was offer a listening ear. She'd kept her distance as Jayne struggled through therapy and searched for a job. Her twin needed to dig her own way out of her giant hole.

". . . shooting yesterday."

Ava blinked as she realized she'd let her mind wander. "I'm sorry. What'd you say about the shooting?"

"It's just horrible. How can anyone feel safe in public?" Jayne asked with an appropriate amount of concern, in contrast to her out-of-control emotions from six months earlier. "That's the second shooting this summer."

Ava didn't mention she'd been at the mall. There were a lot of things she didn't tell her twin—like her new address. Jayne and her drugged-up ex-boyfriend had broken into Mason's old home and stolen personal property.

Once burned.

Ava no longer revealed anything personal in conversations with Jayne. She'd mastered the art of being "specifically vague." Jayne didn't know Ava was on vacation, she didn't know she'd bought a new house, and she didn't know Ava had dreams of marrying Mason on a beach someday.

Theirs wasn't the typical twin relationship; Jayne had crushed Ava's trust over and over. Now Ava operated under a new rule: Share as little information as possible.

But she'd discovered she still loved to idly chat with her twin. Lately the conversations had been blessedly calm and rational, and they only seemed to improve. Ava's brain took a rest as her twin carried 90 percent of the conversation.

Has Jayne finally harnessed her demons?

Wait and see. Don't trust her. Hard lessons learned from her wombmate, Jayne McLane.

"You can't let the fear of the unknown keep you from your regular life," Ava advised. "Yes, the shootings are horrible and they severely traumatize our population. But we can't let them win."

"Our shop has a plan of what to do if someone is shooting."

"Every business should."

Jayne was silent for a moment and then changed the topic to describe a watercolor painting she'd recently admired. Ava relaxed and pretended she was a normal woman with a mentally healthy twin.

Much better than watching an autopsy on a gunshot wound to the head.

8

"Traffic," Mason muttered in excuse for his lateness as he entered the autopsy suite. "The 205 freeway was a parking lot."

Ray rocked back on his heels and grinned. "Shoulda left home earlier."

Mason glared at him. Ray knew he was anal about being on time. He was going to hear about this for the next six months.

Dr. Seth Rutledge was speaking into the microphone over the autopsy table. He held a hand up at Mason, but didn't pause in his recitation. Glancing at the white body on the table, Mason realized he'd missed the whole thing. That was fine with him. An autopsy wasn't a surgery of tiny, delicate incisions. It was strong, long gashes and skin ripped from half the face. There was no need to be careful around arteries or worry about causing harm to the patient.

An assistant was stitching closed the big Y on the shooter's chest, and the corpse's scalp had clearly been folded back into place after Rutledge finished with the subject's brain, except the hair didn't look right. The young man's hair and scalp dipped in concavities where hard skull should have provided support. Part of Mason wanted to walk over and straighten it. The rest of him wanted to turn around and go back to his car. The odor of burned bone from the skull saw lingered with other odors he didn't want to think about.

"Anyone else make it in time?" Mason asked Ray.

"Two investigators from Washington County just left."

Shit. No doubt the Washington County sheriff would hear that he'd missed the autopsy.

"We've got a good lead on an ID," Ray said eagerly.

"Whatcha got?" Mason asked.

Ray pulled his notebook out of his shirt pocket. "Justin Yoder. Age twenty. His mom called in after hearing about the tattoo this morning. She says he didn't come home from work yesterday, but his work claims he never showed up. Lives in Beaverton."

"Only twenty? Did he look that young?" He looked back at the body. "What's Rutledge think?"

"Says it's possible."

"What about dental comparisons?"

"His mother gave me the name of his dentist and they were open at seven this morning. They immediately emailed over current X-rays. Lacey is looking at them in her office and doing a comparison to the films she took earlier."

Mason nodded, knowing Dr. Lacey Campbell was the odontologist for the medical examiner's office. "Let's go find her." He glanced back at Dr. Rutledge, who was still recording his findings. "Anything else I should know about right away?"

Ray jerked his head toward the doors and they walked out of the suite. "Healthy kid. Fit. Had eggs and hash browns for breakfast along with orange juice."

"Jesus Christ. You make it sound like he had an ordinary day planned."

"Maybe he did."

"You don't walk into a mall and start shooting on a regular day."

"So he should have done it on an empty stomach?"

Mason rolled his eyes. "Tell me something else Dr. Rutledge found out about the shooter."

"He blew a big hole in his brain and out the back of his skull." Ray looked down at the floor as they strode down the hall, his usual vigor subdued.

Mason glanced sideways at him and mentally searched for the age of Ray's son. He couldn't be over fifteen . . . probably closer to twelve. He shoved all thoughts of his own son, Jake, out of his head. If anyone's kid was close to the age of the kid on the table, it was Mason's. "What kind of tattoo was on his upper arm?"

"Some sort of tribal thing. Rutledge photographed it. We couldn't make heads or tails out of it. Sometimes there's a name or letters hidden inside the shapes, but I couldn't see it."

"Could just be a pattern he liked," Mason said. "Did the mother send a photo of her son's tattoo?"

"She was trying to find one. Said she knew her son had pictures of it, but she didn't. The description and location sounded right."

They stopped outside an open office door, and Mason tentatively knocked on the frame. "Dr. Campbell?"

The woman at the computer spun around and smiled warmly. "Mason! Ray said you were on your way. And you know better than to call me Dr. Campbell. It makes me look around for my father."

He couldn't help his grin. He'd first met Lacey ages ago when she was a young athlete in college, and their paths had crossed again a few years back in a serial killer case. Now he considered her a good friend. She was in her thirties and shone with a beauty that made every man dream his dentist looked like her.

"Your father's enjoying retirement?" Ray asked. Dr. James Campbell had been the chief medical examiner before Dr. Rutledge.

"He's in Australia as we speak. I'm pretty sure he's coming back."

"Rutledge seems to be holding down the fort pretty well," Mason said, forcing his tongue to work since he was slightly dumbstruck, as was usual when he was in her presence.

"He's fantastic," Lacey agreed. "You'll want to know about Justin Yoder?"

Mason nodded.

Her smile vanished. "I haven't finished my report, but it's a match. That's definitely him."

Silence filled the small office, and she looked from Mason to Ray. "Too abrupt? Do you want me to show you how I know?"

"Please," Mason asked. He trusted the petite dentist's findings, but he liked to know the why.

She turned back to her computer. "The top films are from his dentist and the ones along the bottom here, I took this morning." She pointed with a pencil. "We're lucky he had good dental care. These top films are only three months old. As you can see, he's had composite restorations placed here, here, and here." She touched three teeth in the first film in the top row and then moved her pencil to the film at the bottom of the screen on the left. "Compare those three restorations to the same teeth down here. They're identical in shape—all three of them. Another body *might* have composite fillings in the same teeth, but the shape will always be different. On the other side of his mouth he has a good-sized gap between his first and second maxillary molars. The film from his dentist shows decay starting on the distal of number fourteen." She touched the tip of the pencil to a dark spot on a film on the right side of her screen, and then moved it down to the corresponding film at the bottom. "On the film I took, the decay is gone and replaced by a composite filling. I called the office and they confirmed that they placed the filling after taking the films." She tapped the film. "There's still a gap between those teeth that will continue to catch food. He's going to need . . ."

She stopped speaking and lowered the pencil. She slowly turned her chair around to face the detectives, her brown eyes soft. "I guess he won't be needing anything," she said quietly.

Mason sympathized. Beside him, Ray shoved his hands in his pockets.

"Thank you, Lacey," Mason said. "This will give us a jump start on figuring out why he did what he did."

"It's terrifying," she answered. "I shop at that mall all the time. Where will someone strike next?"

"Our goal is to make sure there won't be a next time," answered Mason.

• • •

Ava sipped at her coffee, not tasting it, as she studied the bustling room at the community center. Sergeant Shaver had called, asking her to come back to Cedar Edge for a second interview. In her opinion someone had set up a decent investigation center. Lots of room, neatly arranged tables, a dozen computer stations, timelines, maps, and photos on the walls. The atmosphere was slightly different from that of centers she'd been in before. The urgency she associated with big cases was missing. Here the bad guy had already been brought down, and now police were searching for the why. Investigators were more relaxed, not saddled with the stress of finding the shooter before he hurt someone else.

Mason had called during her drive and told her the shooter had been positively identified. He and Ray were on their way to update the Washington County sheriff and then would be paying a visit to the young man's family.

Twenty years old.

Why?

She chewed on the edge of her paper coffee cup. *What drives a twenty-year-old to murder strangers?* Dark eyes behind a mask flashed in her mind. He'd stared right at her and decided not to shoot.

Why?

On the wall across the room Ava recognized the layout of the Rivertown Mall. Labeled pins tracked the shooter's path. She couldn't read any of the notations, but she could see the colors and markings. She had a good idea what the three large red Xs stood for. She scanned the room for Sergeant Shaver. He'd promised to be right back five minutes ago. She stood and went across the room to study the map.

A small rectangle was labeled SUNGLASSES KIOSK and directly next to it was a blue X and a green X. The green one was labeled with her name and a line that traced to a mini-bio and her picture. She looked exhausted in the photo. She faintly remembered the sergeant's snapping it at some point yesterday. Misty Helm was the blue X. Her photo had been taken as she lay on a stretcher. Ava touched Misty's picture, wanting to wipe the blood from her cheek. A small dotted line led from where Misty had been shot to their waiting place by the kiosk. Not far from the kiosk was a larger red X next to a wall. A line led to a description.

Ava wiped at the sweat that abruptly formed on her upper lip and noticed that her hand felt like ice. Her vision tunneled slightly.

Uh-oh. She recognized the symptoms of her blood pressure dropping. *Sit. Before you end up on the floor.*

She grabbed a chair and sat. That was better. She bent over and rested her head between her knees, sucking in deep breaths.

Anthony Sweet. She hadn't known the name of the third victim until this moment. His photo was of his crumpled body against the wall. The man who'd left the safety of his store to try to help her and Misty.

Does he have a family?

She didn't want to know. Her vision cleared and she sat up, but she couldn't look back at the map. Frustration shot through her. The person who'd caused the deaths and pain was gone, but how many people would suffer for years because of what he'd done? A need to fight back and strike out overwhelmed her, making her hands shake. Something raw deep inside her longed to make the killer hurt.

But he's already dead.

She ached to bring him to justice; she could taste the need to do so, but knew it would never be satisfied.

What can I do?

"Sorry to keep you waiting, Ava," Sergeant Shaver said. "Things keep popping up around here. I guess that's good—it means we're getting closer to answers. I found this guy sticking his nose in things, too." He pointed at Zander Wells with a thumb.

"Hey, Ava." She felt the agent take a hard look at her, and she fought the urge to run a hand over her ponytail. *Do I look like someone who nearly fainted a minute ago?*

"I heard you have a positive identification," she said, tossing out a small bone to take the focus off her.

Shaver's mustache twitched, and Zander lifted a brow.

"Mason didn't tell me the name," she clarified. "But he said it's solid."

"It is. But I asked you to come in to look over some videotape with me." Shaver neatly changed the subject without revealing the name. "I had our techs patch together some different clips that I'd like your opinion on." He waved for her to follow him to a bank of computer monitors. She sat as he logged in and opened a file. Zander stood behind them, his arms crossed on his chest. Ava tensed as the monitor showed a color recording of her and Misty walking down an aisle of the mall. The angle of the video was steep—probably shot from a rooftop camera. The two of them walked past the children's play area, where one mother guided her son down the slide. Neither she nor Misty glanced at the two of them.

I didn't give them a second thought when the shooting started.

Dread swept over her, and sweat beaded at her temples. The carefree boy and his mother were oblivious to the fact that death was about to strike. *Thank God I already know the ending to this movie.* She had no recollection of seeing the woman and boy after the shooting began. She blew out a breath and, out of the corner of her eye, saw Shaver take a close look at her.

On the video she gestured with her hands as she spoke to Misty. She couldn't recall what they had been discussing. They moved out of the camera's range, and the feed jumped to a new view. Still steep but from the opposite side of the mall walkway. She and Misty stopped as Misty lifted her arms in a yoga pose and Ava stepped in front of her to adjust Misty's arms. Ava nodded, her memory returning. They'd been discussing a new position. On-screen, Misty silently jerked as Ava jumped, and then she shoved Misty to the ground, covering her with her body.

Ava looked away and wiped her cheeks. "Jesus H. Christ." Her hands iced over, and her heart raced.

Shaver paused the video. "Your reactions were spot-on. You got her down."

"He's right, Ava," Zander added. "Some people would give you a medal for that."

"Where'd the mother and boy go?" she whispered. *I don't want a fucking medal.*

"Watch." He hit PLAY.

Ava watched the woman sprint into the camera's view. She had the boy clutched to her chest and was running toward the parking garage. She barely glanced at Ava and Misty on the ground. *Mother's instinct. Protect her child.*

"You do a good job here," Shaver commented. "You calm Misty down and immediately get her leg taken care of and get the two of you out of view."

"Everything was locked," said Ava. "I wanted to get her out of there, but I couldn't carry her and she couldn't move."

Several minutes ticked by. The shooter came into view, and Ava leaned closer to the screen. Her impressions of him had been accurate. He moved like a hunter, searching and watching. Twice she saw him check his watch. "He looked at the time right before I thought he was going to shoot us," Ava commented. "Does he do the same on the earlier views of his shootings?"

"Don't know," Zander said with an edge in his voice. "Two of the cameras in front of the theater area weren't functioning. We don't have any video of the first two shootings."

"What? How?" Her mind raced. *Was that deliberate or lucky? Maybe the point of the shooting was to take out the jewelry fence's brother-in-law.*

"We're trying to figure that out," said Shaver. "The cameras appear to have been tampered with. I've got a team printing them and checking the roofs right now to see if any evidence was left behind. Along with officers combing through video for how the shooter entered the mall." He pointed at three people at another bank of computers. "We don't know if he came on foot or parked in the garage. I wouldn't mind finding his vehicle or figuring out where he got the weapon, either. So many things to get done."

"No one's talked to his family yet?" she asked.

"Working on it."

"What about witness video? Didn't anyone pull out their phone?"

"Not that's been reported from this shooting," answered Zander. "There weren't a ton of people there that early in the morning and most of them left immediately when the shooting started."

"He had it all planned," Ava breathed, staring as the figure strode out of the camera's view. "He was supposed to be in the bathroom by a certain time. Why?"

"I was hoping you could shine some light on that," said Shaver. "Everyone else who encountered him immediately got the hell away and didn't look back. You were stuck and forced to watch him in person for longer than anyone else. What else can you tell us?"

Shaver leaned closer, his gaze boring into the side of her face. She didn't look away from the computer screen. The video had cut to the shooter walking the last twenty feet to the bathroom. He vanished inside.

Ava's brain ran the scene through instant replay, watching his long strides and confident bearing as he neared the restroom. Something tickled the back of her brain. "Replay that last part, please."

He touched a few buttons, making the piece continually loop, and Ava watched a few more times. The shooter never looked back, never glanced over his shoulder to see if someone was coming. "He's so confident," she said. "His movements aren't of someone who's even slightly nervous. Is that because he achieved his primary goal?"

"Like killing my witness?" muttered Zander.

Shaver tilted his head. "They say these guys know this is an endgame. They're committed once they put their plan into motion, fully aware they'll probably die either by police or their own hand. Everything is showing us he thoroughly thought out his plan. The cameras, the clothing, the weapon."

"Very thorough," Ava said. "Like someone who's rehearsed this over and over. There's got to be earlier footage of him at the mall walking this route. I'd imagine within the last week. He'd want to know if there were recent changes along his planned path." She looked at Shaver and Zander. "How many people do you have reviewing footage? You're going to need a whole lot more."

9

Mason knocked on the door of Justin Yoder's parents' home.

"Nice house," Ray muttered. "Not where I expected to end up today."

Mason understood. Someone who'd committed the type of crime that Justin Yoder had should have lived in a hellhole, his life a hot mess of stress and anger and unfulfilled need. The gorgeous Tudor home in front of them in the quiet, well-groomed neighborhood indicated peace and prosperity.

Appearances could be deceiving. There was no reason to assume the mini-mansion didn't house stress and anger.

A tall woman answered the door. Mason introduced himself and Ray, and Sally Yoder invited them into her home. Mason knew she'd spoken with the medical examiner within the past hour. Justin's mother's voice shook, but she kept her chin up. Her eyes were bloodshot and her nose looked raw and red from too many rough tissues. Despair flowed from her, but her gaze was controlled. The two men followed her through the house to a huge great room with bright sun streaming in through tall windows. The room was

oddly cool. She offered the detectives a beverage, which they passed
on, and then asked them to sit at the table.

She seemed to shrink as she waited silently at the table. She didn't
look at the men but proceeded to tear a tissue into tiny damp bits
on the tablecloth in front of her. The home was silent. A quick scan
of the room didn't show any family pictures, and the house looked
as if it'd been decorated from that unusual furniture store that Ava
was fond of. Solid pale-colored furniture with glittery accents. No
homey touches at all. Mason's preliminary work had revealed that
Justin was an only child, his mother divorced and remarried, and
his stepfather a bigwig at one of the Northwest banks in their downtown Portland office.

"Will your husband be joining us?" Ray asked.

"He's on his way, but he's driving from downtown. I don't know
how long it'll take him to get here." She paused and added in a near
whisper, "I told him it's been confirmed." Her gaze begged the two
men to tell her she was wrong.

"Yes, the dental findings were very clear," Mason said gently.
He watched her swallow hard. "Is there someone else who can be
here with you right now?" He found it odd that she was alone in the
house after finding out that her son was dead. "A neighbor or rela-
tive?"

She shook her head. "I've been on the phone with family all
morning. No one lives close by, and I prefer to do this alone until
Eric gets here." She glanced nervously at the other men and gave a
shaky laugh. "You must think I'm odd, but I'm a private person. I
don't like people fawning over me."

Mason understood but was disturbed by her laugh. *Is this how
she deals with loss?* "When did you last see Justin?"

She took a deep breath. "The day before yesterday. He left for
work in the early afternoon. He usually works three to midnight at
Big John's several days a week."

"The huge bowling and game place?" Ray asked. "What's he do there?"

"Everything. Sells tickets, handles prizes, waits tables. Whatever is needed."

"You didn't see him yesterday morning?"

Sally shook her head. "I assumed he came home after I went to bed. I'm rarely up that late, and I'm used to not seeing him until the next day. Yesterday morning I figured he was sleeping in . . . he often does. I showered, dressed, and went to the grocery store and ran a few errands. It wasn't until I got back to the house that I saw the shooting on the news at noon."

"What about your husband?" asked Ray.

"He leaves for work at six thirty. I was asleep when he left."

Mason made a note. "Was Justin's car here?"

"No," said Sally. "Eric told me he noticed it wasn't parked on the side of the driveway, but he wasn't concerned. Justin often sleeps over at one of his friends' houses. Especially if they've worked the late shifts together."

"A red Toyota Corolla, correct?" Mason asked. "You must have noticed it was gone when you went to the grocery store."

"Yes, it's red, and I did notice. But my thoughts were the same as Eric's . . . that Justin had slept somewhere else. He does it about once a week." Her fingers moved from shredding the tissue to picking at the pattern in the tablecloth, tugging at a loose thread. "It wouldn't have mattered. Even if I'd noticed that he hadn't been at home that morning, the shooting had already taken place." She looked up, fresh moisture in the corners of her eyes. "I should have checked him first thing yesterday morning, maybe—"

"Mrs. Yoder." Ray leaned forward. "You couldn't have stopped it."

Her eyes indicated she wanted to believe Ray, but Mason knew she'd be doubting and carrying guilt for a long time.

Her shoulders hunched, and she buried her face in her hands. "I can't believe Justin did this . . . I can't believe he's gone. Nothing makes sense." She looked up, and her gaze pleaded with both men. "He wouldn't hurt anyone! I know my boy . . . are you sure it's him? I wanted to go to the morgue and see but they told me to wait until they had him ready." Her voice dropped to a whisper. "The medical examiner told me he shot himself in the head. Is that true?"

The pillar of strength that'd answered the door was starting to crumble, and Mason wished her husband would hurry up. Sally Yoder shouldn't be sitting alone with the police. "He did," Mason answered. "I've seen him. I don't think he suffered."

"Of course he suffered!" she shouted, rising out of her chair. "He shot himself! Something drove him to that point! Something so bad he couldn't live with himself, so he must have been suffering! Don't try to sugarcoat this for me. My son is dead." Her voice cracked, and she slowly sat back down. "And he took other people with him." She looked at her hands knotted in her lap, and her head swayed back and forth as a low raw wail erupted from the depths of her lungs. "He was my only child."

Mason froze, but within a second Ray had moved next to the mother, his hand on her shoulder and words of comfort streaming easily from his lips. Mason didn't have that skill. He knew he had compassion: his heart *overflowed* with compassion for victims, their families, lonely children, and sad pets. But he sucked at expressing it. Feeling as inadequate as generic toilet paper, he waited. This was Ray's territory. His partner knew Mason's shortcomings and how to cover them.

A door slammed and a tall, angular man strode into the room. "Sally?" Eric Yoder looked dressed for the golf course, not the bank.

Ray caught Mason's eye.

Golf or casual Friday?

Ray backed off as Sally stood to meet her husband. They embraced, and she hid her face in his neck as he rubbed her back and his dark eyes glared at the investigators over her shoulder. Eric Yoder looked like a stereotypical banker. Tall, silver-haired, and imposing.

Mason introduced himself and Ray. Sally Yoder pulled herself together and made her husband sit down. He sat heavily and studied the two men. Now that he was sitting, Mason could see he was exhausted. His gaze seemed heavy as he made eye contact. As if he could barely keep his gaze off the floor.

Or as if he was self-medicating.

"Mr. Yoder—" Mason began.

"Eric, please."

Mason summarized what Sally Yoder had told them. Eric nodded. "Justin sometimes sleeps over at Paul's house. I assumed that's where he was when I left yesterday morning."

"Do you know where Justin got the weapon? Do you have guns in the house?"

Both parents shook their heads. "No guns in the house," said Eric. "We've never owned any. I took him to a range a couple years ago to shoot, but I don't think he cared for it that much. He never asked me to take him back."

"What about his friends? What about his friends' parents? Where could he have gotten the rifle?" Mason pushed.

Sally and Eric looked at each other. "I'm honestly not sure if any of his friends have guns," Sally said. "He's never mentioned anything. I can't say I've heard a parent mention it." Her voice cracked. "I probably don't know his friends as well as I should."

"He's twenty," said Ray. "He's an adult. You aren't expected to watch over every move he makes. Is he in school, too?"

"He tried," Eric said. "He went to the community college after he graduated, but after one term he didn't want to go back. His grades weren't that great in high school, and he wasn't interested in any particular field of study except his acting classes. We weren't about to pay for him to go flunk out of an expensive college somewhere or pay his rent in LA to be an actor or join a band."

Sally studied her hands as she picked at the tablecloth. She didn't look up while Eric discussed school and had flinched almost imperceptibly when he mentioned not paying for college. *A sore point between mother and son? Or between mother and stepfather?*

"Do you know why Justin would do this?" Ray asked calmly, finally asking the question that'd been the elephant in the room.

Sally's chin went up. "We don't know. We talked and talked about it on the phone, but we keep coming up with no reasons. He's had some depression issues for the last five years or so, but nothing has ever indicated that he'd do something like this."

"Does he take medication?" Mason asked. *Now we're getting somewhere.*

"Yes. I'll get it." Sally left the room. Eric shifted uncomfortably in his chair in the silence.

"How long have the two of you been married?" Ray asked. "Justin is your stepson, right?"

"Nineteen years," said Eric. "I adopted Justin immediately. His biological father has never been a part of his life."

"Is he around?"

"He lives in Texas," answered Eric. His mouth tightened as he answered. "He's a useless bum."

"You never had more kids?" asked Ray.

"No." His mouth went even tighter. "Sally can't."

"Any behavioral issues with Justin that you saw leading up to this?" Mason asked. "A kid with poor grades and depression doesn't indicate that he'll go shoot up a mall. Something big happen in his life recently?"

Sally reappeared and set an orange pill bottle down next to Mason. He copied the drug name, pharmacy, and prescribing doctor's name down on his pad. "I was just asking your husband if Justin had anything big happen in his life."

She sat back down and gripped her husband's hand. "All he does is sleep and go to work. I'm not aware of anything new . . . good or bad."

"Girlfriend?"

"No. Not in a year or so."

Mason looked at the doctor's name on his notepad. "Is this a general doctor or a specialist? Was there other treatment for his depression?"

"Dr. Beck is a psychiatrist. He's been treating Justin for about a year."

"Treating? How often does he see him?

"Justin goes in for counseling every two weeks."

"And that's been going on for a year?"

Sally pressed her lips together. "It started off every week. That lasted for about three months. Recently they were talking about going to a longer interval between sessions."

Mason didn't know if a year was a long treatment time or normal. From his understanding the disease was unpredictable and difficult to treat at times. Things constantly changed. And life events or chemical production in the body could worsen or improve the patient's outlook on life. He imagined it was a lot like trying to shoot a moving target in the dark with occasional flashes of sunlight.

"When was his last appointment?"

"Last week. Wednesday."

"How was his relationship with the two of you?" Ray asked. "What was your latest argument about?"

Sally wiped at her eyes. "I got on him for leaving an open box of cereal in his bedroom a few days ago. The damn thing was attracting ants. I've told him a million times that he can't do that, but he never remembers. Seems so stupid now."

"Garbage cans," answered Eric. "He's to put the bins back in the garage before I get home on garbage day. I pulled in that evening and they were still at the curb."

The same kind of arguments Mason had had dozens of times with his teenage son.

"Kids are the same everywhere," said Ray. "I'm not sure at what age they figure that stuff out. I suspect it doesn't happen until they have their own home and ant problem."

Sally nodded through fresh tears. "He wanted to move out. He wanted to be on his own and we wanted that for him, but he doesn't make enough. He and three friends were discussing moving in together. They thought that between the four of them, they could afford a good-sized house. But I didn't like the idea. I asked him what would happen when one of them lost his job and couldn't pay the rent anymore. Then the other three were on the hook to make it up. How long would they carry a friend?" She rambled rapidly, her words spilling over one another. "One roommate, I told him. One responsible roommate is all he should try to handle. He may have been a little upset with me that I didn't think it was a good idea." Her voice cracked.

Eric slid an arm around her shoulders. "That wouldn't drive him to do what he did." He looked at the investigators. "I assume you want to search his room? You've been very polite sitting here and talking with us, but I imagine you're itching to look around," he said bitterly.

"We do have a warrant," Mason said. "But we appreciate you letting us look. The two of us will take a quick look, but there will be an evidence team arriving soon." He paused. "The warrant covers the entire house and your vehicles. Electronics, too."

Sally and Eric stared at him.

"I have work stuff on my desktop." Eric started to stand. "I need to back it up."

Mason stood, holding out a hand to slow him down. "It'd be best if you didn't get on your computer right now."

Eric froze. "You think I'm going to hide something." Anger flushed his face. "We've got nothing to hide."

"I didn't say that. But for your protection and to guard any evidence, let's stay away from anything that Justin might have accessed before yesterday's shooting." Mason held Eric's gaze, trying to be nonconfrontational as he slowed his words and softened his tone.

"He doesn't use my computer," Eric snapped.

"Then we won't need it for very long." Mason raised his brows. "I'm not trying to be an asshole. We're searching for answers about the deaths of four people, including your son. Our investigation is going to cause some havoc in your lives and routines, but I think you want an explanation as much as we do, right?"

A murky and heavy aura descended over the table. The atmosphere in the room had started with sorrow and confusion but now distrust and anger bled through them.

"Are you going to tow our cars?" Sally asked, breaking the stalemate. Her nervous gaze darted between the investigators; she was uncertain whom to ask.

"I don't know. That'll be up to the evidence team. I suspect not," said Ray.

"Did you find Justin's car?" asked Eric.

"Not yet. We just got the description of his car a few hours ago. We'll find it," said Mason. They hadn't released the car's description to the public. If it had been in the parking garage, they should have heard by now, but there were plenty of side streets where the young man could have parked to walk to the mall. Someone must have complained about a strange car parked on their street in one of the thousands of leads called in since the shooting.

"Are you going to publicly say who the shooter is? Is it going to be all over the news?" Sally whispered.

Mason took a deep breath. "He's an adult. We've got no reason to hold back that information. Yes, everyone is going to know. You've contacted an attorney, right?" Eric gave a quick nod. "Huddle up tight with the people you trust," Mason advised. "Elect a family spokesperson or use your attorney to talk to the media. Stay away from the windows. I'm sorry, but it's going to be ugly for a while. The media can be vultures. I've been close to a situation like this and you need to be prepared to cope. Avoid the news and unplug your landline."

Sally paled. "Can we leave town? Can we go away for a while?"

Mason exchanged a glance with Ray. "Not yet. Let's get some answers first. How about you show us Justin's room?"

10

It smelled like a teenage boy's room. Old tennis shoes, leftover food, and sweaty sheets. Even though Justin Yoder was twenty, he hadn't abandoned any habits or interests from his teenage years. A big-screen TV that rivaled Mason's hung on one wall. Two gaming systems, a cable console, a Blu-ray player, and three sets of headphones filled the shelves of a wooden unit below the TV. A rack held four guitars and a dusty keyboard was pushed against one wall. Ray took a series of photographs before they started. All they needed was to do a quick once-over. They'd leave the in-depth digging for the evidence team.

"How do you play more than one guitar at a time?" asked Ray. "This is my son's dream bedroom. He's been begging for a drum set. Like that will ever happen, but maybe a guitar with headphones is the way to go. But I gotta watch his hearing," said Ray as he picked up one of the guitars with gloved hands. "I swear my nephews are going to be deaf by the time they graduate high school. My sister doesn't get on them about the volume on their iPods. Wow. Look at those babies." Ray gave a low whistle as he set the guitar back and stepped closer to two crossed swords hanging on the wall. "Shiny."

He ran a finger along a long blade. "Also completely dull. Just for show. And fantasies."

"With enough strength behind them you could hurt someone," Mason pointed out.

"You could say that about a broom handle, too," said Ray. "Help me lift the mattress." He stepped over a small pile of towels and shoved aside the balled-up sheet and blanket. The two of them bent and lifted the awkward pliable king-size mattress.

"Isn't this one of those spendy foam things?" muttered Ray. "Even I don't have one of those."

Mason kept his mouth shut. He wasn't there to judge and didn't let Ray know that he and Ava had a "spendy" mattress because sleeping on springs hobbled his damned back every morning.

Nothing under the mattress. Ray produced a flashlight and they knelt to take a look under the bed. "Jesus Christ," muttered Ray. "I need to go inspect under my son's bed."

They couldn't see a thing under the bed; there was too much crap in the way. Shoe boxes, books, shopping bags. Mason reached out to move a sock and changed his mind. "Leave it for the evidence team." He pointed at Ray. "You take the closet. I'll go through the dresser."

He squatted at the dresser and pulled out the bottom drawer. He squeezed and thoroughly shook each item of clothing and then tossed them in a pile on the floor. As he finished each drawer, he dumped the unfolded clothes back in and moved on to the next. Not that the clothes had been folded to start with.

Every home has a unique odor that develops over time from cooking smells, cleanser scents, pets, and everyday cleaning habits . . . or lack thereof. A person acclimates to the smell of his or her own home, but is often slapped in the face by new odors upon entering someone else's house. The Yoders used a strong-smelling floral laundry detergent that made Mason's throat itch, and it wafted in huge waves from the drawers. He'd caught a faint scent of it when he'd first met Sally Yoder and assumed it was a perfume. He wondered if Eric's coworkers thought he smelled like a flower shop.

He breathed through his mouth.

The dresser yielded nothing of interest. There was some loose change in the drawer corners, and old baseball cards and a half dozen condoms in a tin in the top drawer. Mason studied the arrangement of mementos on top. Two baseball trophies from six years ago. A most-improved certificate from a theater camp in July. Three Iron Man figurines. One Incredible Hulk. More loose change and four name badges from Big John's that read JUSTIN. Six empty Mountain Dew cans. Three CD cases from groups he'd never heard of—no surprise there. He opened the CD cases. They were all empty. *I thought kids didn't use CDs anymore.* He glanced around for the silver discs and wondered if they might be in Justin's car . . . or loaned to friends.

He moved to the desk. Justin had a desktop computer with a big monitor. Mason looked back at the shelving near the TV. Yep, he thought he'd seen a laptop over there. An iPad lay on the floor next to the head of the bed. He would have let his son know what he thought of expensive electronics left on the floor, begging to be stepped on. An empty docking station perched on one end of the desk and Mason wondered where the boy's cell phone was. Justin hadn't had ID or a cell phone on him at the mall.

Probably all in his car.

He didn't touch the computer. He knew to leave it to the experts. Even simply unplugging it could mess up something. He moved over by Ray. "Find anything in the closet?"

Ray shook his head. "No weapons outside of those decorative swords on the wall. There's a hammer and a screwdriver in a shoe box on the floor in here. But it also has a level and tape measure. A mini-toolbox, I guess. Here's a score." Ray held out a plastic baggie holding about a quarter cup of what looked like dried parsley. "I found it in the inside pocket of the very last suit jacket."

Mason was more surprised by Justin's having a suit than by the sight of the pot. "He has more than one suit?"

"Four, actually. Probably hasn't worn them in a few years, judging by styles."

Mason wondered what Ray would say about Mason's ancient suits.

The two men stepped out of the closet and stood studying the room. They hadn't messed it up too bad if you didn't count the unfolded clothing in the drawers. "Did we miss anything?" Ray asked softly.

Mason stepped over to a poster of a dark-haired siren whom he recognized from one of the *Transformers* movies. He pulled out the lower thumbtacks and checked the wall behind the poster. "No escape routes."

A chorus of new voices in the house told him that the evidence team had arrived. The men turned the bedroom over to the team, and Ray filled out an envelope to catalog the marijuana. Mason's cell phone buzzed in his pocket and he looked at the screen. Zander Wells.

"Callahan."

"Wells here. I'm at the center with Ava, and we've been watching video of Justin Yoder. Can you ask the parents if they know if he was spending a lot of time at the mall in the weeks before the shooting? Maybe there're some items he purchased from the stores? If we could pinpoint a time frame of when he was previously here and what stores he'd shopped at that'd be a big help to hunting down some previous video."

"Will do." Mason turned his back to the other people in the bedroom. "How's Ava doing?" he asked in a quieter tone.

"Good. You'll be stunned when you watch the video. It was amazing to see her get that teen out of harm's way."

His stomach turned. "I don't know if I care to watch that," muttered Mason. He ended the call and asked the evidence team to keep an eye out for receipts from any stores at the Rivertown Mall, and then stepped out with Ray to talk to the parents again.

"Who are Justin's closest friends?" Mason asked Sally. "You mentioned he'll sleep over at someone's house. Can you give me some names and numbers if you have them?"

She agreed and pulled out her cell phone, skimming through contacts and writing down some names. "Have you found his phone?" her husband asked. "We tried using the locater app we have on our phones to find it last night. It's not connecting. It must be turned off."

"We put in a request to your wireless provider," Ray said. "I'll let you know what we find out."

"Did you find anything in his bedroom?" Sally asked, handing Mason a list of three names and numbers. The paper quivered in her hand.

"Nothing obvious," said Mason in a kind voice. "Looks just like my son's room when he's home from college."

She attempted a smile, and he saw she was on the verge of tears again.

"Do you know if Justin had done any shopping at the Rivertown Mall in the last week or so?" Mason asked. Both parents shook their heads.

"Did Justin know the shooter from the Eugene incident in June?" Ray asked.

Both parents froze. Eric started to speak, changed his mind, and shot a questioning look at Sally. The mother blinked at Ray.

"The shooting in June?" she repeated.

Mason held his breath.

Her head moved back and forth. "He never mentioned it. I followed it in the news, of course—I didn't recognize the name—but I never talked about it with Justin. Perhaps an 'Isn't that terrible?' type of comment or two with him." She looked at Eric, who was nodding.

"Same here. My immediate reaction was to say no, but I didn't know if he'd said anything to Sally about it." He pressed his lips together, scowling. "Wasn't he older than Justin?"

"Four years older," supplied Ray.

"We don't know anyone from that area," said Sally. "If Justin does . . . did . . . I didn't know about it." Her voice wavered.

Mason raised a brow at Ray. *Anything else?* A subtle shake of the head answered him. "We're going to head out. There will be at least one Washington County deputy in front of your house for the next few days to help with any crowd control—"

"Crowd control?" Eric grabbed at his wife's arm to steady her. "You think that's going to be necessary?"

"I hope not," Mason lied. "But if you need them, you'll be glad they're there. They can keep media away, too."

Mason took a breath and pushed out the words that'd been on his brain for the last half hour. "A word of advice from my experience in this sort of situation. Stay away from social media sites and reading any comments on news articles. This sort of thing brings out the trolls and haters posting bullshit, looking to stir up trouble. You won't find any information there that you can't get from us. You'll only find heartbreak and anger."

An awkward silence filled the room. He'd had to say it. They deserved to be warned.

"Call us if you think of anything else," he added, placing his cowboy hat back on his head. He touched the brim and nodded good-bye to the couple. Ray followed him out the door.

Mason welcomed the slap of heat on his back. The Yoder house air conditioning had been running at full blast. He was relieved to see no media vans or trucks on the street.

"They're holding back the name as long as they can," said Ray, looking down the quiet street. "This neighborhood is going to be in shock in a few hours."

Mason thought of Sally Yoder's fragile mask and the cracks that'd opened during the interview.

Losing her son was just the beginning.

11

"They found his car!"

Sergeant Shaver rose out of his chair at the officer's announcement and started to leave the video he'd been watching with Ava and Zander, but Zander stopped him. "I'd like to go."

Ava opened her mouth to chime in. And then closed it.

Not my case.

That's not going to stop me.

She knew how to make herself indispensable. Or invisible. Whichever was needed to get a look at Justin Yoder's vehicle. Shaver glanced at Zander and nodded. Ava said nothing, but she caught Shaver's gaze. She saw him take a quick look around the room and then give a tiny jerk of his head toward the door.

Yes!

The three of them rode in Shaver's car to a quiet neighborhood roughly a half mile from the mall. "They got the history of the weapon, too," said Shaver on the drive. "It was reported stolen two months ago."

"Two months?" Ava repeated. "Has he been planning this that long?" Her mind raced. So far every movement that had been made by Justin Yoder spoke of extensive planning.

"Who knows how long he's had the fantasy," answered Shaver.

"Where was the weapon stolen from?" asked Zander.

"A private party. The owner has an extensive weapons collection. All aboveboard according to my investigator who talked with him. He's not positive of the exact date when the weapon was stolen. He has a special locked room for them in his basement and returned from vacation to find his house broken into. Several items were missing, including three other weapons and some small electronics. According to my investigator, he could have lost a lot more, including several large flat-screen TVs. They theorized the crooks took what they could carry."

"If they were on vacation, the crooks could have come back and cleaned them out," commented Ava. "Where does he live?"

Shaver met her gaze in the rearview mirror. "Less than a mile from the Yoders."

"The other weapons haven't turned up?" asked Zander.

"Not yet. The burglary investigation went cold. No prints, no witnesses, no leads."

"Until now," said Ava. She looked out the window. It couldn't be a coincidence that Justin lived so close. "But that many missing items could indicate more than one thief. Has anyone talked to Justin's friends?"

"Not yet. We're putting together a short list based on his parents' suggestions and asking his boss who Justin hung out with at work."

So many threads to follow.

"Zander, the link to your international jewelry fence is looking weaker and weaker," Ava said. "I don't think they hire guys who work at Big John's to do their dirty work."

He turned in the front seat and gave her a wry grin. "Never say never. Until we have a motive for Justin I'm not ruling it out."

Her mind continued to race through possibilities. "What about the shooter in the Eugene incident in June? He was about Justin's age, right? Has that connection been explored?"

"That's been assigned to Callahan," answered Shaver. "He'll follow up on that lead."

Zander scowled. "That shooter was a bit older." Ava watched his fingers tap a rhythm on his thigh. "Were the weapons stolen before or after the shooting in Eugene?"

"Can't tell. The owners were gone for a week over the date of the June shooting. It could have happened right before or after, but the weapon in the Eugene shooting didn't belong to him. The leads on that weapon have gone cold."

"Dammit," muttered Ava. "I'd like to know what Justin was doing during the time of that shooting."

"We'll get there," Shaver promised.

The sergeant parked along the curb behind three Washington County sheriff's vehicles. Ava could see a small red car surrounded by evidence tape.

"How'd they find it?" Ava asked.

A few observers who looked as if they belonged in the small retirement neighborhood watched closely, whispering to each other behind their hands. "Someone called it in yesterday," said Shaver. "We didn't make the connection until we had Yoder identified and a description of his vehicle. Actually a half dozen residents called it in. I guess a strange car stands out here."

Ava wasn't surprised. The Fall Oaks community was a "fifty-five and better" neighborhood. A coworker had shared stories about her grandparents' move into the community. The couple had felt as if they were under a microscope. Neighbors commented on their visitors, complained about the new color they'd painted the front door (even after association approval), and discreetly moved landscaping rocks back to their original places after the couple had altered an arrangement . . . in their own yard.

They'd moved out after six months.

An unusual car parked overnight would have tongues wagging like crazy. She studied the small groups starting to gather. No media yet. Anyone with half a brain would put the large police presence around a strange car and the proximity to yesterday's shooting together. "Have they released Justin Yoder's name yet?" she asked Shaver in a quiet voice.

He grimaced. "Soon. There's a news conference in a few hours. We're trying to keep it quiet to give his parents a few hours to acclimate, but something tells me finding this car will get the word out early." Shaver showed his identification to a cop and pulled on a pair of gloves, handing a second pair to Zander. "Touch as little as possible. I want a preliminary look before they tow it away."

"It's unlocked?" Zander asked.

"Yep," said Shaver. "Lucky for us."

Ava shoved her hands in her pockets and tried to look invisible. Shaver hadn't offered her gloves—a clear message that she wasn't officially there. She saw a few cops give her curious looks. She was wearing shorts, a T-shirt, and flip-flops in deference to the predicted heat for the day. Nothing about her said "official."

The men each opened a front door, and Ava peeked over Zander's shoulder. He borrowed a flashlight from one of the patrolmen and quickly went through the glove box and looked under the seat. On the driver's side, Shaver did a similar quick search. They opened the rear doors and looked some more. Zander asked a patrolman to snap a picture of the mess in the backseat before he dug through it. Ava saw crumpled tissues, gas receipts, Mountain Dew cans, and a pair of tennis shoes.

Shaver popped the trunk and gestured for the same patrolman to take a few pictures. Inside was a duffel bag, a lacrosse stick, and a helmet and shoulder pads that she assumed went with the stick. The men rustled through a few empty paper bags and pushed aside two college textbooks. One for math and one for biology.

"Nothing obvious," Zander said to Shaver, who agreed. "Odd thing is that it was unlocked. Someone could have stolen his shoes and lacrosse gear. Apparently he didn't care."

"Who leaves their car unlocked in a strange neighborhood these days?" asked Ava. She looked around and noticed two women with white hair filming the search with their cell phones. "Even if the neighborhood seems safe."

Shaver slammed the trunk and said to Zander in a low voice, "You saw the empty prescription bottles?"

Zander nodded. "I counted six."

"Where?" asked Ava. "In one of the bags in the trunk?"

"Didn't want to give the neighbors anything to leak to the media," Shaver said with an answering nod. "We'll let them think nothing interesting came up in our search." He gestured to the patrolmen. "It's ready for the evidence team."

An increase in observer whispers made Ava look over her shoulder. A satellite truck with a news station number on the side had stopped down the street.

"Let's get out of here," said Shaver.

• • •

Ava grabbed a cup of iced coffee from the big dispenser at the back of the command center. The discovery of Justin Yoder's car had given everyone a bit of an energy boost, but now impatience set in as the car was being officially processed. It could be days before anything interesting came out of the forensic examination of the car. Lunchtime had come and gone hours ago. She'd had a few texts from Mason, who was with Justin Yoder's parents, but she really wanted to hear his voice. Across the room she saw Zander crook his finger at her.

Bless him for keeping me in the loop.

"I've been assigned to take another statement from Steve Jordan," he told her.

The name floated briefly in her brain and then dropped anchor. "The man who ran out of the mall bathroom with the child," she said. The boy's confused face was permanently imprinted on her brain, along with the father's expression when he realized he had to leave her and Misty behind. "I'd like to thank him for offering to help us. I didn't see him later that day."

"He went home. His son was in full meltdown mode. He gave an officer his name, number, and a brief statement. This will be his first in-depth interview." He indicated she should follow him. They walked down a short hallway to a small room. "Holding up okay?" he asked.

"Yes. The activity today has helped keep my mind off of things. If I was sitting at home, I'd be going nuts wondering what progress was being made."

"You're on vacation," Zander pointed out. "Why don't you go hiking or something?"

"Uh-huh." She shot him a sideways look. "That's exactly what I need to do. Give me something to do with my brain, please."

He pushed open a door and let her pass in front of him.

Steve Jordan turned around. He'd been studying a child's finger painting displayed on the wall. Apparently the room was used as a preschool art department of some sort. Steve looked from one of them to the other and his gaze homed in on Ava as his eyebrows rose. "*You* were there! Oh, thank God you're okay. What happened to the other girl? The one that was bleeding?"

"Misty is fine. She had surgery and is recovering."

Steve slumped down in a chair. "I told every police officer I saw about the two of you once I got Chase out of there. You don't know how shitty I felt about leaving you guys behind. I've been watching the news, and I knew one woman died, but they said she was shot in front of the theater, so I knew it couldn't be one of you. I prayed that you'd made it out okay." He rubbed a hand over his face. "And I'm not a guy who prays."

Ava was touched. "Thank you. I appreciate your concern." He looked like a middle-class dad in his early thirties who spent his weekends mowing the lawn and taking his son to the zoo. Cargo shorts, concert T-shirt, wavy dark hair in need of a cut. He hadn't shaved in a few days and had large bags under his eyes that Ava suspected were new for him.

The shooting had created hundreds, possibly thousands of victims. Victims who hadn't lost blood, but who had lost sleep and peace of mind. People who would forever look over their shoulders at loud noises in malls. Victims who would panic at the sounds of kids lighting fireworks in May. Employees who would study every shopper with an oblong package. People who would never lose the tension in their shoulders while in public places.

Then it would extend to their families and friends who had to cope with the anxiety and odd behaviors.

"How is your son? You said his name is Chase?" Ava asked.

He gave a weak smile. "He's good. He hasn't mentioned the man in the mask or the loud gunshots. But I haven't taken him anywhere in public. I felt like we needed to stick closer to home for a while. I wonder if he'll have flashbacks if we enter an unfamiliar bathroom."

"Maybe you should let more time pass before testing his reactions." Ava completely understood.

"I was supposed to grocery-shop this morning, and I spent an hour stressing about taking him out of the house." Steve leaned forward, his elbows on his thighs and his hands clenched together. "I finally decided to take him to my mother's. She lives forty-five minutes away, but the peace of mind was worth it, knowing he was with her in a place that's as familiar as his own home. She lives in a rural area." He gave a harsh laugh. "And then I couldn't relax in the grocery store. I looked around every sixty seconds and forgot half the things on my list."

Victims.

"You're married, Mr. Jordan?" Zander asked.

"My wife works. I stay home with our son. Best fucking job I've ever had." He paused. "Until yesterday."

Zander and Ava took seats at the table across from the father. Steve studied her and then looked at Zander and then back at her again. "You're with the police." It wasn't a question.

"I'm a special agent with the FBI," Ava said. "I was simply passing through the mall that morning, just like you." She gestured at Zander. "I asked Special Agent Wells to let me thank you for your offer of help; it meant a lot to both of us. I could tell it wasn't easy for you, but your son needed you, and there was nothing you could have done."

His shoulders deflated. "I could have set him down and helped you with the other woman. You don't know how many times I've thought back and wanted to do the right thing."

"That would have been unfair. Chase needed you to get him out. Misty and I would have slowed you down considerably. That wouldn't have been worth the risk."

Steve gave a shuddering sigh and turned his gaze away. "If something had happened to one of you, I don't know how I would have handled it."

"And if something had happened to your son if you'd stopped?" Ava asked.

His gaze shot back to hers; his chin came up. "I'd be in hell."

"Don't play that game with yourself," she emphasized. "It's over. You made the right decision and everything worked out. Don't waste your time worrying about something that didn't happen."

"What were you doing at the mall that early?" Zander asked, subtly shifting the subject.

"I'd taken Chase to play on the little playground. And there's a good water fountain for kids at the other end of the mall. I try to get him out of the house to burn off some energy every day during the summer before it gets too hot." He grimaced. "He's up by six A.M. and full of energy. Our days start early."

"And you were using the restroom when the shooter entered?"

"I was washing my hands and Chase's at the time. I remember he calmly walked in the door, and I glanced up to acknowledge him and did a double take."

"What did he do?"

Steve closed his eyes, his palms flat on the table in front of him. "He swung the gun directly at us and stopped next to the first sink. I swear he was startled to find us in there because he seemed to hesitate. Then he yelled for us to get out. He fired his weapon into the ceiling. Chase started to cry. I grabbed him up, and the shooter stepped to the side and gestured with his weapon for us to move past him to the door." He opened his eyes, and Ava realized he had tears running down his cheeks. "I thought we were dead. All I could think about was holding Chase as tight as possible to me, that maybe my body would block most of the bullets and he'd survive."

Ava's stomach tightened into a hard mass.

"I ran. But when I saw the hurt woman with you"—he nodded at Ava—"I had to stop. But she couldn't walk, right? She couldn't move?" His eyes pleaded with Ava.

"She couldn't put any weight on that leg. Even when I bumped it, she'd nearly pass out," Ava assured him.

"I couldn't carry her. I might have been able to help you get her upright and between us . . . and maybe we could have—"

"No," said Ava. "It wouldn't have worked."

He swallowed audibly. "So I ran with my son."

"Was there anyone else in the bathroom?" Zander asked. Ava thought the agent affected the perfect amount of concern in his tone. He skillfully kept the witness on task and focused.

Steve nodded. "An older guy came in and went in one of the stalls. He was still in there when I left. I briefly spotted him in the police area afterward and was relieved that the shooter had let him out."

"Anyone else? What about in the back half of the restroom?"

"I don't know. I didn't hear anything, but I wasn't paying attention. I had the impression we were the only ones when Chase and I first entered, but I didn't walk to the back part and look. Plus Chase was singing so loud when we first went in—and it echoed like crazy. I remember thinking we were clearly announcing ourselves to anyone else in there."

"Any other impressions of the shooter that you could share with us?" Zander asked. "You mentioned he seemed startled that someone else was in the restroom. Do you remember getting any other emotions from him?"

Steve's forehead wrinkled. "I'm not sure what you mean. Like did I think he was upset and about to shoot himself?" He looked from Zander to Ava, a touch of sarcasm entering his gaze. "I thought he was going to kill me. He fired a gun in a small enclosed space and yelled at my son and I didn't take the time to wonder if he was depressed or suicidal." The sarcasm evaporated, leaving anger seething in his dark eyes.

An ache shot through her heart for the man. *How damaged is he? Will his son be all right?*

Zander studied him and then pulled a business card out of his folder. He wrote something on the back and slid it across the table. "That's my card. Email or call me if something occurs to you that you'd like to share." He paused. "There's the name of an excellent mental health group on the back."

"I don't—"

Zander held up his hand to silence Steve. "Hear me out." He leaned forward, holding Steve's gaze. "You've been through a traumatic experience and people who go through that shit can easily end up with post-traumatic stress disorder. You don't have to be in a war to become a victim. *For your son*, you need to take steps so it doesn't manifest in your home. It can sneak up on you and most of the time you can't see it until it's ripped a big hole in your life." His voice quieted. "This group knows their stuff. You got health insurance?"

Steve nodded.

"Then go. Don't do it for you, do it for your wife and kid. Catch it early or get a clean bill of health. Can you do that?"

The father picked up the card and read the back. He lifted his gaze to Ava and then met Zander's.

"Yeah, I can do that." He tapped the card on the table. "Thank you," he whispered.

12

"Only old people eat this early," Mason stated, tossing the menu to the side.

"I don't let stereotypes affect my hunger," answered Ava, biting back a grin. "You know as well as I do to eat when you can when a case is heating up. And I'm starving."

She'd asked him to meet her at a restaurant on the edge of downtown Portland, where the foot traffic morphed from people in business suits to tourists in shorts. The pub offered a nice outdoor seating area with a great view for people watching. It was a bit out of his way, but they both knew the service was fast and the place was quiet. There were two other tables of diners, and the quiet created an insulated pocket of peace from the intensity of the investigation.

Taking time to connect was priority number one for their relationship. Their careers could easily swamp their lives, squeezing aside precious minutes spent with one another. She'd seen too many law enforcement relationships in which the marriage came second to the career. No marriage yet . . . but maybe someday. Mason had already walked the marriage path, and they were both stepping cautiously with this relationship. Nothing was hurried.

"How'd it go at the Yoders'?" She'd reviewed the entire menu even though she knew it by heart and always ordered the same Asian salad. She knew Mason would get the burger with the jalapenos and not touch his fries.

Are we in a rut?

Nothing wrong with routine and knowing what you enjoy.

She listened to his description of Justin's home, interjecting occasionally with a question.

"I can't get a feel for this kid yet," Mason said, his eyebrows coming together. "Usually by now I have a picture with lots of pieces. So far all I can see is a typical twenty-year-old who doesn't know what to do with himself and isn't getting much guidance from his parents. They seem to let him float along, doing as he pleases."

"What about his history of depression? They got him help for that."

"Yes, but I wonder if they were scared to push him into more independence. It really was odd over there. It was like he was sixteen, not twenty. When I was twenty, I'd been out of the house for two years. I studied hard in college, worked a part-time job, and got an apartment with friends. We were lucky that one of us had an old TV, otherwise we wouldn't have had one. Kids today believe they *must have* every piece of updated electronics."

"Careful, your old man is showing," she teased. "Next you'll be telling me you didn't get a new car for high-school graduation."

He snorted. The waiter took their orders and left them with a basket of dark warm bread. Ava tore off a piece, slathered it with butter, popped it in her mouth, and sighed, closing her eyes in bliss at the happy sparks emanating from her tongue. She opened her eyes to find him grinning at her.

"What?"

"You look happy. That makes me smile. I didn't know someone could enjoy bread so much." His brown gaze held hers, and she wished she weren't heading home alone after their meal.

"I told you I was hungry. So Justin's room turned up nothing? His car looked pretty clean, although we did find some of his prescription bottles in the trunk. It was the same medication his mother showed you."

"Who keeps old pill bottles? Most people throw them out once they've picked up the refill."

"Maybe the evidence teams will find something more interesting in his car or the home. Is his psychiatrist next on your list?"

Mason swallowed his mouthful of bread. "I hope so. Ray's contacting him because we want to talk to him tonight. Was Zander still at the command center?"

"Yes. Although the connection to his jewelry fence is looking weaker and weaker. Justin Yoder doesn't seem like the type to get involved in millions of dollars of stolen gems."

"Agreed. The kid collected Marvel action figures and had a weakness for Mountain Dew. Doesn't say international assassin to me."

A group of people strolled by their outdoor table, and Ava fought the urge to hide as her gaze locked on a slim platinum-blond woman dressed in too-short shorts.

Jayne?

The woman laughed in the center of the group; her head turned and Ava caught a clear view of her profile. *Not Jayne.*

"Jesus Christ," said Mason. "What was that?" He studied her, his brow wrinkled. "You looked like you were about to dive under the table." He turned to follow her gaze, and watched the group continue down the sidewalk. "Oh." He looked back at her. "It was the blonde, wasn't it?"

Ava gave a shaky nod.

"What went through your head?" His expression showed nothing but concern.

"I wanted to hide," she said, her heart still pounding. "I didn't want her to see me or see us or stop to talk to us." She briefly covered her eyes. "Oh, my God, how wrong is that?"

"Not wrong at all. I'm pretty certain you prefer your calm life instead of the spinning mess that Jayne creates. I don't think your reaction was overboard."

Ava took a long drink of her ice water and set it down. "You don't know the jolt it sent through my system." Her limbs still tingled.

"I saw it clear as day on your face." He scowled at her. "Stop beating yourself up about it. You haven't seen her in months. And the last time you did see her, she wasn't fit for human companionship."

"I'm sorry," she muttered. The waiter brought their food and she took a few bites of her salad, not tasting it.

"Screw this." Mason set down his knife and looked at her earnestly. "I thought you'd learned not to let her affect you. We've got a good chance for a nice meal here. I don't want Jayne McLane messing with my burger."

He was absolutely right. She shook her head at him. "It snuck up on me. I talked to her on the phone this morning, and she sounded great."

His brow rose and he popped a piece of bread in his mouth.

"I know it's temporary. But I do like to talk with her when she's normal."

"You miss her."

She sucked in a breath. "I miss the normal Jayne, but normal has always come with a large piece of crazy. I don't think there's been a time in our lives when she's been one hundred percent normal."

"What was your mother like?" Mason carefully buttered another piece of bread.

His casualness didn't fool her. *Was your mother mentally ill, too?* "Other than two years of hell with her ovarian cancer at the end of her life, she wasn't like Jayne. Ever."

"And you never knew your father."

"Right."

"You've looked." It wasn't a question.

"I did after my mother died. I suspect she didn't give us accurate information about his name and where he lived. The question is, was that deliberate or an accident? Maybe he was never honest with her." It wasn't a new discussion for her and Mason. They'd skirted around her family history a few times. Her past was like a partially healed scar. It'd been ripped open too many times, and she'd discovered the only way to let it mend was to completely avoid it. Mason had pressed her a few times about her parents, and she'd been brief. If she dug too much, the scar might tear wide open.

"I miss my mother," she said softly. "She was a hardworking woman who never gave up. She knew Jayne wasn't right in the head, but she didn't believe in coddling her . . . or giving her special treatment when she was younger. She set expectations and we were to meet them. If we didn't, there were consequences."

"Sounds like my kind of woman."

"She would have liked you," Ava said. "She didn't take crap from anyone . . . including Jayne."

"Smart."

"I rarely saw a soft side of her." A small pain started at the site of the scar. "Her chin was always up. Looking back, I think she had to fight for everything. Her job, her independence, us."

"She raised you well."

Ava looked out the window. The passing group was long gone. Her emotions had been triggered as if by a ball in a pinball machine. It bounced off raw grief, anger, tenderness, and guilt. This was why she didn't like talking about her family: it was exhausting.

"Someday we'll look for your father."

The pinball vanished as all her emotions dried up. Her father was an empty dry well in her brain. A place she avoided. She didn't know how to feel toward a man she'd never met, so she didn't dwell on it. There was no point. How could she be angry at or disappointed in someone she knew nothing about?

Does he know Jayne and I exist?

The question was like a tiny rock dropped into the well. It hit the dusty dirt at the bottom and then . . . nothing.

"We'll see," she answered noncommittally. She didn't know if she wanted to explore that pit of nothingness. Some things were best left alone. They spent a few minutes eating in comforting silence. There was no need to fill the air with useless conversation. She and Mason were both fans of avoiding empty conversations; they didn't waste effort or breath on small talk.

His phone buzzed, and he reluctantly looked at it. Usually they had a no-phones rule during meals, but with the urgency of this case, it was suspended. "Text from Ray. Address of the psychiatrist. We're to meet with him in an hour." He took a large bite of burger. "Plenty of time to eat and get over there." He set the phone back on the table, facedown. "Let's pretend for a few more minutes that no one died yesterday, and you had an uneventful morning at yoga."

"Agreed." She smiled at him and welcomed the peace that enveloped her. It'd been that way from the first moment they met. When they were together, the air around them settled into a relaxing harmony. It was rare and precious, and something she wanted for the rest of her life.

13

Dr. Colum Beck's office was in a small office building that'd seen better days. From the odd architecture, Mason guessed it'd been built in the late seventies. It was all angles and round windows. He and Ray bypassed the elevator and took the wide staircase three stories to the top floor. According to the directory in the small lobby, it housed several doctors' offices, an architect's, an accountant's, and a remodeling agency. The building smelled like old dust. Poor insulation or design allowed the roar of the traffic on the highway out front to echo through the building. Dr. Beck's name was on a plastic placard on the wall next to a glass door that Ray pulled open. Mason noticed he specialized in "psychiatry for children and young adults."

The waiting room was empty. A tiny sign next to the inside door asked them to "press button and have a seat." Ray pressed. Neither of them sat.

There was no television or music piped into the room and it felt ominously closed in to Mason. He wasn't claustrophobic, but the silence and still air made the hairs on the back of his neck itch.

Ray picked up a magazine. This waiting room didn't offer the usual magazines of gossip, sports, and home decor. Instead they were a mishmash of unfamiliar journals that appeared to be targeted to children and teens. The inner door opened and Dr. Beck stepped into the waiting room. He introduced himself and shook hands. He looked like an athlete, not a psychiatrist, and reminded Mason of the group of younger guys at his gym who played basketball every day. He was tall and lean with biceps that bulged out from under his short-sleeved shirt. Mason already knew he was thirty-six and had been practicing for eight years. Mason liked him immediately and bet that the doctor's young patients did, too.

"Please take a seat in here." Dr. Beck gestured them into his office and Mason felt as if he'd stepped out of a closet into a sunny day. The office was bright and open and had huge windows. The view was of the highway, but now Mason couldn't hear the cars.

"Nice office," said Ray. He sounded as stunned as Mason felt.

Dr. Beck grinned. "I know that waiting room is a bit glum. I felt this space made up for it when I was looking for a place to set up shop."

"You heard about Justin Yoder." Mason didn't want to waste any time.

The doctor's face sobered instantly. "I did. I was crushed. It's not the first time I've had a patient pass, but it's certainly the most violent."

"Justin's parents gave you permission to speak with us?" Ray confirmed.

"Yes, I don't see any issues. I'll try to tell you whatever you need."

"Did this incident surprise you?" Mason asked.

"Absolutely. I'd never have guessed Justin would have shot those people and then himself. But there's a lot of things about the workings of the human mind that we don't understand."

"When did you last meet with him?"

A shadow crossed his face. "Today would have been his standing appointment. So it's been two weeks."

"Did anything seem different at that last appointment?"

"I reviewed my session notes. Nothing odd had jumped out at me then."

"You record all sessions, correct?"

"Yes, I didn't review the recordings yet, just my notes."

"Tell us how Justin came to be your patient, Doctor. How long has it been?" Mason knew the parents' answers to these questions. Now it was time for the doctor's.

Dr. Beck leaned forward over his desk and propped his chin on one hand. It made him look extremely young. "I've been working with Justin since he was sixteen. He originally came to me through a referral from his medical insurance company, I believe. His parents were very concerned with his attitude and physical well-being. According to them, in a matter of months he'd gone from being a three-sport athlete with solid grades to sleeping nonstop and letting school and sports slide away."

"Teens sleep a lot," said Mason, thinking of weekends he'd spent with Jake. Sometimes he'd been annoyed that his son had slept away three-quarters of his visitation time.

"They do. And they're supposed to. But not nonstop and not to the detriment of themselves and the people around them."

"You diagnosed him with depression?" Ray asked.

"He was a textbook case."

"What triggered it?"

"Someone doesn't need an inciting incident to have depression. Sometimes the chemicals in their brains simply aren't acting the way they should. It's tricky in kids and teens. Their bodies are growing and constantly changing. Sometimes the chemical balance gets off and it takes time to get it back in sync."

Jayne danced through Mason's mind. Ava had once told him that she'd changed significantly around puberty. "Sometimes they don't ever get back in balance."

Dr. Beck met his gaze. "That is correct. For some it's a lifetime of management. For others it's temporary."

"What sort of things would Justin tell you?"

"What do you mean?" The doctor looked at him calmly. Mason didn't get the feeling he was trying to be difficult, but after four years of therapy he imagined they'd talked about everything under the sun.

"What was on his mind? I mean . . . did he struggle with girls? His parents? His job? If I asked you what he hated most about his life, what would it be?"

Dr. Beck leaned back in his chair, his expression turning thoughtful. "Priorities change from age sixteen to twenty."

"No doubt," said Mason.

"But the only constant struggle I'd say was his relationship with his stepfather."

"You mean his father. Eric Yoder adopted him, correct?"

"Yes, that's true," agreed Dr. Beck. "But Justin always called him his stepfather. He had a lot of questions about his biological father, and I know he tried to find him at one point, but he didn't get any support from his mother . . . or stepfather. They both told him his father wasn't worth looking up. Even for his medical history."

"You'd wondered if his biological father had a history of depression?" Ray asked.

"Of course. I was curious. It'd be nice to know if it was something his biological father battled all his life or if it never touched him at all. Of course, everyone will encounter depression at one point or another in their life."

"Back to Eric Yoder," Mason stated. "I had the impression from the parents that the relationship was . . . normal. If there is such a thing between a father and teenager."

"I've talked with Eric and Sally several times over the years," said Dr. Beck. "More at the beginning of the therapy. I guess I haven't actually seen either one of them in at least a year. I'd agree that their relationship seems quite normal, but from Justin's point of view, Eric has never supported him or showed him affection or bonded with him."

Mason waited a few beats. Then he asked, "Is that true?"

"I don't know. When I met with the parents they appeared supportive, but when I talk with Justin, I hear a different story."

"But shooting up a mall isn't 'I don't get along with my stepfather' anger," said Ray.

"Absolutely not," agreed Dr. Beck.

"It's 'I hate the world'–type anger," said Mason.

Dr. Beck looked at him thoughtfully. "I don't know if it's classifiable. I never saw that sort of anger in Justin. He was more of the type of person who closed in on himself, hesitant to leave the house or talk to people. Once we got him on medication, he seemed to become the teen his parents remembered. But it took constant monitoring. What worked well for him one month, six months later was suddenly ineffective."

"Did you ever see him have a bad episode?" Mason asked.

"A bad episode? You mean like ready to rage against the world? Shoot people?"

Mason could hear the sarcasm. He didn't know the right terminology, but Dr. Beck knew exactly what he meant. He waited.

"When I was first put in touch with Justin, we—meaning his parents and I—agreed he needed to go away for a bit. He spent two weeks in a facility at the coast that treats teens and adults for depression or addiction. Justin wasn't battling addiction, I simply felt he needed a change of scenery. He seemed extremely overwhelmed by life, and I wanted to get him into a brand-new environment where I could talk with him and monitor his medication."

"Is that normal treatment?" Ray asked.

He shrugged. "What's normal? I have to look at every case with fresh eyes and suggest what I think will work. Justin was unable to function around his parents and house. A different set of stimuli seemed a good idea to try."

"Sounds expensive," commented Mason. *A clinic for two weeks? Probably cost more than an NYC hotel. A luxurious one.*

"It was. But his mother told me it was one of the best decisions they ever made."

"Did he ever go back to the clinic?" asked Ray.

"No. He responded very well to medication after that. We had to make adjustments from time to time, but overall it was smooth."

"Then why has he been seeing you for four years if everything is so good?" asked Mason.

Dr. Beck smiled. "I'm not soaking him for the money. We've discussed cutting back his therapy several times, but I've left the primary decision up to Justin and his parents. I've told Sally several times he doesn't need to come in so often. But Justin likes it and feels he benefits from it. So it goes on."

An odd prickle made the hairs rise on the back of Mason's neck.

Dr. Beck's eyes lit up and he laughed. "Detective, you should see the look on your face. No, there's nothing sexual or predatory about our visits. It's all clean."

Mason's face flushed, and Ray shifted in his seat as he said, "Maybe Justin thought differently."

"Girls were a big topic of ours. Justin was a perfectly normal male when it came to thinking about sex and girls every ten minutes."

"Dr. Beck." Mason paused to get his thoughts in order. "I can guarantee no teen talks to their parents in depth every other week for a solid hour. It sounds like no one knew him better than you. What is your answer to why he committed suicide in such a violent way?"

The doctor straightened in his chair and looked right at Mason. "I have no idea."

14

Mason surveyed the park. Fire trucks and police cars crowded every inch of the street around the grassy area in Troutdale.

"What the fuck is happening?" asked Ray.

"Wish I knew," answered Mason, slamming the door to his vehicle. The ambulances had left. Five bodies remained behind, screened from the mass of onlookers and TV news cameras.

It'd happened again. Another morning mass shooting. This time in a popular lake park at six A.M. Again the shooter was reported to be a young man who'd taken his own life in the public restrooms.

"If I was a parent with small children, I'd never leave the house," said Mason.

"My kids aren't small, but I'm sure considering it," replied Ray. "This is bullshit."

Mason looked sideways at his partner, and noticed the slight tremor in Ray's hands as he made a notation on his pad of paper. Sometimes fatherhood sucked. A person became a parent, assuming they could teach their kids how to be good members of society and stay out of trouble. But what did one do when trouble struck out of nowhere in locations that were assumed to be safe? The three shootings this summer had sent a shock down every parent's backbone. How could they protect their children?

"We don't live in a third-world country," Ray muttered. "This isn't supposed to happen here."

Mason stared at the line of swings and curving slides. "Damn right."

The children's play area was set under big firs at one end of the man-made lake. A sandy beach sloped down to clear water where a small section of the lake was cordoned off for children. Mason recalled bringing Jake here when he was about three. The water in that area wasn't deeper than twelve inches. Beyond that was a larger area that was marked by buoys for regular swimmers. Far across the lake he could see the place that rented small paddle boats and canoes. Good circulation and regular maintenance kept the lake clean and bacteria-free. It was almost like a giant pool.

"I've brought my kids here," said Ray. "It's absolutely packed during the summer. We're lucky it happened so early in the day."

Or was that a careful decision made by the killer?

"They have to all be related," mumbled Mason.

Ray shook his head. "All three of the shooters are dead. Unless they had some sort of suicide pact that we haven't discovered yet, I don't see it. I think they've been copycats."

"No one had considered that they were tied together until this morning," said Mason. "The first two were far enough apart in time and distance that we made the stupid mistake of assuming they were separate incidents. We're going to have to look at everything again."

Ray pointed at a news van. "That's our problem right there. These shooters are getting glamorized on television and all across social media. It's putting the idea in the minds of others whose brains aren't working quite right. For some reason they want the same attention and that's what's driving this. I swear these types of shootings happen in groups."

Mason knew Ray had a point, but he was still going to push to find a relationship among the three shooters. "We'll consider everything."

"Of course."

They signed in and headed toward the restrooms. Troutdale fell under Multnomah County's jurisdiction. Each shooting had occurred in a different county, and the Oregon State Police hadn't become involved until the Rivertown Mall shooting. With the cities, the counties, the state, and the FBI's interest in the Rivertown shooting, there were a lot of cooks in the kitchen.

"Crowded," mumbled Ray, and Mason knew he wasn't referring to the park. Ray's brain was traveling the same path as Mason's.

"We'll make it work. We got everything centralized with the Rivertown incident. We'll convince Multnomah County that we've got a good system going and ask them to join. We'll dangle the FBI's hardware and assistance in front of them. That'll make everyone play nicely together."

"Depends."

"Yep." Mason knew he was referring to egos. They rarely encountered a situation in which a smaller department didn't appreciate OSP's or the FBI's man power, but it was known to happen.

"There's Rutledge," said Ray, raising a hand at the medical examiner, who was headed in the same direction.

"Just getting here," Dr. Seth Rutledge said after a quick greeting. He shook his head. "I don't know what's happening to our state."

They continued toward the restrooms. "Who's the incident commander?" Ray asked one cop who blocked their path as they drew closer.

The cop looked at their IDs and waved a hand toward the rustic-looking bathrooms. "Chief Deputy Arnold Bishop. He's inside."

"Where are you doing your interviews?" asked Mason.

"Local church. It's a block that way." The officer pointed again.

The three men stopped outside the bathroom. The rustic look was a facade. Mason saw the restroom was a solidly built structure with clean concrete flooring. They stopped to slip on booties and two cops came out. One had a green tinge to his face as the other slapped him on the shoulder. The second cop looked amused at his friend's nausea, but Mason saw the pain flash in his eyes and knew the amusement was forced.

The scene in the restroom must be bad.

They stepped inside, the odor of copper touched his nose, and he swallowed hard. They followed a hall for ten feet and then it opened up into a wide room with sinks and urinals. Three people looked their way as they entered; the fourth person stretched out on the floor didn't move.

Black clothing—again. Full face mask—again. AR-15—again.

And blood and brain matter sprayed all over one wall.

Chief Deputy Bishop introduced himself. The two crime scene techs went back to work after a brief nod at the newcomers. Dr. Rutledge squatted next to the body and gently opened the mouth to shine his flashlight in the dark cavity.

Mason looked away. "What's the story?"

Bishop hiked up his jeans with a thumb in his belt loop. He looked to be pushing sixty, but his eyes were sharp as he scanned the two OSP detectives up and down. "You two work with Denny Schefte?" he asked, referring to their supervisor.

Mason nodded.

"I've known Denny for years. Our wives go way back." He turned to the body. "Don't know who he is yet. But the story from the witnesses who were in the area say they saw him walk around the lake from the boating side. Once he got close enough he simply raised his gun and started shooting. One guy said it was like he was calmly shooting at targets."

"Christ," breathed Ray.

Bishop nodded. "We're just glad there weren't any kids here. That hour of the day had early birds out for walks or exercisers."

"Are the victims identified yet?"

"We think so. Three of the four had identification on them. The fourth was identified by the women she was walking with. Three men, one woman. Talk about being in the wrong place at the wrong time."

"How many witnesses?" asked Mason.

Bishop grimaced. "Eight have come forward. Three women from the walking group and five others who were at the park when he started shooting. But according to these eight, there were more people here than that. So some took off. I'm hoping they come back."

"No cameras?" Ray asked.

"None. We're canvassing the nearby homes to ask about security systems to see if they caught anything."

"What about on the side with the rentals? Don't they have cameras to watch their gear?" Mason asked.

"Nope. They padlock everything into sheds at night. We're searching that side, trying to figure out where he came from." He looked down at the body. "I took a look under his mask. Looks about the same age as the one who shot up the mall the other day. What the hell is wrong with kids these days?" He shook his head.

"We want to look at the three shootings as a whole," said Mason delicately. "There could be a history between these three young men. The FBI was looking at the Rivertown case with us, and I think we need to loop them in on this one to try to see the big picture."

Bishop gave him a sour look. "I'm not an asshole who's going to turn down federal or state help. Clearly something is messing with these kids' heads. We'll take all the help we can get. Something needs to be done to figure out how to stop this from happening. We'll do whatever you need."

Dr. Rutledge stood up.

"Whatcha got, Doc?" Ray asked.

"I've got nothing new," Dr. Rutledge said shortly. "He did exactly what the last shooter did. Placed his rifle in his mouth and fired. You already know the time and manner of death. Once he's on my table I can run the tox screens and see if he had anything chemical in his system and look for something to help get him identified." His gloves snapped as he yanked them off. "I can tell you I'm sick of this sort of case. If you'll excuse me, I've got four victims to examine and confirm that they were shot to death." He nodded at the investigators and stalked out of the bathroom.

"I don't blame him," said Ray. "Frankly I don't know how he does that job."

"He probably says the same thing about us," Mason added.

Bishop sighed. "If he's tired of seeing dead people, he's in the wrong business."

"I don't think it's the dead people. I think it's the murdered ones," corrected Mason.

"We could all do with a lot less of that," agreed Bishop. "But what has kept me going all these years is my thirst to hunt down every bastard who does shit like this." He eyed the black figure on the floor. "When the perpetrators are handed to you on a silver platter, it loses some satisfaction. There's no reward in this one. All that's left is to find his family and ruin their day."

"And four other families' day," added Ray.

Mason stepped closer and bent over, eyeing the label on the shooter's lightweight jacket. "There might be more to these shootings than there first appears." He pointed at the small white swoosh. "Our last shooter wore the same jacket. Let's find out what the guy in the June shooting in Eugene wore."

15

Ava wondered how Mason's morning was going. He'd left very early, whispering to her that there'd been a shooting and that he'd call later. After she got up, she'd watched the early news reports of the shooting and caught a glimpse of Dr. Seth Rutledge over the shoulder of a reporter's "breaking news" announcement at a park east of Portland.

Four dead. Plus the shooter.

She realized Mason's callout had been for another mass shooting, similar to hers two days ago. Had he known and purposefully not told her? Or had he been told only that there'd been a shooting?

Zander called minutes later. She begged to accompany him when he told her he had an interview with Justin Yoder's best friend. "I'm good with young people," she argued. "If I wasn't on vacation, I'd probably be going with you anyway."

"Do you not get the concept of vacation?" he asked. "It means *no work*."

He gave in. She dashed out of her house as he turned into her driveway. "Do you think it's related?" she asked him, craving information. If she'd been officially working the case, her email inbox would have been full. Instead she had to ask questions to get caught up.

Zander's eyes didn't leave the road. "Don't know yet. Copycat would be my guess. Someone wasn't brave enough to try a public mall. They went for a park where they could be almost certain no cameras would be around."

She suspected he'd wanted her to go along and that had been the reason behind the early phone call. She didn't know if he hadn't been able to find anyone else to go with him or if he wanted her insight into the case. Didn't matter. She was here now.

She glanced at the printout he'd given her on Justin's friend. Cole Hooper was twenty and had gone to school with Justin Yoder since the seventh grade. Cole lived in an apartment downtown, not far from Portland State University, where he studied business. Currently on summer break, he waited tables at two Portland restaurants.

"Two jobs," Ava commented. "He has a little more drive than Justin did. And it looks like he expects to graduate on time."

"I had two jobs at the same time during college," said Zander.

"I had at least that. And I sent money home. Ugh. He's got three male roommates. I can tell you right now his apartment is a sty."

"If he and Justin were such good friends, why wasn't Justin living there?" Zander asked.

"He wasn't in school. Makes perfect sense to me. Looks like these other guys are students."

"It does work better if everyone is on the same page," agreed Zander. "Hard for students to live with nonstudents. It would have driven me crazy to be studying hard and living with someone who slept all day."

"Uh-huh," Ava agreed, thinking of the short period of time in college when Jayne had lived with her. Jayne hadn't been in school and had worked when she pleased. She'd gone out every night and pleaded with Ava to come, ignoring her excuses about homework. The arrangement hadn't lasted.

Zander circled the quiet block, searching for elusive street parking outside the brick apartment buildings. Ava studied the architecture, not knowing the name for the style. Old. Slightly crumbling red brick. White curly trim that needed paint. She had a strong hunch the rooms inside would be small and the hallways narrow. College students had probably lived in the buildings for the last fifty years. Zander found a spot and they walked two blocks back to the address. The glass was broken out of the security door to the lobby of the building, but it was still locked. Zander carefully reached through the sharp glass edges and opened the door. The lobby was dark and the elevator was out of order.

"Christ," muttered Zander. "At least we're only going to the third floor."

"That's got to be some sort of code violation," said Ava. "I wonder how long it hasn't worked."

They found the apartment and knocked. And waited. Zander knocked again. Ava watched the peephole darken briefly and then listened as three locks clicked. A tall, impossibly skinny male with bedhead opened the door. "Sorry," Cole apologized after introducing himself. "I overslept. I worked really late last night." He yawned, and Ava wanted to suggest he brush his teeth. Cole gestured for them to follow him and led them to a living area crammed with three Goodwill couches and a huge flat-screen TV.

It smelled like stale beer.

He pointed to one of the couches. "I'll be right back." Cole vanished down a hallway.

Ava carefully sat and after a moment Zander sat next to her. "I remember this," he said with a big grin. "I loved living with roommates in college. We didn't care how we lived; the best part was the independence. The worst part was dealing with lazy roommates. No one wanted to scrub the toilet or clean up after themselves in the kitchen. I remember some really nasty toilets."

Ava's bladder reminded her of the coffee she'd just drunk. *Hell no.*

Cole reappeared, his hair damp and flattened. He'd changed his T-shirt to a slightly less wrinkled one.

"Is this a good time?" Ava asked. "Where are your roommates?"

"One is sleeping, the others are at work. We're good," he said. "I need to start a pot of coffee. Would you like some?"

Both agents declined and Cole moved into the kitchen, talking to them over the breakfast bar. "I can't function until I get some caffeine. I haven't slept well since Justin died." His voice quivered the smallest bit on the name.

"When did you see him last?" Ava asked.

Cole poured water into the top of the coffee maker. "Uh, let's see . . . it was on a Saturday. Not this past one . . . the one before. We met up at a sports bar down by the river that night."

Zander made a note. Ava met his gaze and took it as permission to continue with her questions.

"Did you get together very often?" she asked.

"About once a month. Maybe more during the summer."

"Did anything about him seem off to you? Or was he the same Justin you've always known?"

Cole scowled and focused on scooping coffee into the filter. "There's no easy answer to that. Justin's always been a changing type of guy."

"What do you mean?"

He shoved the pot into the machine and hit a button. He leaned on his hands on the counter and studied the machine for a few seconds until it started to rumble and release coffee. "I mean, of course he's not the same guy I've known since we were twelve. Or age fourteen, or sixteen, or eighteen." He looked across the counter at Ava and Mason. "Yes, he's always been my friend, but I never know what his interests are going to be. One year it's sports; the next year he hates sports, and he goes all out taking acting classes and auditioning for parts. He went goth for a while, convinced he'd be in a band, but then he discovered skateboarding, and I swear he slept with his board for six months. Then one day he didn't want anything more to do with it. You see?"

Ava did. And it sounded hauntingly reminiscent of her twin.

"What was he into recently?" Zander asked.

Cole looked longingly at the pot but left the kitchen and perched on a stool in front of the breakfast bar. He slouched and ran a hand through his hair. "His job, I guess. Kept saying he was going to work his way up to management and then he'd make a ton of money."

"You don't sound convinced," Ava commented.

"I wasn't. I felt like he only said it because he felt he was slipping behind by not going to school. He sees us studying nonstop and taking classes and feels left out. I hope to get a decent job one day, but my degree won't guarantee that. Takes hard work and a bit of luck, I think. But my dad always said the degree was important to have anyway. It'd give me an advantage against other applicants without one in most positions." He looked earnestly at Ava and Zander, seeking agreement.

They both nodded. "Some places won't even look at a résumé unless you have a bachelor's degree," said Ava, wanting to encourage him. *Although there's no substitute for experience.*

"So when you saw him two Saturdays ago, what was his mood?" Zander asked. "Did he ever talk to you about being angry with someone? Did he mention the shooting in Eugene in June?"

Cole bit his lip and looked at the ceiling. "Nah. His attitude seemed normal. I don't remember talking about shootings." He looked at the agents. "But he'd handled guns. I think he took classes at a range somewhere. And I think he went with some friends out to the mountains to go target shooting or something."

"He owns a gun?" Ava asked. Small alarms were ringing in her head. According to the family and the state, no one in the Yoder household owned a weapon.

"Nah, he'd borrow a friend's. Said he had to buy the ammo."

"Who's the friend?"

"Dunno. No one I've ever met. Maybe someone he works with? I think his dad might have taken him shooting once or twice also."

"How'd he get along with his parents?" Zander asked. Ava watched Cole's face. Last night Zander had shared a few key points with her from Mason and Ray's interview with Justin's doctor. She knew the doctor's opinion of Justin's relationship with his father didn't quite jibe with the parents' opinion.

Cole shrugged. "Fine. Usual shit. Sorry, ma'am," he said politely to Ava.

She bit back a laugh. "Not a problem."

"I know it was hard for Justin, still living at home at his age. But at least he didn't have to pay rent. He doesn't know how good he has it—" Cole stopped. "I mean . . . how good he had it. He could spend his work money on his car and stuff. Didn't have to worry about the gas bill or tuition." A hint of envy colored Cole's tone.

"Yes," said Ava. "I remember that first apartment. All the costs add up quickly. Did Justin ever talk about depression?"

"Oh, yeah. All the time. You know he was seeing a doctor for that, right?" Cole asked. At their nods he continued. "He hated going. Said he only went to make his parents happy. Said the doctor was an asshole who always wanted him to talk about his feelings. Drove him crazy. And kept prescribing all sorts of medication for him. Justin never took it."

"What?" Ava's back straightened. "He didn't take his meds?"

"Nah, he didn't need them. He'd just dump them out after picking them up. His mom gave him money to get the prescriptions and the pharmacy automatically refilled them. He'd pick them up just to keep everyone off his back."

Ava couldn't speak.

"So everyone thinks he's taking meds and he wasn't?" Zander clarified.

"Stupid, huh? You know how many people can't afford their medications?" Cole asked. "I told him once he should give them to someone who needed them." He shrugged. "I don't know if he did."

Ava thought of all the empty bottles in the back of Justin's car. *Did he give the drugs to someone? Or just empty the bottles into the trash? Why keep the empty bottles?*

"How long do you think he'd been doing that?" Ava asked. She could always tell when Jayne stopped taking her meds. Her mood swings were epic.

"I remember him doing it in high school," said Cole. "I don't know if he always did it. Maybe he took them some of the time. But for the last year or two he was really into clean living, you know?"

"Explain," stated Zander, his pen ready.

"Organic. No chemicals. No processed food. He shopped at one of those fancy supermarkets where a shriveled apple costs you five bucks. Turned up his nose at McNuggets . . . that sort of thing. Except he couldn't give up his Mountain Dew. He was addicted to that stuff and drank it by the case. And he was always running. He was into parkour."

"What?" asked Ava and Zander simultaneously.

"It's like natural obstacle courses. Like climbing fences and jumping off roofs. Well, maybe not roofs but getting some height."

Ava remembered seeing it on TV. Basically using the world as your freestyle gym and obstacle course. "He lived in the suburbs. Where would he do that?"

"I didn't say I saw him doing it. He talked about it a lot. Said he did it."

"So he could have been lying . . . or talking about something he wanted to do," Zander clarified.

Cole shrugged as an answer.

Ava and Zander exchanged a look. "What did you think when you heard what had happened?" Ava asked slowly, watching Cole's expression. "What were your first thoughts?"

Cole dipped his chin, lowering his gaze to the floor. He shook his head. "I didn't believe it. There was no way the Justin I knew could do that," he said softly. "But then the more I thought about it, the more uncertain I was. *Could he have done it?*" He looked up, doubt and misery in his eyes. "I couldn't be sure that he wouldn't. I look at myself and know the right set of circumstances could probably push me to do anything if I was desperate enough, right? I could lie and say I'd never kill another person, but I suspect we all have that line that we can be pushed across. Maybe someone pushed Justin."

The truth of Cole's words rolled across the ratty carpet like giant boulders, imposing and unavoidable, and stopped at Ava's feet. They couldn't be ignored.

Even I have a line. She'd be lying if she said otherwise. She sat frozen, unable to breathe or look at Zander for fear of his seeing every thought in her head. *Considering my genetics, my line might be closer than most people's.*

"So maybe he wasn't working alone," Zander said. His voice yanked Ava back into the conversation.

A partner?

"I don't know," said Cole. "Like I said, he didn't talk about it. We were all shocked as hell when we heard the news. I've asked people who knew him. No one saw it coming." His brows came together, making his young face suddenly ten years older. "I never saw anger issues, he didn't talk about killing people, he didn't act suicidal, he didn't talk to me like he'd never see me again or try to give me his car. *I didn't see it coming!*" He slammed his fist on his knee.

The coffee maker beeped.

Cole exhaled and looked away. "Would you like some coffee now?"

He sounded exhausted.

Zander raised a brow at Ava. She gave him a tiny shake of her head. *I don't have any more questions.* Zander stood up.

"Thanks, Cole. You've been a big help. We'll pass on the coffee." He handed the young man his card, and Cole accepted it without looking at it. The angry mature-looking man had vanished, leaving an uncertain college kid in his place.

Ava said something polite and headed for the door. The small apartment suddenly felt too warm.

They stepped out into the hall, and she abruptly missed the scent of the coffee. It'd taken over the room without her noticing. Now she smelled old carpet and a subtle odor of cat boxes.

"What did you think?" she asked Zander.

"I think that's a very confused young man who was probably the best friend Justin ever had. He didn't care what sort of changes Justin went through; he stuck by him every time. A lot of guys would have bailed."

"Could Justin have hid something as big as plans of suicide and murder from Cole?" she asked as they jogged down the creaking wooden stairs.

"I don't know," said Zander. "Sounds like he was hiding a lot of things from several people. According to the briefing Ray Lusco sent me about their conversation with the psychiatrist last night, the doctor saw his relationship with Justin as very solid and said the professional visits continued because it was what Justin wanted. According to Cole, that's not true."

"And his parents?"

"I think they said Justin asked to continue the visits. I don't know who to believe."

"We need the toxicology reports from the autopsy," said Ava. "I want to know who was telling the truth about Justin's medication."

Zander raised a brow at her.

"I mean *you* need to get those reports, since this is your case," she corrected herself. They moved out of the building and into the morning sun. Ava raised her face to the rays and slipped on her sunglasses. "I'm on vacation."

16

Mason held the Troutdale church door open for Ray.

"Feels different this time," Ray commented as he passed by. "The shopping mall shooting was a mass of hysteria for a half an hour. This shooting in the park was over almost immediately and under control within minutes."

Mason fell into step with Ray as they headed down the hall to where police were interviewing Troutdale witnesses. Ray was right. The incident had been over by the time the first responders arrived on the scene. The public had momentarily panicked but then taken back its park. Was it because this was the third occurrence? People had had time to think about how they would react? Or was it because the attack had happened in the open and people saw the threat was over minutes after it had started? Personally, he hadn't felt the same stress about this shooting that he had about the Rivertown Mall shooting. Probably because he'd known Ava was home and in bed.

Are they related?

That damned Nike logo on the jacket and pants of the Troutdale shooter stabbed at his brain. He needed to check, but he was 99 percent certain investigators hadn't released to the public what the

Rivertown Mall shooter had been wearing. Someone close to the mall investigation would know, but had anyone leaked the information? It wasn't top secret. They'd identified the mall shooter within twenty-four hours. There was no reason for anyone to be interested in what the Rivertown Mall shooter had been wearing . . . unless they wanted to imitate the shooting.

He'd made a call on the way to the church, trying to find out what the Eugene shooter had worn in June, and was waiting for a return call. He'd Googled every article he could on his cell phone, but the description hadn't gone beyond "dark clothing." It wasn't good enough for Mason. It seemed every damned mass shooter in history had worn dark clothing or camouflage.

Did they have a rash of copycats or an organized group of young men bent on killing themselves as publicly as possible?

Inside the church, he and Ray checked in with Chief Deputy Bishop and his organizers. They were assigned a witness to interview. Shirley DeMarco. One of the deaths, Anna Luther, had been in her regular walking group. They met in a quiet room where the woman made constant use of a box of tissues. Shirley DeMarco was seventy-three and widowed, and had walked the lake park five days a week with the same group of women for years.

"Not all of us can make it every day," Shirley stated. "But we all aim for five days. I haven't missed a day all summer. Even in the rain we walk." She dabbed at her nose.

"I'm very sorry for your loss," Mason said. "How long had Anna Luther been in your group?"

Shirley nodded, her bloodshot eyes clouding for a second. "Anna joined us three years ago. We all live close to the park and she made almost every walk." She blew her nose. "Sweet woman, quiet, but always had a nice smile and a positive word for everyone. One of those perpetually happy people, you know?"

Mason and Ray both nodded.

"She was the type you almost didn't believe was real. The glass was always half full and she knew how to make everyone laugh. No fakiness going on at all."

Ray slid a map of the park across the table. "Show me where you walked, where you were when Anna was shot, and what you saw the shooter do."

Shirley took a deep breath. "We always do two laps around the lake. It's almost four miles and takes us about an hour. We'd finished the first lap and were close to the play area here." Her finger circled the lake once and stopped at the south end. "I heard three or four shots . . . all close together. We all stopped and looked around. My first thought was fireworks. They do a big display at the park for the Fourth, and it seems like some people continue to shoot off fireworks at least for a week after that, but they're always at night." Her finger slid an inch west. "He was here. He'd been behind us . . . I don't know if he followed us from the far side of the lake . . . but I didn't see him until after I heard the shots. I looked behind me, saw his mask, and he was aiming directly at our group."

"What did you do?" asked Mason.

"I hit the ground," she said simply. "I could either run or get down. I can walk just fine, but running was out of the question and there was nowhere to take cover within fifty feet. The slides were the closest, but my brain told me to get down." She shuddered. "Everyone else ran. Including Anna. I heard more shots and saw her fall. He shot her in the back," she said angrily, her eyes narrowing. "God damned young kid shooting a woman in the back. A woman with a family. I don't know whether to cry or scream."

"What happened next?" Ray asked. "Did you look at the shooter?"

"I did. I looked back as I belly-crawled to Anna. By the time I got there she wasn't breathing." Tears rolled down her soft cheeks, but Shirley kept her gaze on the men. "The shooter shot at another man, and I saw him fall, and then he vanished into the restroom. I think there was some shouting, and I know there were more shots."

"Did anyone come out?"

"Yes, someone was yelling that the shooter shot himself. I remember wondering if I was safe now, but people were still screaming and running around. One woman from my group appeared right after that and helped me check Anna again, but there was nothing else we could do for her." She wiped at her tears with a tissue. "I stayed with her until the police arrived. I didn't leave until they placed her in one of those bags."

"That was very kind of you," Ray said.

"They say one's spirit hangs around after death. I hope she knew I didn't leave her alone. I told her husband I stayed with her. I can't bear the thought of dying alone." Her demeanor changed and a hardness settled over her features. "Except for that man . . . the shooter. I hope he was miserable and terrified when he stuck his gun in his mouth. I hope he knew the world wanted nothing more to do with his kind. Hell was waiting for him."

Mason blinked, stunned speechless by the rapid change in the kind woman.

She nodded at him. "Close your mouth, Detective; you're going to catch flies. I've lived a long time and believe we're here to make other people's lives happy. I have no sympathy for people who want to destroy."

Mason shut his mouth and looked down at his notes. "You didn't notice anyone on the far side of the lake when you were doing your first lap?"

"No. No one was over there that I saw. It's usually very quiet on that side in the mornings. A bit creepy. I wouldn't walk over there by myself that time of day."

"But he was behind you when you heard the shooting. On the path that led from that side of the lake? Did you have the impression he'd come from that direction?" Ray asked.

Shirley thought for a moment. "By the time I looked back, yes, he was on the lake path, but he could have come from one of the side streets. I honestly don't have an opinion about where he'd been. He was simply *there* when things went to hell."

"Had you seen him before that morning? Did his physical presence remind you of someone you'd seen in the park before? I imagine you run into the same people a lot," Mason asked.

She shook her head. "I saw a tall man when I looked back. We see a lot of men each morning, usually runners, some familiar, some not. Nothing in my brain said, 'Hey, that reminds me of . . .' I've lived in the lake neighborhood for a long time, but I won't claim to recognize everyone in the area."

Mason tapped his pencil on the table. The shooter must have done some reconnaissance of the area. But did it matter? They had the shooter. Just not his identity. Yet.

"I think we're done here." Mason stood and held his hand out to Shirley. "You've been very helpful."

She looked him in the eye as she took his hand. "Figure out who's doing this," she said firmly. "Please find who is driving our young men to kill others and then themselves."

17

Zander skimmed Justin Yoder's autopsy report and admired the ME's thoroughness as Ava studied the computer screen over his shoulder. They had left Cole Hooper's apartment and headed back to the community center where joint law enforcement agencies were still analyzing what had happened at the Rivertown Mall.

There had been no medications in Justin Yoder's system.

"Did they look specifically for the medication he was taking?" Ava asked.

"Yes. They had to run some different tests, and I called Dr. Rutledge myself to ask about it. But according to this, Justin Yoder didn't have a trace of anything in him. Not even Advil. Maybe Cole Hooper was right about Justin's clean-living commitment." He glanced over the ME's notes about the physical condition of the body. The twenty-year-old had been in excellent shape with good muscle tone. Maybe he had been doing the urban obstacle courses.

"This is someone who took care of himself," said Ava. "So why end it all?"

"And does it lend more credibility to Cole's story that Justin didn't want to go to therapy?"

"I would think that a twenty-year-old could convince his parents that he was finished with something. Especially if he'd been doing it for four years. I have a hard time believing he went just because his parents made him."

Zander nodded. "We're missing an element of the story." He pressed his lips together. "I wonder how long he'd been off his medication. I'll check with his psychiatrist and see if he'd made any changes to his prescription. Although I would guess he wouldn't change anything unless Justin complained that he wasn't feeling right. And if he wasn't taking his meds, he must have been feeling okay."

Ava snorted. "That's the problem with going off that sort of medication. Trust me, my twin did it all the time. Jayne would feel great so she'd stop taking it, but she couldn't see the personality changes that I could. I always knew when she'd switched something up."

Zander sympathized. Jayne McLane was a piece of work. She and Ava stood on opposite ends of a spectrum. He'd witnessed Jayne blow up a house with her impulsive behavior and abandon Ava with a killer as she chased after her abusive boyfriend. Ava claimed Jayne was currently stable and capable of rational conversations; Zander would believe it when he saw it.

"She's doing okay now, right?" he asked.

"For the moment." Ava gave a wry grin. "It makes me suspicious. When things are crazy, I'm relaxed because that's normal. During the calm times, I'm constantly waiting for something to explode. It's nerve-racking."

For identical twins, the women were night and day. How had they emerged from the same genetics? Last time he'd seen Jayne, her hair had been as brown as Ava's and the resemblance had been startling. But in her dozen mug shots, she was blond. The main difference was in their eyes. Both had blue eyes, but Ava's felt like calm seas. Jayne's were more like a hurricane. Even in her photos, restless energy leaped out of her gaze.

"Is there any news on Justin's vehicle?" Ava asked.

Zander scanned through his emails and opened one. "This says there was nothing unusual in the car. They've sent several things to trace, but who knows how long until we hear back on those. There was a gym bag in the backseat with dirty shorts, T-shirt, and running shoes. Only thing of interest was a receipt for ammo from the county shooting range. It was two months old."

"Doesn't he need to have his own weapon to be allowed to shoot there?" Ava asked.

"Yes, but remember Cole said he thought he went with a friend. I bet the friend owned the weapon." Zander scratched a note to visit the shooting range and follow up with Justin's workplace friends and his parents. One of them should know whom Justin had gone shooting with.

He read further down the report. "This is odd."

"What?" Ava asked.

Zander kept reading and the hairs on his arms stood up. "Justin's car was wiped down. Everywhere. They couldn't find a single print of Justin's in it. Someone was very thorough."

Ava sucked in a breath. "Would he wipe down his own vehicle before going into the mall? That says he assumed the police would find it—"

"He didn't hide the vehicle. Of course he expected it to be found. But why wipe it down?"

"Maybe he wasn't the one who left it there?"

Zander was silent as his brain searched for an explanation. "Then who? And why?"

"Has his cell phone turned up?" Ava asked.

Zander rubbed at his forehead. "Not that I've seen. We got back his records from his wireless company. There were no calls or texts the morning of the shooting. The company lost contact with the phone during the night at some point. His mother tried to contact him several times the day of the shooting, wondering when he was coming home. The calls went nowhere."

"I don't get it."

"You and me both. The wiped-down car really confuses me. Did Justin think he could get away after the shooting? Removing his fingerprints doesn't hide who the car belongs to."

"Logic dictates that it wasn't his fingerprints he was hiding . . . or someone else was hiding. Someone doesn't want us to know who else was in that vehicle, right?" Ava asked slowly. "You said a minute ago that we're missing an element of the story. I think there's a big glaring one missing here. It's almost as if the things that are missing are what's creating the path. Missing medication in Justin's system . . . missing fingerprints . . . things that we expect to be there, aren't."

"You're saying someone else is involved. Could it be the shooter who died this morning in Troutdale?" Zander glanced up at the silent television someone had tuned to the local news station. It'd canceled all regular programming and was running constant reports about the Troutdale shooting, interspersing them with details from the Rivertown and Eugene shootings. The reporters had already connected the similarities among the three shootings, commenting on the ages of the shooters, the weapons, and the suicides at the end.

"When's the briefing on the Eugene shooting?" Ava asked, her gaze following Zander's as a high-school picture of the shooter from Eugene flashed on the TV screen.

"In an hour. They moved it up. Lane County Sheriff's Department is presenting. They handled the entire investigation two months ago." Zander pulled up a news article from June about the Eugene shooting. "Joseph Albaugh. Age twenty-four. Grew up in Eugene. Did both high school and college in the area. Was an employee at Home Depot. Opened fire early morning in a park. Four adults killed. Two children injured." The same high-school senior photo from the newscast accompanied the article. Joe Albaugh was fresh-faced, with blond hair and a heavy coat of freckles. His smile was infectious. "Shot himself in the restroom. The usual comments from friends and family that it shocked the hell out of them that he'd done it."

"This is giving me the creeps," muttered Ava. "It's like they belong to the same herd of sheep."

"Word out of Troutdale is that the shooter is a young male, too. No ID yet."

"There has to be a connection between the three of them," Ava stated. "There're too many similarities."

Zander took the devil's advocate role. "It could simply be generational. They could have all been disgruntled young men. Once they saw the first one do it, they decided to follow suit. Something about shooting innocents and the media coverage feels glamorous to them."

"There's nothing fucking glamorous about it!"

"It might be similar to the mind-set of the young men who are willing to blow themselves up to kill their enemies. Or the Japanese pilots who were willing to make their planes into torpedoes. They think they have a higher purpose."

"Then what is the goal?" Ava waved a hand, encompassing the hub of the investigation. "What are these young men trying to achieve? A hundred virgins in paradise? Notoriety? Revenge?"

Anger washed through Zander. *Don't they realize that life is a gift? And the people around them will forever mourn their loss?*

"That's what we need to figure out."

Will there be more?

• • •

Ava turned away from the photo on Zander's computer screen, disturbed by Albaugh's all-American looks. Blond hair, blue eyes, white teeth, sun-touched skin. He looked as if he'd grown up on a corn farm and should be starring in an ad for Ralph Lauren denim.

What had driven him and Justin Yoder to murder and suicide? Two young men who seemed to have the world waiting in front of them? They should have been looking forward to picket fences and taking their kids to the river to fish someday. She knew she was jumping to conclusions based on his looks. Perhaps the briefing would present a history of mental illness. The few newspaper articles she'd read hadn't alluded to it.

Would the Troutdale shooter turn out to be more of the same?

Glancing at her phone, she saw it was midway through the afternoon and that she'd missed a call from Jayne. She excused herself to Zander and headed out into the blazing heat to return the call. Spotting a bench under a tree a dozen yards from the back entrance of the community center, she sat in the shade. The front parking lot of the community center was still packed with media, anxiously waiting for news of what had driven young men to murder. Out back it was calm and peaceful. She eyed the face of her phone. If she called Jayne, would the peace continue?

"Dammit."

How does making a simple phone call cause so much distress?

She hit the missed call and waited, one-handedly cracking her knuckles as she anticipated Jayne's voice.

Is it a good day or bad?

"Ava? Where are you?" Jayne howled as she answered.

Bad day.

"I'm at work," she answered calmly. "What's wrong?"

"You're not here! I came to visit because I knew you were on vacation and our calls have been so good and I wanted to see you in person, but *you're gone!*" The words flew out of Jayne's mouth as if they couldn't keep up with the speed of her brain. She noisily sucked in a deep breath.

Ava's mind shifted into calm-her-twin mode. "Slow down. I'm unofficially following up on a case today." She repeated Jayne's outburst in her head. "What do you mean you came to visit?"

"I'm at your house but *you're not here.* The woman says you mooooved!"

Her heart slowed. "Are you at my condo?"

"No! The house. The one where you lived with that guy! How could you not tell *me*?"

You mean the house you broke into last spring? Thank goodness the new owners had been home. Would Jayne have broken in again? "His name is Mason. What made you go there?"

"Because every time we've talked on the phone, you've mentioned you're at *the house.* I assumed you got rid of your condo and lived with him now." She paused. "Are you at the condo? Did you break up?"

"Jayne, I haven't seen you in person in almost five months. I did sell the condo, but things—"

"I came all this way to see you, and you didn't tell me you'd moved! What are you hiding from me?"

"I'm not hiding—"

"I can't believe you did this to me! Are you ashamed of me? Because I used drugs? I'm clean now." She burst into fresh tears. "I just wanted to see you. I needed to talk to you and you're not here!"

"Now, Jayne, I *never* know where you're living. You flit from one place to the next."

"But you're different! You're a rock, *my rock.* As long as I know where you are, I know there's someplace I can *go*!"

"Do you need to go somewhere? Is something wrong at your house or with your job?"

"No! I just wanted to see you!" Rapid breaths came through the line.

She's out of control. Nothing could calm Jayne down when she got worked up.

"You moved and weren't going to tell me. Were you going to change your phone number next? Is that what you'd do to me? I know where you work, Ava. I could find you if I needed to. I'm not stupid," she snapped.

And her mood wildly swings to anger.

"Jayne, what was so important that you needed to talk to me in person?"

"Are you saying I'm not important? Your own twin? I'm all the family you have left, Ava. Don't make me feel guilty because I wanted to see my sister." Her words stabbed deep.

"I'm not—"

"Were you planning on never seeing me again?" she breathed. "Do you hate me that much?"

"Jayne, you haven't let—"

"You do hate me. You've always hated me and believed you were better than me."

Ava froze. It wasn't her sister speaking. It was as if something had taken over her body. *Did she stop taking her medication? Did she find some drugs? Or is this just an episode?*

"You wish I was dead, don't you?" Jayne whispered. "Wouldn't your life be easier if I was simply gone?"

Yes.

"Jayne, I don't think like that. You're my—"

"Just think, Ava," she said in a hushed voice. "No more crazy Jayne. No one to wreck your cars, steal your men, or break into your house."

Is this an apology?

Ava couldn't speak.

"You'd like that, wouldn't you?" Jayne's tone grew louder. "You wish I was dead! Well, I do, too! My only sister moves away and doesn't even let me know. I get the message, Ava. I'm too messy to have in your life."

"Are you threatening to kill yourself *again*, Jayne?" A red haze crowded her vision. "Because I've heard it too many times."

"You—"

"This isn't about what *I've* done. This is about *you*. *I'm tired of hearing you're going to kill yourself!*" Ava sucked in a deep breath as all rational thoughts flew out of her head. "Do you know what that does to *me*?"

"You don't know what—"

"Here's what I know, Jayne. Your brain works differently than mine—differently than ninety-nine point nine percent of the human population. But it's time you thought about someone else for once. Hearing you want to kill yourself, *kills* a part of me." She slapped her hand over her heart. "And then you say it again. And again. Until I have giant dead holes in my heart. And you know what? They don't heal very fast. Hell, some of them don't heal at all."

Jayne was silent.

Am I getting through to her?

"To you, you're venting your frustration and trying to stir up some excitement in your life. But for me, you're ripping out my insides!" She paused. "You've got to stop doing this to me."

"This isn't about *you*, Ava," she whispered.

"Well, this time I'm making it about me." Her heart pounded in her ears. "What you say and do affects me like no other person in the world. You're my twin and I love you more than life . . . so I go out of my way not to hurt you. But you don't think about anyone but yourself. You're not going to kill yourself, Jayne. We both know that."

"You hate me," she hissed.

"I hate how you make me feel. Can you see the difference? I hate your actions and your words, but you're threaded through my soul. Hating you would mean I hate myself." Clarity shot through her. "Oh, my God. You really hate yourself, don't you? That's why it's so easy for you to hurt me. It's yourself you're striking out at."

"You are such a bitch," Jayne cried. "You've got the perfect life, and you're stomping all over me when I'm down."

Calm flowed through her. *I know I'm right.* "You need help, Jayne. You need to stay on your medication and continue to see your therapist."

"*I hate you!*"

The rage physically punched her in the gut. Her lungs seized.

"You'll regret it when I'm gone," Jayne shouted. "You'll want to take back every awful word you said to me. You're going to cry and scream and feel the pain that I've felt for decades. And I'll be laughing at you from the other side!"

"You're threatening to kill yourself again?" Exhaustion swept through Ava.

The call ended.

Ava pulled her phone away from her ear and stared at the screen, feeling another piece of her heart decay and die. *What just happened?* She started to call Jayne back. *No. She's clearly not rational at the moment.* She took a deep breath and called the halfway house where Jayne lived. She got the manager's voice mail and left a request for her to call back. She didn't relate what Jayne had said to her, but asked if everything had been okay with her sister recently.

She shoved the phone in a pocket, moved back to the bench, and sat, feeling as if the world had been ripped out from under her feet. During the conversation she'd stood and walked a dozen steps away from the bench as if she could move closer to Jayne. *There's no reasoning with her when she's like that.* She took three deep breaths, forced out one long exhalation, and stared up at the blue sky.

What am I supposed to do?

Tears burned in the corners of her eyes, and she angrily brushed at them. *How do I hate and love the same person simultaneously?* Her heart ached for Mason to sit beside her. She needed his solid arms around her and his neck to bury her face in. She shivered, suddenly cold even though the air was over ninety degrees and the bench felt like a heating pad. Mason was better at these moments than she. He could calm her with a touch and help her rationally see what'd just happened. *How unfair that I bring that into his life.* She snorted, immediately seeing the error in her thinking. Mason had told her a dozen times he wasn't affected by Jayne. He was affected only by watching what she put Ava through. *I'm the one who needs to handle it better.* Every time she thought she had her feelings and relationship with Jayne balanced and controlled, Jayne attacked from out of the blue.

Like today. Ava thought back through the conversation. *That wasn't a conversation: that was Jayne venting and me trying to keep up. Will she try to kill herself?*

It wouldn't be the first time she'd made the threat. Twice Ava had called local authorities when she believed Jayne was about to hurt herself. Both times had turned out to be false alarms. One time Jayne had gone through the motions with a knife, but never seriously cut herself. A second time she'd claimed she'd taken an overdose of medication, but stomach pumping and lab tests proved she'd lied. She knew how to push Ava's buttons and get the attention she wanted. Sirens and flashing lights outside her apartment building made for a healthy dose of notoriety. Or unhealthy dose, depending on how one looked at it.

Now what?

Ava wondered how long it would take the manager to return her call. Could be hours. Until then she needed to get Jayne out of her brain and go back inside and focus on the case. *Easier said than done.* She took several deep breaths and studied the sky, emptying her mind of Jayne's words. She concentrated on the absence of fingerprints in Justin's car and the lack of drugs in his system.

What drives a person to do what he did?

Are they missing something in their brains? Like Jayne?

So far no one had questioned her presence in the investigation. Zander was deliberately including her, and she suspected it was out of pity. He knew she'd go nuts looking at this case from the outside. *Time to go back in.*

She stood, her muscles aching as if she'd lifted weights for the past eight hours. She didn't want to go inside. She wanted to close her eyes and let the heat bake away her chill. Jayne's call had drained her. Ten hours of sleep and a glass of wine sounded heavenly. Footsteps sounded behind her . . . no, *boot steps.* She spun around and all thoughts of the call fluttered away. Warm brown eyes smiled at her and a schoolgirl giddiness filled her lungs. The crinkling of skin at the corners of his eyes filled her with love.

This was how someone who loved you made you feel. Not guilty, not confused, not exhausted.

He stopped in front of her, still holding her gaze, and slid his hands around her waist, pulling her tight to his chest. She melted into him and sighed.

How does he do that with a simple touch?

"You look like you need something," Mason quietly said into her ear.

"Not anymore. I found it."

18

Mason studied the photos of the Eugene shooter on the overhead screen. The Lane County sheriff had accompanied two of his deputies to make the presentation to the Rivertown Mall shooting task force. Mason had seen Multnomah County's chief deputy, Arnold Bishop, slip into the room before the briefing started. Their task force was growing. Now they had three large crimes from three different counties to look at. During a quick meeting before the briefing, there'd been a discussion about who would oversee the coordination of information and investigation among all the law enforcement agencies, and the ball had landed firmly in the hands of Sergeant Shaver from Washington County. He was the most centrally located among the crimes and had the organizational skills and resources to keep things flowing.

Mason thought Shaver was perfect for the job. As long as no one had volunteered Mason himself, he was happy. People-pleasing and ass-kissing weren't things he did well. He preferred to be left alone to get his job done. Not to be assigned a chair with everyone looking at him to guide the next step.

"He looks so happy," mumbled Ava, eyeing the photos of Joseph Albaugh.

Mason didn't say anything. He'd seen too many smiling killers. People lied. Lied with their mouths and with their expressions. He didn't trust any of it.

"Albaugh was a local boy from one of the more rural areas," said one of the Lane County deputies, gesturing at the screen. "Grew up knowing how to shoot and hunt and ride dirt bikes. Family has lived in the area for generations. Graduated from the University of Oregon with a degree in economics and had been working at the Home Depot for the last four years.

"On the day of the shooting, Albaugh left his apartment by four A.M. He had a roommate who woke up briefly when he left; he assumed Albaugh had an early shift at work. Just before seven A.M. Albaugh pulled into the lot of Green Lake Park. Witnesses noticed his car arrive but said he didn't exit immediately."

"Who else was in the park at seven in the morning?" asked one of the Cedar Edge cops.

"People were putting their boats in at one end of the parking lot for a day of fishing. There were a few people running or walking the trails that crisscross that area. Parents and a few kids. There's a children's play area that's one of the best in the state. Original stuff for kids to play on. There's a gigantic set of dinosaur bones, an automatic river with a sand bed, and unique climbing structures of the like I've never seen before.

"Once Albaugh stepped out of his car, he immediately began to shoot." The deputy changed the overhead display to a map of the park. "He'd parked at the east end of the lot, far away from the boat ramp." He pointed with a red laser pointer.

The children's play area was directly beside where Albaugh had parked. Mason tensed in his chair. *Asshole. Why next to the kids?*

"The first victim was a jogger; he went down here. Second and third victims were two parents in the play area. The fourth was an older gentleman simply sitting on a bench. Two children were injured but not by gunfire. One of the murdered parents dropped her toddler daughter when she was shot and another child fell off the slide in the aftermath."

Ava sucked in a breath and discreetly slipped her hand into Mason's between their seats.

Mason knew she was going to see a counselor arranged through the FBI's Employee Assistance Program tomorrow. She'd been sleeping really crappy for the last two nights. Her chin was up and she seemed to be coping okay, but he didn't want to take any chances. There'd been no protest on her part about talking with the psychiatrist; she knew the drill and accepted it.

"Albaugh then headed to the restrooms here." The red pinpoint of light circled a square on the map. "He chased two men out of the restroom and then shot himself. We estimate the entire episode took less than two minutes."

"Cameras?" asked a voice.

"None."

"History of mental illness?" asked another cop.

The deputy shifted on his feet and glanced at the Lane County sheriff. "Here's where it gets a bit dicey. By all accounts he had a normal childhood and teenage years. But Albaugh had been complaining of headaches for two years or so before the shooting. He'd seen a few specialists who couldn't locate the exact issue and he'd tried every medication available. We pulled every medical record of his for the last four years. He's been to naturopaths, chiropractors, ear-nose-and-throat docs, psychiatrists, and done every brain and head scan available looking for the source. His mother said he'd tried an elimination diet, thinking it was something he was eating, but couldn't find the source of his pain. As far as she knew, he'd never solved the problem."

"The pain in his head drove him to shoot?" muttered Ray on the other side of Ava.

The deputy up front heard him. "Believe me, we've discussed that possibility to death. Your guess is as good as ours."

"Any results on his vehicle?" Zander asked from the back of the room.

"You need to be more specific. What kind of results?" the deputy answered.

"Justin Yoder's car outside the Rivertown Mall was completely wiped down. No prints of any kind left," said Zander, causing a murmur through the room.

"Did you know that?" Mason asked Ava.

"Just found out a little while ago," she whispered back.

The deputy stepped to the side of the room to confer with the Lane County sheriff and the other deputy. The three men shook their heads. He looked back at Zander. "We don't know the immediate answer for that. I'll pull the forensics report on his car as soon as we're done here. But I'll be honest with you . . . we had our shooter; we weren't looking for a suspect. I'm wondering if the car was even examined in that way."

"Do you still have the car?" Zander asked.

The deputy raised a brow at the sheriff. The sheriff nodded vigorously. "We still have it."

"Can we get a team on it tomorrow if you find it wasn't printed?" asked Zander.

"Absolutely," said the deputy. "I'll make the call tonight."

"What was the consensus from his friends and coworkers about the shooting and suicide?" asked Ray.

"I'd say they were all stunned. Everyone was completely surprised and claimed this behavior made no sense. This was a popular guy. Lots of friends . . . although he had broken up with his girlfriend about a month before. Everyone said he'd gotten over it."

"Maybe he hadn't," muttered Ava. She raised her voice: "And what did the girlfriend say about that?"

"She said she hadn't heard from him since the breakup."

"Who ended it?" Ava asked.

"She said she did because she was moving to Seattle and didn't want a long-distance relationship. They'd been dating about three months. Albaugh's friends backed her story and said Albaugh had been down for a while but seemed to recover."

Mason wondered if she'd asked him to move with her or seen the move as a chance to break things off.

"We thought this was an open-and-shut case," the Lane County sheriff spoke up. "There was no evidence he wasn't acting alone. What bugged us the most was the lack of motive. I don't like to think that people simply start shooting for no reason. We picked apart his background. Nothing even hinted that he'd try such an action. No broken family, no bullying, no drug abuse, no depression. The tiny indicators we all look for in cases like this." He paused. "But now . . . two more . . . I really hate to think that we missed something that could tie these three young men together." He scanned the crowd of law enforcement. "Who contacted me about what he was wearing?"

Mason put up a hand.

The sheriff nodded at him. "When you told me the other two shooters had been wearing the same black athletic wear, I could barely believe it. I had to look in Albaugh's file. I knew he'd been wearing black, but when I saw it was the same brand and style as the other two, I wanted to puke. I spent the next hour confirming that that information hadn't been released or mentioned in the press. The only way your Rivertown shooter could have found out was if someone privately leaked some photos and he chose to wear the same. I don't think there was a leak. I think it's all part of a plan."

The sheriff's keen eyes studied the group. "And if this many investigators can't figure out how the hell this all happened, I don't know who can."

"Does the media know about the clothing yet?" asked a voice.

Sergeant Shaver stood up. "No. What we've said in all three cases is that the suspects wore black. I've reviewed the witness accounts and none of them state the brand or even that it's athletic wear. I don't think they were looking at his clothing."

"Is there an ID on the Troutdale shooter?" asked a Washington County deputy.

Shaver turned to look at Bishop, from Multnomah County. "Not yet," Bishop replied. "Tips are coming in, but I haven't had word from the medical examiner on a confirmation. We don't know much of anything yet about the shooter. I'll make certain his vehicle is thoroughly processed once we find it."

Thirty minutes later the meeting wrapped up.

Ava was silent as she and Mason left the building. The sun had set two hours ago, but the heat radiated up from the blacktop as they walked through the parking lot. They stopped at her car and looked at each other.

"Another romantic evening," she whispered, one side of her mouth curled up.

He stepped closer and cupped a hand around her jaw. In the dim light of the parking lot he could barely see the light shower of freckles on each of her cheekbones. He rubbed a thumb over them. The freckles were a reflection of her. She was completely professional in her dress and grooming, but she couldn't cover up the small bit of playfulness that danced across her cheeks. Just so, her personality was calm and rational, but she had that hint of flirtatiousness that she couldn't keep hidden.

She had spark. And he couldn't stay away.

"Every evening I spend with you is romantic," he said. "Doesn't matter if we're looking at a corpse or walking on the beach."

Her eyelids flickered and uncertainty shot across her face.

"Jayne?" he asked.

"I'm worried." She leaned into him. "I'm sorry," she whispered.

He held her tight and his own worry increased—but not for her twin.

Would he ever have Ava completely to himself?

19

It felt as if he'd had an hour of sleep.

And that hour had been patched together from brief periods of dozing with the bedroom light on and Ava tossing in bed beside him.

After a dose of a prescription antianxiety medication she had on hand, Ava had finally crashed. He'd had to threaten her to get her to take it. "You don't have to be anywhere in the morning," he'd told her. "It doesn't matter if you sleep in or are groggy most of the day. But I need sleep and I can't sleep until you do."

The stress of the shooting had finally caught up with her. Combined with her disturbing phone call from Jayne earlier in the day, it'd made for a night from hell. First Ava had paced around the bedroom, complaining that she wasn't tired. He'd suggested a glass of wine, and she'd agreed, but then barely drunk it. She'd set down the glass and moved away, forgetting that it existed. She looked stressed, with smudged half circles darkening the skin below her eyes, and she kept losing track of their conversation.

Mason knew the signs of mental and emotional exhaustion. But Ava had kept moving. She'd run two loads of laundry and dug around in the kitchen boxes. Reorganizing, she'd said. Physically she was running on nervous energy, but her brain had shifted to pause, protecting itself. "I can't think straight," she'd said. "My thoughts keep skittering about in my head as if everything is covered in ice. I can't get purchase to focus on one thing—everything keeps pushing the other thoughts out of the way. Important facts from the shootings that I feel like I need to remember and follow up on. Then I start thinking about what Jayne said to me and everything spins away again."

"There're plenty of sharp brains working on these murders," he'd told her. "We'll cover everything. It's not on you to solve these cases."

"I know, but—"

"You've forgotten you're not assigned to work on them. You're a witness. That's it," he'd said sharply.

The look she'd given him could have frozen fire.

At midnight he'd bargained her into bed, promising a foot and back rub.

It'd taken over an hour, but she'd finally fallen asleep. Only to jolt awake later, scrambling out of the bed.

It'd scared the crap out of him.

He'd seen the vein pounding in her neck and her dilated pupils. "The shooter?" he'd asked. She'd nodded, unable to speak and her gaze wide and blank. He'd pulled her back to bed, held her close, and stroked her back until she drifted off to sleep again. After two more identical heart-stopping episodes, she'd taken the medication.

Her appointment with the counselor today couldn't come fast enough.

This morning Mason had awakened to a six A.M. call. The Troutdale shooter had been identified overnight and they wanted his presence at the shooter's apartment ASAP. He'd plugged the address into his GPS and hit the Starbucks drive-through after kissing Ava good-bye. She'd been half-asleep in their bed. He'd written her a note and taped it to the bathroom mirror, uncertain if she'd have any memory of his leaving.

The name of the Troutdale shooter was AJ Weiss. Weiss had lived in an apartment basement in his parents' home in Gresham, a city that bordered Portland to the east. And an easy jaunt to Troutdale.

Mason parked on the street and spotted Ray talking on his phone as he leaned against his car, waiting for Mason. Two patrol units were parked in front of the house and one officer stepped out of his car as Mason walked across the street toward the home. No evidence team yet.

Mason identified himself and showed the officer his badge. He glanced at the other patrol car. "Expecting trouble?"

"They're going to release the name of the shooter soon, but I think they're trying to wait until the morning news shows are over to give the family some time to take this in. Who knows what kind of nuts that's going to draw out of the woods," the officer replied. "The parents seem like nice people. Hope it doesn't turn ugly here."

"Make the media keep their distance," said Mason. Ray wrapped up his phone call and joined him.

"That was the medical examiner," said Ray.

The two men headed up the long walkway to the older home. It was a ranch-style home on a raised lot with huge oak trees in the front yard that made Mason cringe to think about the leaf maintenance. A low white iron fence separated the front patio from the yard. Rust spots dotted its joints. Mason lifted the latch. The screech of the hinges made him shudder.

"Argh," said Ray, jerking his shoulders. "*Now* I'm awake."

"What'd Dr. Rutledge say?" Mason asked.

"The identification came in last night. A girlfriend who was convinced it was AJ Weiss called it in and then went to the examiner's in person this morning to visually make the ID."

"Why didn't the parents do it?"

"The girlfriend told Dr. Rutledge she didn't want to disturb them unless she was positive. She says the mother has a heart condition."

"But they know now?"

"Yes, the girlfriend and an officer informed them about an hour ago."

"Shit. They just found out?" Mason looked at the faded silk flower wreath on the door. It had a small wooden heart in the center that said WELCOME. He took a breath and knocked on the door. "Anything else I need to know?"

"Don't think so. Rutledge did the autopsy late yesterday. Healthy twenty-six-year-old."

A young woman with swollen red eyes opened the door and warily studied them. The men held out their identification as Mason made introductions.

"I'm Kari. I was dating AJ," she said softly. Mason wanted to lean forward to hear her. She was tiny and slight, with long straight dark hair and dark eyes. "His parents aren't handling this well." She glanced over her shoulder. "I don't know if this is the best time to talk to them." She hadn't opened the door more than a foot.

"We understand," said Ray. "But we need answers as quickly as possible—"

"Why? He's dead. It's not like you're trying to track down a suspect." Her eyes narrowed at them, reminding Mason of a protective mama cat. "You have all the time in the world to talk to his parents. Let them mourn first."

"Kari," said Mason, wondering how much to reveal to her. "I know this incident feels like it's over to you, but it's not. Yes, AJ is gone, but we need to find out why this happened. We don't want it to happen again."

The young woman looked from Mason to Ray. "What are you saying?"

"We'd like to look through AJ's apartment and see if there's anything that he's left behind that will clear up this picture for us." Mason frowned. "Has anyone else been in there?"

Kari visibly stiffened. "I went in yesterday. We were supposed to meet yesterday afternoon, but he never answered my texts, so I stopped by and let myself in. His parents said they hadn't heard from him. I called and texted him several times. Then I started thinking about the shooting on the news."

"Can we come in, Kari? We need to hear what steps you took to figure it out and to talk about AJ." Mason held her gaze. "I bet you knew him better than his parents." He held his breath. She didn't have to talk to them. Neither did the parents, but things were much easier when people simply wanted to help.

She looked over her shoulder again and then back at the detectives. "Just a minute. Let me talk to Pauline." She closed the door.

Mason and Ray took two steps away from the door. "She better not slow this down," said Ray.

"I think she's just overprotective," said Mason, hoping it was true. "Even the uniform mentioned that the parents were nice people. They must trigger something that makes everyone want to shield them."

Kari stepped out of the house and closed the door behind her. "Pauline is resting. Roy says he'll have her ready to talk in about thirty minutes and that you're welcome to look through AJ's apartment until then. But he asked that you don't remove anything without him knowing. It's this way." She gestured to the men and pushed open the screeching gate, ignoring its scream. The detectives followed her back to the sidewalk, where she turned into the driveway and then headed down a narrow walkway alongside the house. She stopped at the lone side entrance on the lower level and opened the ancient aluminum screen door. She slipped a key in the doorknob and pushed the door open. She stood back, holding the screen, allowing the detectives to enter first.

Mason removed his hat and stepped inside. The ceilings were low. Claustrophobically low. He didn't turn on the light switch. Plenty of light was coming in from the kitchen windows that faced east. The apartment was tiny. One bedroom, one bathroom, and a micro-kitchen.

"Shouldn't you be wearing gloves and foot thingies?" Kari asked, standing outside the open door.

"It's not a crime scene, right?" said Ray. "Does AJ invite a lot of people over?"

She snorted. "No. More than two people in there and it feels too crowded."

Mason agreed. "Let's sit and talk for a few minutes," he suggested. Kari studied him, and he believed she was about to refuse, but she shrugged and entered.

The three of them sat around AJ's glass-and-brass dining table. "We'll put on some gloves before we look around," Mason said, noticing Kari hadn't stopped frowning as she watched their hands. "We don't have a lot of information about AJ yet. Why don't you tell us how long you've known him and what kind of person he was?" Kari looked surprised by the open-ended request. Mason could tell she was a very cautious girl, and distrust continued to radiate from her. His friendly attitude hadn't won her over.

"We've been dating for about a year and a half. He's a good guy, and I'm in shock that he'd do something like this. If I hadn't gone to the morgue to see him myself, I'd never believe it." She clamped her lips together, holding back her tears.

"What made you think that it could be AJ?" Ray asked. "You said you started thinking about the news broadcasts. It was enough to make you reach out to the medical examiner's office, right?"

"AJ's very reliable. Always. I knew something major must have happened to make him vanish and not return texts or calls. Especially with his mother so ill. He's not like that."

Mason tilted his head. "But to think he could have shot several people? That's pretty extreme."

"I didn't look at it that way," she said earnestly. "What I couldn't get out of my head was that an unidentified young man was also dead. The initial description fit. My mind wasn't going to rest until I asked." She looked from Mason to Ray, sincerity on her face.

"Okay," said Mason. "Then why do you think he did it?"

She slumped in her chair, her gaze going to the floor. "I have no idea. He'd been looking for a job for a while, but things weren't that bad. He gets free rent and didn't have any debt."

That you know of. Mason made a mental note to double-check the Weiss financial situation.

"His parents and I have been asking each other why since we found out. None of us has an answer."

"What kind of job was he looking for?" asked Ray.

"Marketing. It's competitive right now."

"He couldn't find anything?" Ray asked. "Was he holding out for something in his field or would he be willing to make coffee for a while?"

"We've both stood behind a coffee bar," Kari answered. "We don't mind doing whatever it takes when bills need to be paid. He also studied drama in college and falls back on that when he needs to. Last week he went shopping for the outfit he needed for an acting gig."

"He had to buy his own costume?" Mason asked. *Sounds like a scam.*

"No, he was given an allowance. It paid well. Some years he made more money through small acting gigs than *real jobs.*" She made air quotes with her fingers. "My point is that he's not the type to sit around and wait for a job to land in his lap. He was looking." Her voice rose. "He was *responsible.* This wasn't something he would do!" She buried her face in her hands. "I don't understand why he did this. Nothing makes sense!"

Mason sat silently as Ray moved next to the girl and patted her on the back. "We'll figure out what happened. There's some sort of explanation."

Kari raised her head and sniffed as she wiped at her wet nose with the back of her hand. "It's not like him. He was so sweet and funny and knew how to make everyone laugh. He's not a killer."

"Not upset with anyone or angry about anything?" Ray asked.

Kari shook her head. "He was too easygoing. He liked to please people and never got upset with anyone."

"No guns?"

"I don't think he's ever touched one in his life."

Mason stood. "Mind if we take a look around now?"

She waved a hand toward the back of the apartment, resentment shadowing her eyes. Beside Ray, Mason poked through AJ's drawers and closet, but Kari's bitter eyes kept flashing through his brain. Their search yielded nothing of interest. No weapons, no drugs, no suicide notes.

One more mystery shooter.

20

A shudder shot through Ava as she stared at the pavement where Misty had been shot.

No trace of blood. Someone had scrubbed away every speck.

She squatted down next to the sunglasses kiosk to get a closer look at a dark spot. *Is that blood?* She blinked and the spot faded. She stood, shaking her head. What would be the point of finding some blood? She knew what'd happened here; she didn't need to find proof.

"Ava!"

She turned at Zander's voice. The agent had agreed to meet her at the mall for another look. Yesterday had been the first day it'd opened for business, and she wondered how the sales had been. Would people avoid shopping here now?

She hoped not.

Zander approached her and glanced at the ground. "What are you doing?" Worry crossed his face.

"Just looking. Not sure why."

"Uh-huh." He studied her face.

"Don't worry, I'm good." She looked away at the entrance to the men's restroom. It seemed much farther away than it had the day of the shooting. "Feels like this happened weeks ago."

"Three days. When's your first appointment with the therapist?"

She gave him a wry look. "Did Mason sic you on me? It's this afternoon. I won't forget."

"He may have mentioned it." Zander looked away, and Ava wondered how much Mason had told him. Did Zander know about the nightmares?

"I just want to sleep better," she admitted.

His raised eyebrow told her he knew she was downplaying the situation.

"A lot better." She started toward the men's room. The mall didn't officially open for another two hours and it felt eerily similar to the morning of the shooting—mostly deserted. A few walkers strolled by, but Ava noticed they looked carefully at her and Zander, studying them for any threat; the opposite of the usual casual mood of the exercisers. She passed the area where the police contact team had made its stand. "I hated seeing Walter have to get down on his knees for the team. I knew how much it was hurting his joints," she commented. "And the fear on the face of the father who was carrying his son—what was his name?"

"Steve Jordan," Zander promptly replied.

"I never heard the third guy's name," Ava mentioned, recalling the last stranger who'd offered to help her and Misty.

"He hasn't come forward," Zander said. "When he reached the perimeter, he didn't tell anyone that he was a witness. He was simply searched and released. I guess he didn't want to be involved."

Ava frowned. "Most people are willing to help. He was very concerned for Misty and me. I'm surprised."

"Maybe he has a reason for staying out of the spotlight. He could be an ex-con or he owes child support."

An ex-con? Ava froze as Zander's words echoed in her head and she tried to recall the third man. Shorts. Cap. T-shirt. A tiny burst of an idea poked at her brain, and she held her breath, terrified she'd lose it. *What if...?*

"Let's get this over with." She strode toward the door. *What if someone wanted to stay under the radar and make us see...*

Before she reached it, the door opened, and a janitor pushed out a garbage can on wheels while pulling a mop and bucket behind him.

"Good morning," said Zander, showing his ID. The janitor stopped and looked them up and down.

"Still investigating?" The young janitor spoke with a Mexican accent.

"Yes, notice anything new?" Zander asked.

The young man shook his head. "No, but your cleanup crew sucked. They did a lousy job getting the blood out of the floor—but I got it all."

"Ah . . . thank you," said Zander.

"Is there a ladder somewhere that we could borrow?" Ava asked. She ignored Zander's questioning look. *Make us see what we want to see . . .*

The janitor shrugged. "Sure. I've got one over there." He nodded to a nearby door with a placard that read EMPLOYEES ONLY.

"Thanks. Anyone in the men's room?"

"No."

Ava pulled open the door and stepped into the brightly lit bathroom.

"What do you want a ladder for?" Zander asked as he followed.

"A hunch."

The men's room looked like all the photos she'd studied at the command center. Except clean. Blood no longer covered the floor and stalls. "Walter Borrego said the shooter kept walking back and forth between the two sides of the restroom." She walked around to the back half of the restroom: a duplicate of the front half where the shooter had shot himself. Same layout of stalls, urinals, and sinks.

"Right. He'd told someone to get on the floor back here. Our third witness who has vanished."

Ava nodded. "I assume all the trash was collected by the techs."

"Yes. There were only a few paper towels. The restrooms had been already cleaned for the day and been barely used."

If there's no place down low . . . She looked up at the ceiling. It was the standard drop ceiling she'd expected. A network of white metal frames and lightweight panels resting on the frames. Zander caught his breath.

"Surely they looked in the ceiling," he said.

"I don't recall seeing it in any reports, but that doesn't mean it wasn't done." A low buzz had started in her brain as she looked at the ceiling. *I could be on a wild-goose chase but that third man . . .*

The door to the bathroom flew open and the janitor came in with a six-foot stepladder. Zander took off his sport coat and hung it on a hook on the wall in one of the stalls. He took the ladder from the janitor and looked at Ava. "Where to start?"

"There wasn't a ladder in here so he would have stood on a toilet or the sink."

Zander nodded and set the ladder up to sprawl over a toilet in the first stall. He started to climb.

Itching to look, Ava eyed the sinks. Would one hold her? She leaned her weight on her hands on one edge and bounced. Seemed solid. She was about to try when an image of it ripping out of the wall as she stood on top stopped her. *Have some patience.* She turned around and watched as Zander pushed up on a ceiling panel with his fingertips. He moved it up and to one side inside the open space above the false ceiling. He stepped higher on the ladder and stuck his head inside.

"It's too dark. I have a flashlight in my car."

"Here," said the janitor. He'd been silently watching and moved forward to hand a flashlight to Zander.

Zander thanked him and shone the flashlight into the space above the panels.

"Well?" Ava asked.

Zander carefully rotated on a step on the ladder, invisible from his shoulders up. He was facing in the direction of the sinks when he stopped turning. "I think there's something in the far corner. It'd be above the sinks."

"I knew it," Ava exclaimed. Not patient enough to wait for the ladder, she climbed on top of the last sink, her worry about its holding her weight gone. *It obviously held someone heavier than me.* She balanced her feet on the sides and slowly stood, looking above her head. She pushed up on the farthest panel, copying Zander's movements. The panel seemed heavy. She pushed harder and one side shot up while the other tipped down and dropped through the metal frame, dumping clothing onto the floor as the white panel crashed beside them. "Aha!" She jumped down.

Zander grabbed her shoulder before she could touch the black clothing, thrusting vinyl gloves into her hands. *Dammit.* She yanked them on, her hands swimming in the huge gloves, and lifted a black Nike jacket from the floor. Thrills shot up her spine and she grinned at Zander, who smiled back, his eyes dancing. "Nice job, Special Agent On Vacation."

She picked up the black athletic pants. "Our shooter changed out of these clothes, shot Justin Yoder who had been hiding in this part of the bathroom—already wearing the same outfit—and ran out, posing as a victim, and left Justin to accept the blame. He strolled right out of the mall—after stopping to talk to me and Misty—and no one blinked."

"We'll have him on camera," said Zander. *"And you've seen his face!* You could recognize him."

Ava caught her breath, thinking hard. "I can't remember him that well—I couldn't see the color of his eyes under the brim of his cap. I had so much adrenaline pumping through me. I was mainly worried for Misty."

"We need to check the restrooms of the other shootings."

"Has he done this before?" Ava could barely breathe as implications flooded her brain.

"We'll find out."

21

He'd been following her for forty-eight hours and knew her name was Ava.

The woman had first appeared on his radar as the police swarmed around Justin Yoder's car in the quiet subdivision close to the mall. He'd been surprised it'd taken them that long to find it. He'd thought the neighbors in that senior living neighborhood would quickly report a strange vehicle. Maybe people were more tolerant than he. A few times he'd left the spot from where he'd watched the car to make food and coffee runs, expecting to return and have missed the show. But the police had finally turned up. He'd watched as the patrol unit pulled up behind the car parked on the street. One officer had stayed in the car, running the plates he assumed, while the other peered in the windows.

He'd seen the cops' body language change as they realized what they'd found. Movements were faster, chins jerked up, and a sense of urgency appeared in their actions in stark contrast to the measured caution of their arrival. More units had arrived within minutes.

But it'd been the investigators out of uniform who had caught his attention. When they'd arrived, the other police had deferred to them immediately. Two men and a woman. The two men had explored the car, careful of what they'd touched. As she should, the woman had stayed back a bit, almost trying to appear inconspicuous, but he'd noticed that both men kept speaking to her and pointing out aspects of the car. She clearly carried some authority and the thought made his skin crawl.

He'd watched her every move—something about her seeming very familiar.

She had a tendency to tuck her hair behind her ear and crack her knuckles, and it'd driven him crazy that he couldn't see her eye color at this distance.

After they'd all looked in the trunk of Justin's car, she'd turned, giving him a direct view of her face through his binoculars.

He did know her.

Ava had been at the Rivertown Mall. He'd offered to help her with the bleeding girl.

Her eyes had been dark blue.

Relief had swept through him as he realized she was with the police because she was a witness. The men were simply being polite in their deference to her; she wasn't in law enforcement.

But something compelled him to follow her, and his misconception had lasted less than a day. Witnesses didn't continually go in and out of the police command center. After he'd seen her enter and leave many times, he started to wonder. She didn't carry a gun or wear a badge, but she moved and conversed like someone in charge. An inappropriate role for her. He'd called a friend to check the plates on her car and discovered it belonged to the federal government.

"Can you be more specific?" he'd asked his friend as a loud buzz started in his brain at the phrase *federal government*.

"I'd guess the car belongs to the Justice Department or the FBI," his friend had answered.

"How do you know?" he whispered.

His friend had paused. "Experience."

He'd offered to help a federal agent that day at the mall? A female federal agent?

Anger shot through him, cranking up the static in his head. She'd refused him. At the moment he hadn't cared, he'd wanted to put as much distance as possible between him and the crime. But when he'd seen the two women on the ground, he'd known it'd look odd to anyone later viewing the video if he didn't offer to help.

Did she think she was so powerful that she didn't need help from a man?

Arrogant bitch.

Through his surveillance he'd learned Ava lived with a man, clearly one of the investigators on the case. He appeared to be a strong alpha type. *How does he put up with her pretentiousness?*

The woman was attractive and probably a good fuck if she left her badge out of the bed. He figured she probably knew where to toe the line if her relationship with the man was successful. But he hadn't seen wedding rings. The relationship was probably new. *How long before she destroys it? Or he gets tired of her true nature?*

Women shouldn't carry a badge. Any sort of badge. Common sense. Females weren't meant to order men around; it went against nature. Everyone knew women were made to nurture and serve.

He'd followed her to the Rivertown Mall earlier this morning and seen her pause as she stared at the ground where the young female had lain bleeding. Then her head had gone up, and she'd marched in an arrogant manner toward the men's room, the other investigator trailing in her wake.

She needed to be taken down a notch.

They'd come out of the men's room and ordered it closed to the public. A security guard had been stationed outside after they'd left and had directed all users to another restroom. He'd gone close enough to hear the guard tell a shopper the police were still recovering evidence in the restroom.

Did they find the clothes?

He'd followed Ava and the other investigator back to the community center and then he'd returned to the mall. He'd bought a hot dog and drink and picked a bench in the shade, pretending to read a book as he kept an eye on the guard at the bathroom.

He'd tried to retrieve the clothing a few times but people were always in the men's room. He had to get the clothes out. Today.

The guard kept stretching his back and shifting his feet. The sun beat directly on his dark-blue uniform and he wiped his forehead several times.

Go get a drink.

The guard checked his watch. Fewer and fewer men were deflected from using the restroom as the heat chased people indoors to the stores.

He sucked hard on his straw, making the last drops of soda slurp in the cup. Across the mall aisle, the guard looked his way. He focused on his book. The guard glanced at his watch, looked around, and walked away from his post.

He waited until the guard had turned the corner before tossing his cup in the garbage. He jogged to the restroom, yanking open the door, welcoming the air conditioning. He strode to the back of the bathroom and hopped up on the last sink and lifted the large tile in the ceiling.

Empty.

His heart sped up and sweat pooled under his arms. He checked another ceiling tile, hearing his pulse pound in his ears, knowing the clothes hadn't moved of their own accord.

Still empty.

He hopped off the sink, leaned his weight on his palms on the sides of the sink and stared in the mirror, ignoring his scars. Why had he waited?

Maybe the police don't know what they have.

Maybe the janitor removed the clothes not knowing what they were.

Maybe . . .

He'd left the clothing at the Troutdale scene, too.

"God damn it!" he roared at his reflection. Angry reddened eyes stared back at him, and he wiped the spit off his lips.

He'd been overconfident.

There's no link to you. Nothing. They have some clothes. That's it.

He slammed his forehead against the mirror. Pain ripped through his skull as cracks shot across the mirror. But the pain softened the sounds pounding in his ears. Blood welled and trickled down his forehead, and he angrily brushed it with his fingers.

It was that female. Ava. She found the clothes. He knew it in his gut.

22

"How can someone convince three young men to go along with plans like these?" Mason asked the group of investigators at the community center, knowing no one had an answer. His question was rhetorical.

Ava and Zander's discovery in the Rivertown Mall's bathroom had stunned all the investigators. A quick search of the Troutdale park bathroom had revealed an identical stash of clothing in the restroom's ceiling. But the bathroom at the Eugene park had an open ceiling. No clothing had been found.

Standing next to him, Ray hadn't stopped shaking his head since he heard the news. "Could he have shoved them in his backpack and walked out?" asked Ray. "Just like at Rivertown Mall, the reports from the Eugene shooting say that a male had run out shouting that the shooter had shot himself—but this witness never came forward. Is there a description of this witness anywhere? Was he wearing a backpack or carrying a bag?"

"Again it was convenient that the last guy out of the restroom never stayed at the scene to give a statement to police," muttered Mason. "He takes full advantage of the panic and terror to blend in."

"I want to review all the Eugene witness statements again," said Sergeant Shaver. "I want special attention paid to the reports where someone saw anyone go in or out of the restrooms. I want these people interviewed again."

"We've got him on camera at the Rivertown Mall," Mason pointed out. "Let's get some stills made of his image and circulate those."

"I don't know," said Zander. He sat down at one of the computers at the center and started tapping. "My recollection of that particular guy is that we never get a good shot of his face."

"There has to be at least one good angle." Mason crossed his fingers as the detectives and agents crowded behind Zander's chair. The discovery of the clothing had given the investigation a shot of energy. He'd watched over and over as each person had digested the news and then reacted in confusion and awe as their minds followed the same thought process.

The killer isn't dead.

Possibly three innocent young men are dead.

Is there one mastermind behind all three shootings?

How did he get these men to participate?

"How could we have missed this?" asked Ray, waiting for Zander to cue up the videos from Rivertown. "Was it the same shooter every time? With a victim waiting in the restroom? How did he convince them to wait for him to come kill them?"

"Don't jump to conclusions," said Zander. "Let's find some proof that our dead shooters didn't do the shooting first."

"I want to find the guy from Rivertown," stated Mason. The third witness from Rivertown had walked right up to Ava and talked to her. *Cocky son of a bitch . . . offering to help them out.* Knowing that she'd been that close to the shooter was making the back of his neck sweat. It was like finding out that the cookies the nice old lady next door had brought you were laced with arsenic.

It's already happened. She's fine. Get over it.

He glanced across the room to where she was deep in discussion with another FBI agent. Looking closer, he realized it was more of an argument. Ava was shaking her head, her back ramrod-straight, with her left hand clenched in a fist.

Uh-oh. *Is she getting her marching orders?*

She'd been flying under the radar in the investigation, getting a lot of leeway from Sergeant Shaver since she was a witness. But officially she was on vacation. Looked like word had gotten back to the office. He glanced at Zander to see if he'd noticed, but Zander had found the video he wanted and a familiar view of the Rivertown Mall filled two screens.

Zander sped it up to where the third witness burst out of the bathroom. His cap was pulled low, covering shaggy hair, the brim hiding his eyes and a large portion of his face from the camera view. Mason leaned closer.

"That asshole. Look." Mason pointed at the screen. "He knew exactly what he was doing. He keeps his head tipped down the entire time. Doesn't matter which angle you switch to. The damned cameras are too high. How about shots of him leaving the area? He has to be caught from a few more angles as he leaves."

"We'll have to go through all that footage again," said Zander. "We weren't focused on those sections."

"There should be footage of Justin Yoder heading into the bathroom," Ray pointed out. "If that's not him with the mask and gun heading into the bathroom, then he had to walk in at some point. He wasn't teleported."

"Fuck me," said Shaver. "We didn't review the hours of video before the shootings, did we?"

"We went back a little ways," said Zander. "Probably not far enough. I know I've seen the clips with Walter Borrego and Steve Jordan with his son heading into the bathroom. We need to back up further. No telling how early Justin Yoder went in—if that's what really happened."

Mason bit his lip. His instinct told him that was exactly what'd happened. Yoder and their mystery witness had been working together. The witness did the shooting while Yoder waited in the bathroom.

But had Yoder known his job was to be a dead body and take the blame for the shootings?

Or had he expected a different role?

"What was Yoder thinking?" Mason asked. Several of the investigators nodded; they'd wondered the same thing.

"I'll guess this didn't play out as he assumed," said Zander. "He probably expected to join in the shooting."

"One weapon," Ray pointed out.

"But he was dressed to shoot," countered Zander.

"Dressed for stealth," clarified Mason. "He might have been told something completely different from what went down. Perhaps he expected to participate in a robbery or some sort of weird fantasy game."

"He stayed silent in the back of the bathroom while the shooter confronted Borrego and Jordan. He was aware of what was happening," argued Ray.

"This is making my head hurt," said Mason. "Let's examine more views of Yoder and our witness before we follow any theories."

"I need to make a statement to the press," said Sergeant Shaver. "Do we let them know we might be looking for another guy?"

"Hell no," said Mason. "Right now he doesn't know we're looking for him. Why give him a heads-up?"

"But it might stop another shooting," said Ava.

She'd silently appeared beside Mason. He studied her face. Stress showed in the new tiny veins that reddened the whites of her eyes. She cracked a knuckle, and he noticed her nails were bitten to the quick. *When did that happen?* An image of a wineglass in her hand from two nights ago popped into his brain; her nails had been trimmed short but not . . . gnawed on.

"How many of these shootings could one person engineer?" asked Ray.

"We don't know that we're looking for one person. Could be a group. Perhaps this is much larger than we realize," added Zander.

The group looked at one another, and Mason felt the stress level rise. Everyone was already exhausted and now the appearance of stashed clothing had opened up a dozen other questions about mass shooting incidents in which they'd believed the organizer was dead.

"I wouldn't say anything about these leads to the press," Mason said slowly. "If our brains are spinning in a million directions now, the press will make it worse. We'll have every armchair detective coming out of the woodwork with theories."

"I'll keep it quiet for now," said Shaver, making eye contact with each person. "But I need answers. Today. I want to see the video of Yoder entering that bathroom and every shot we have of the third witness after the shooting. He went somewhere. Figure out where. And the Eugene witness statements need to be reviewed and new interviews set up."

Everyone nodded.

"We've called these three young men murderers, and now it looks like they might be victims." Shaver shook his head. "If we've done injustice to their families, I want it cleared ASAP."

"This doesn't put them in the clear," said Zander. "It's placed a big question mark above their heads."

"I want it figured out. *Soon*. And the next shooting prevented."

Ava winced, and from the corner of his eye Mason watched her slip a stubby fingernail between her teeth. He turned his head toward her, and she whipped the finger out of her mouth, never taking her gaze off Shaver. She swallowed hard.

Does she need distance from this investigation?

He'd thought being involved would help her, but maybe it'd done the opposite.

Shaver made assignments and Ava wasn't included. Mason wondered what she'd say if he told her to go home. She'd probably just smile and ignore him. He shoved his hat on his head. He and Ray were to look over the Eugene interviews. The group broke apart, and Ava followed him and Ray. Zander had been assigned to oversee the search for more video clips of Justin Yoder and their third witness—the possible shooter.

"I think we need to travel down to Eugene," said Ray. "We're going to want to talk to several people face-to-face."

"Agreed," said Mason. He eyed Ava, wondering if she'd fill him in on her discussion with the other FBI agent in front of Ray. He lifted a brow at her.

"I'll stay here," she said. "Zander can use another pair of eyes."

"Your car or mine?" Ray asked.

"I get carsick if I read in a car," Mason said. "We could get a lot of files covered on the ninety-minute drive down there if you can stomach it."

"Not a problem." Ray looked from Mason to Ava and back again. "I'll meet you out front in a bit."

Mason jerked his head toward a door, and she followed him out of the main room into a quiet hallway. She leaned against the wall with a sigh. He stepped close and lifted her chin until her gaze met his. "What happened?"

"Nothing happened."

"I saw your *discussion* with that agent. What's up his ass?"

One side of her mouth curled up. "He was questioning my presence here. He knows I'm not assigned."

"Did Ben Duncan send him?"

"No. If Ben wanted to tell me to go home, he'd call me."

"Are you going to get a call?"

She frowned. "I don't know. I've been half expecting it."

"How'd you think to look in the ceiling?"

"I've been wondering if these young men were under orders from some cult-like figure who directed the shootings. But then Zander mentioned that maybe the third guy hadn't come forward because he was an ex-con that didn't want to be noticed. Something about the word 'ex-con' made me think about repeat crimes and how if the shootings *were* repeat crimes, how else could one person accomplish it? We'd seen a person in black go in and not come out. Suddenly I knew he'd have to take off the black clothing and hide it because I talked with him when he left. He was empty-handed. It had to be somewhere."

Mason didn't question the way her mind had jumped around. It'd happened to him dozens of times. When his neurons started firing he didn't question how they worked.

"Maybe you should go home and relax for the rest of your vacation. Read a book or binge-watch something."

Her wary dark gaze held his. "What are you saying?"

He lifted one of her hands and lightly touched the ragged nails. Her gaze followed his touch. "This isn't like you," he said. She tried to pull back her hand, but he held on and clasped it between both of his. "Look at me," he said.

Insecurity looked at him through her blue eyes.

"I know you want to help. I know how good it feels to lose yourself in work when there's something stabbing at your heart. I've done it a million times. But I think you need some more downtime. Didn't you have an appointment today?"

"Crap!" She yanked her hand out of his and dug out her phone. "I missed it! Finding those clothes put all rational thoughts out of my head today. Dammit!"

A lecture about letting work overtake her life was on the tip of his tongue. But he couldn't do it; he was just as guilty—if not worse.

Kettle, meet pot.

"Call them. Now. Get in as soon as you can. I don't like you tossing and turning all night." *Or lunging out of bed in terror.*

"You're not the only one," she muttered. "I feel like only half my brain is engaged these days. But I had to wait for this appointment. I'm afraid they won't get me in until next week."

"I'm heading to Eugene. If they can't see you today then go home. Get away from this for a while."

"I will," she promised.

He looked hard at her.

"*I will.*"

He hugged her and kissed her good-bye. "I'll be back late tonight," he said. He and Ray could stay in Eugene overnight, but he didn't want her alone tonight. She probably didn't mind, but the thought of her alone in their bed bothered him. A lot.

"I'll be waiting."

• • •

Ava wanted to bang her head on the steering wheel. The therapist couldn't see her until next week.

I knew it!

She hadn't sounded pleased that Ava had missed her first appointment, and Ava knew the woman had no interest in taking on flaky patients. "This really isn't like me," she'd pleaded. "We had a hot hit on a case today."

"I thought you were on vacation," came the therapist's reply.

Ava backtracked and acknowledged that she wasn't supposed to be working. She was a poor patient. She might be a prompt and responsible person, but everything went out the window when one of her cases suddenly grew legs. It'd happened several times when she'd worked Crimes against Children. Her cases had been all-consuming and she'd often missed appointments and social events with friends.

I don't mean to be irresponsible.

The problem was that she saw other people's lives as more important than her own well-being. She had it good. She lived in a nice home and had a great guy and a good job. She lived the American Dream. But when she saw someone else was being victimized and she had the power to help, she felt obligated to make it a priority because when the day was over, she could return to her dream life. The victims and their families remained in limbo until answers were found.

Time to take care of myself. She'd promised Mason she'd go home and relax. Maybe it was time to catch up on that TV crime series. *No. Something funny. A show where I can turn off my brain and eat ice cream.* She turned on her car and planned a stop at the grocery store.

Her phone rang.

She glanced at the unfamiliar number that popped up on the screen on her vehicle's dashboard. *Maybe the therapist?* She kept her car in park and pressed the green button on her steering wheel to answer the call.

"Is this Ava?" asked a male voice. He nearly shouted in the phone as voices in the background moaned and cried.

She sat up straight. "This is Ava." She listened hard, trying to make out the words in the background.

"Your sister had me call you. She's bad off. The fire department's here and they're working on her."

"What happened?" She gripped her steering wheel, her foot pressed on the brake, staring at the phone number on her dashboard screen.

"I don't know. I found her collapsed in Jefferson Park and called 911. She was throwing up and there's blood everywhere."

Her heart stopped. "Was she hit by a car? What—what did she do?"

"No car. She was behind the restroom structure." He hesitated. "Her wrists are all bloody."

No. Jayne. Tell me you didn't . . .

"Are they taking her to the hospital?" she forced out.

She heard him question someone.

"Yeah. OHSU."

"I'm on my way." She paused, her mind unable to focus. "Thank you for calling me."

"She's bad. I don't want to scare you, but it doesn't look good."

Ava froze. "I appreciate that."

"Just warning you."

Ava ended the call. She didn't need warnings; she'd expected this day for two decades.

23

Sirens sounded.

He glanced in his rearview mirror. Red and blue lights. His hands tightened on the steering wheel.

Is this it?

He looked in the mirror again. Only one set of lights. If they'd figured out who he was, they'd have sent twenty police cars, not one. He steadied his breathing and flicked on his blinker. Sweat made his fingers slide across the leather wheel as he turned the vehicle down a side street and pulled to a stop. He turned off the engine and wiped his hands on his shorts.

Stay calm. In his side mirror, he watched a woman step out of the cruiser.

Jesus-God-damned-fucking-Christ!

Every muscle clenched, and he ground his teeth, creating a sound as if he were chewing rocks. This wasn't happening to him.

She was small and blond with her hair pulled tightly back. She met his gaze in the mirror as she strode toward his vehicle, and he looked away.

Unacceptable.

"Good afternoon, sir." She stopped a step behind his driver window. Her stomach and weapon visible in his side mirror. "May I see your license and registration, please?"

He didn't answer, knowing she'd had a clear view of the distorted skin on the left side of his neck. He leaned across to the glove box and dug for his registration. He held the piece of paper out the window without looking at her, feeling her gaze probe his scars.

"License?" she asked, plucking the registration from his hand. Her voice was young. She sounded like a middle-school-age child.

"I'm getting it," he muttered. He shifted in his seat to remove his wallet from his back pocket.

"Do you know why I stopped you?" she asked sweetly.

"No." He slid his ID out of his wallet, and turned to meet her gaze as he handed her the plastic. Her eyes were an impossibly light blue and her cheeks were sunburned. Or flushed. *Is she scared?*

A rush of pleasure made him smile at her.

"Your plates are expired."

"What?" Shock rocked through him. He'd been pulled over for that? "Seriously? I haven't received a renewal in the mail."

"Have you moved recently? Perhaps they were lost in the mail. I'm sorry, but that's not an excuse. You can contact the DMV if you haven't received new stickers."

Her tone was like fingers on a chalkboard. Condescending and haughty. "Yes, I moved recently." Anger narrowed his vision to a small point.

She sounded like his mother, pointing out everything he'd done wrong. He'd never done anything good enough for her.

"I'll go to the DMV."

She handed back his registration and license. "I'm going to give you a warning. Your stickers are only a month out of date. Can you make it to the DMV today?"

"I'll go right now. I don't want to be pulled over again." *And lectured by a woman.*

Minutes later he was back in traffic and fighting the rage that overtook him every time he remembered her tone. "Fucking bitch. She's just another woman looking for a reason to talk down to a man. She must really get off on ordering men around."

His mind raced ahead. *What if she'd pulled her gun on me?* He imagined himself throwing open his driver's door and leaping out, focusing on the scared woman. *He strode toward her, never taking his eyes from hers as her weapon shook in her hands. She screamed for him to stop. But he didn't. He reached out and yanked the weapon away as she stepped backward, cowering from him, tears flowing from those light eyes. "Don't hurt me," she said. He released the magazine and removed the round from the chamber, throwing the pieces to the side. He stepped close, pressing her back against her own car. "Don't tell me what to do," he whispered. She tilted her head back to look up at him, nodding frantically, trapped between his body and her vehicle. Fear radiated from her, her trembling passing between their pressed bodies. He tossed the remaining frame of the weapon through the driver's window of her car.*

Hate flooded over him. "Why do you do this?" he roared at her.

Shaking violently, she lowered her gaze. He stepped back, losing the heat of her body, and shoved her aside. "You don't belong in uniform."

He walked back to his car, feeling her terrified gaze on his back.

The daydream made him sigh. *That's what I should have done.* He relived it three more times and each time she cowered more, terrified by his power, acknowledging that she'd been wrong to give him orders. By the time he pulled into the parking lot at the DMV, he was relaxed.

He wasn't taking any more chances with his expired plates.

• • •

He looked at his watch.

I've been here over an hour! He glared around the dingy DMV waiting room, catching the gaze of a child two rows ahead. Her eyes widened and she ducked down behind the back of her seat, peering cautiously at him over the edge. He was used to the horrified second glances and visible recoils. He wasn't pretty to look at; he knew it. At one time he'd avoided people, but now for the most part he didn't give a shit. *Keep staring. Get a good eyeful.*

Most of the time he wore a cap that kept his longer hair in place over the scars. It helped but didn't hide everything.

He'd removed it when he entered the building. An echo of the manners his mother had taught him and it made people keep their distance. As a general rule he didn't like people. He didn't like their small talk and fake politeness. Removing his cap made people avoid him and that was how he liked it. No one sat in the chairs to either side of him even though the waiting room was packed.

He was a monster. And he was fine with that.

Privately he thought of himself as a type of Jekyll and Hyde. But he had full control over his two personas. One side people knew and respected; the other side everyone avoided at all costs. He chose when each appeared. He wasn't dissociative; he decided how he wanted to act each day. It was empowering to know that he could cause people to cower in fear.

But it wasn't satisfying when the scared were children.

He looked again at the small brown eyes studying him. Her fear had dissipated and now she was simply curious. He gave her a half smile and her head rose a few inches above the chair back to smile back at him, a sliver of acceptance in her gaze.

Why don't adults accept? He'd noticed that small children quickly got over their initial scare and moved on. At what age did humans lose that skill? Adults never got past his grafts. Neither did teens. Somewhere in childhood a person lost the ability to accept differences without judgment.

His number was called.

Relief swept over him and he stood, edging his way out of his row. He was moving toward the window assigned to his number when a woman rushed in front of him and slapped her ticket down in front of the agent. "No one called my number," she said. "And now you've passed it!"

He froze midstep.

The woman looked over her shoulder at him. Her heavy eyeliner and bleached hair made her look like a whore. "You don't mind, do you?"

He did. He minded a lot. "Go ahead."

The female agent made eye contact with him, nervously nodded, and focused on the woman's issue.

Fifty sets of eyes burned holes through the back of his shirt. *Do I go sit back down? Or wait?* He looked at the automatic number display that declared his number was currently being helped. Was he going to be skipped now? Fury burned up his spine. He scanned the other agents, all busy with customers. Any second they were going to call another number, and he would have to publicly declare he was next. He shoved his hat on his head and heard his mother's voice berate him for wearing it indoors. *Tough shit.*

That whore had cut in front of him and the female agent had let it happen.

He stood powerless in front of an audience, stripped of his rights. Sweat dripped down the center of his back. He didn't move. He wasn't going to let a woman do that to him again. *I will be next.*

Women first, Son. Always remember that. He tried not to cringe at his mother's voice in his head. A physical blow had always followed the words. Either an abrupt slap to the back of the head or a fist to the ear. His mother hadn't always hit him. It'd started after they had taken away his father—after the cops had taken away his father.

He closed his eyes in the DMV as the memory flooded his brain, clear and sharp as yesterday. But he'd been ten.

His mother had sported bruises and black eyes for years. He'd thought that was normal. Women needed discipline, his father had explained. Their brains didn't function the same way as a man's. Without male guidance and protection, they'd all be whores, living on the street and selling their bodies.

He'd assumed a man would purchase a woman because he needed someone to clean for him, iron his shirts. That was why women sold their bodies. It wasn't until he was in sixth grade that a friend had told him the truth in whispered tones behind closed doors.

Disgusting.

One late evening when he was twelve, the police arrived. He'd been in his bedroom, his music cranked up through his headphones as usual so he couldn't hear his parents fight. But he'd seen the lights flashing outside his window. He'd lifted his blinds and peered out, expecting to see a fire truck or police car across the street. Three police cars were parked in front of his home. He ripped off the headphones and dashed to the kitchen.

His father was facedown on the linoleum. A cop's knee in his back as she wrestled to lock handcuffs around his wrists. A male cop held his mother back as she screamed for them to let her husband go. After a moment's hesitation, he ran to pull the female officer off his father. Hands grabbed his shoulders and another female cop neatly corralled him. "Don't interfere, son."

"I'm not your son!" he shouted, thrashing to get out of her arms. He looked to his mother. Blood ran out of her nose and a fresh cut marred her cheek. "Mom!" He thrashed again, but the officer held him tight.

"She's going to be fine," said the officer holding him. "We'll get him away from her."

Dad did that to Mom? He shook his head. *No. Bruises maybe, but he'd never make her bleed.*

The female officer climbed off his father, leaving him on his stomach with his hands cuffed behind his back. "Fucking bitch!" his father shouted. "You have no right to do this in *my home!*"

The female cop ignored his father and wiped the sweat off her forehead as she turned and smiled. "You won't need to worry about your father tonight."

He stood stock-still, staring at the officer. They were arresting his father for nothing, and she was *smiling*? "Get out!" he shouted at her.

Her face fell, the smile vanished, and her eyes narrowed at him. She pointed at his mother. "Do you see her face?"

"He didn't do that! *You* did it!"

"No, your neighbors called us because your mother was screaming so loud."

"You're a liar!" he screamed. He wrestled to get his arms free, but the female officer holding him was unnaturally strong.

The female who'd lied to him exchanged looks with the other officers and rolled her eyes. His dad was right. Women shouldn't be in power. It went against nature.

"Fucking bitch," he shrieked. He'd never spoken such ugly words.

"Sir? I can help you now." The agent's words interrupted his memory.

He opened his eyes. The female agent was looking at him, curiosity in her gaze. Had she already called him? Anger and embarrassment drove through him and his face heated. Every cell in his body told him to turn around and leave. Walk out. Don't give in to the female.

But he needed his plates renewed.

He swallowed hard and stepped up to her window. The whore with the black eyeliner had left and he hadn't noticed.

How long did I stand there with my eyes shut?

He slid his numbered ticket across the counter. "My plates have expired. I moved recently and I think the new stickers have been lost in the mail."

Her lips smiled but the kindness didn't touch her eyes. "I can help you with that." She was mousy-looking. Fine bones, limp brown hair, and no makeup. She blinked too much, but her fingers moved with precision on her keyboard. This was the correct type of position for a woman. She serves. The public has demands, and she fulfills them.

She reminded him of his mother—in the good years before they took away his father. In the years following his father's conviction, his mother had tried to become one of *them*: a woman who bossed others around. He'd set her straight. If his father had been alive, he would have been proud.

He exhaled and counted backward from ten. His blood still boiled from the place-cutting whore and the childhood memory. The meek woman's actions calmed him as she worked efficiently behind the counter to meet his needs. She didn't stare at his scars.

This is how it should be.

24

Mason knocked on the door of Tana Britton's Eugene home and children's voices immediately shouted. He glanced at Ray.

"She's got three kids," said Ray.

Mason nodded. After a review of the witness statements from the Eugene shooting, Tana's had stood out as giving the best description of the shooter. Over the phone she'd agreed to talk to the investigators in her home. The door opened and the spicy scent of tacos touched his nose. His stomach rumbled, and he was thankful he and Ray had agreed to grab a late dinner after the interview. Tana had a baby on a hip and a larger child clinging to her leg. Down the hall behind her, a baby crawled as fast as he could toward the door, determined to join his mother. Mason looked from the baby on her hip to the baby on the floor.

"Yes, they're twins," Tana stated. Her dark hair was pulled back in a ponytail and her brown eyes were surprisingly calm for those of a mother with three young children. The girl attached to Tana's leg blinked at him with eyes identical to her mother's. A mini-me. Tana glanced behind her to locate the other twin and then carefully stepped back. "Come in."

Ray pointed at the boy on the floor. "Can I?" he asked Tana. She nodded.

He deftly scooped up the boy. "Hey, big guy." The baby stared solemnly at him.

"That's Lane. This is his sister Cora and the big sister, Ellie."

Mason shoved his hands in his pockets. It'd been a while since he'd been around babies. He never knew what to do with one and didn't feel the need to hold one. He was content with just looking. Babies harbored surprises. Usually the kind that made adults change their shirts. He followed Ray into a large family room. The rug was covered with toys and two swings took up way too much space. Mason perched on the couch next to Ray, who expertly balanced the baby on one knee. The baby continued to silently stare at Ray.

All Mason remembered about that baby's age was his panic when Jake started to crawl. Suddenly everything in their home had become a potential threat.

Tana sat in an easy chair across from them and shifted Cora onto her lap. Ellie immediately squeezed herself into the tiny space left in the chair and eyed the investigators suspiciously. Cora grabbed at her mother's tank top strap and pulled before Mason could look away. Tana snagged her strap and her daughter's fist in time to avoid embarrassment all around. "Whoops."

Mason pulled out Tana's written statement from the Eugene shooting. "You were at the park really early that morning," he said.

Tana nodded. "When I've got three kids who can't sit still, getting in the car and going *anywhere* keeps me sane. They were all waking up at five A.M. during that month. I'm glad that's over. This month they've been sleeping in until seven. Well, at least two of them have been." She eyed the oldest, Ellie, who Mason estimated was close to four years old. "I know every park in the area and Green Lake is a good one. It's got a huge sand area and even a clean water feature. It's usually our first choice." Her gaze dropped. "At least it used to be. We haven't gone back since it happened." She ran a hand over Ellie's dark curls. "I don't think the twins will remember, but Ellie sometimes talks about that day. I won't go back because I'm afraid it will reinforce her memories. I want her to forget." She gave Mason a weak smile. "Maybe next summer."

He met Ellie's gaze. Kids were sponges. How much did she still remember? Anger rolled through him at the thought of her terror. "Umm ... maybe ..."

"Ellie, weren't you watching Elmo?" Tana asked.

The child immediately slipped out of the chair and trotted down another hallway. "It's on in our bedroom," Tana explained. "When she's watching she doesn't hear a word I say. It's almost scary."

Elmo had been Jake's favorite, too.

"Can you tell me what you remember from that day?" Mason scanned her statement as she talked, listening for any changes or inaccuracies. He hadn't let her review the written statement, wanting her to freshly recall the incident. Her account matched what she'd written almost perfectly.

"You said he'd sat in the car in the parking lot for a while," Ray stated. "How long would you estimate that time to be?"

Tana looked up at the ceiling, bouncing Cora on her knee as the baby started to squirm. "I remember wondering if he was talking on a cell phone. I couldn't see one," she quickly clarified. "But that's what you expect is happening when someone parks and doesn't get out. I don't know the time. Maybe two or three minutes?"

"You were watching the car pretty closely?" Mason asked.

She shrugged. "I have three kids. Do you know what it's like to have your attention divided into three sections? I don't have much focus for anything else." Her gaze narrowed at Mason. "But when you're a mom, part of your senses are always on the lookout for trouble. I notice when unfamiliar people enter an area where my children are playing. I notice when dogs appear or vehicles arrive. My mind leaps ahead a hundred steps and sees all possible outcomes, and you can be damn sure I take action when I see one of those outcomes start to unfold."

"So your radar went up with this vehicle?"

"A little bit. I could see movement in the car, like someone was leaning over the backseat, and wondered if the person was getting a kid ready."

Wiping it down. They'd received word that the only prints on the vehicle had been around the trunk and the rear doors. The entire front seat area had been thoroughly wiped down, along with most of the backseat.

"Then he stepped out with that gun and I saw he'd put on a mask, so I went into action." Tana closed her eyes. "Cora and Lane were in the sand, two feet from me. I grabbed them and yelled for Ellie, who was over by a slide. She just turned and stared at me, so I ran to her." Wet brown eyes opened and looked at Mason. "I had a twin on each hip, but I shoved them both into one arm and grabbed her hand and we dashed behind the castle. He was already shooting."

Mason had studied park pictures that showed the castle, a solid structure that stood about four feet high with an opening for kids to crawl inside and peer out through narrow slits of windows. The castle was about fifty feet from the restrooms. He doubted it would have stopped a bullet.

"The screams . . ." Tana looked away and tears dripped from her cheeks onto Cora's shoulder. She wiped them off.

Mason leaned forward. "You must have been terrified for your children."

"You have no idea."

I have a bit of an idea.

"I want you to think about when the shooting stopped. You said you heard a man yell that the shooter had shot himself. You got a good look at him?"

Tana brushed at her cheeks and swallowed. "I did. I looked around the corner when I heard him shout. The shooting had stopped."

"What was he wearing?" Mason prodded carefully.

The mother frowned. "Shorts. Tank top. A hat."

"Like a baseball cap?" Ray asked.

"Yes. I can't recall the color. Something dark. Dark longer hair, too. Like just touched his shoulders."

"Was he skinny? Short? Fat?" questioned Ray.

"Tall," Tana said. "Narrow build. Long arms. He was holding them up as he ran like he was surrendering. I remember being relieved when I saw him because he seemed so assured that the shooter was down."

"What did he do next?"

She shook her head. "I don't know. I turned back to my kids and stayed behind the castle for at least a good minute. I couldn't move; I was absolutely frozen. All I could do was hang on to my babies. If the shooter had walked around the castle at that minute, we'd all be dead." She took a shuddering breath. "I was able to react and get them out of the way at the right time. But as soon as I heard it was over, I couldn't do a thing."

"That's pretty normal for a stressful situation," Mason said. "Are you seeing anyone?"

"Yes, I followed up with my pediatrician because I was concerned that Ellie would need to talk with someone. The doctor saw that I needed help and put me in touch with someone." She gave a shaky smile. "Ellie's been fine. No behavior issues at all. I'm the one that's a wreck."

"Did you see the man with the cap afterward?" Mason asked.

Tana thought. "No. I don't think so. My memory is crystal-clear up to where he shouted that the shooter shot himself and then after that it's all a blur."

"Anything else you remember about the shouting man?" asked Mason.

"He was wearing a backpack."

Mason exchanged a look with Ray. *He carried away the black clothing.*

25

Her phone rang through her car speakers as Ava whipped into the parking garage at Oregon Health & Science University. She hit the button on her wheel and flinched as her voice shook as she answered the phone. She'd had thirty minutes to stress over Jayne's condition on the drive to the hospital, and she'd nearly run through two red lights.

"Ava? This is Charlene. I'm sorry I missed your call yesterday."

The manager at Jayne's halfway house.

"Did you hear about Jayne? What happened to her?"

"No." Charlene's voice sharpened. "What are you talking about?"

Ava hit her brakes as she nearly rear-ended a sedan backing out of a parking space. The sound of her pounding heart filled her car. She waited and snagged the space. She turned off her car and leaned her head against her headrest. "I had a call thirty minutes ago. It sounds like Jayne attempted suicide. They took her to OHSU. I just got here."

"What?" The manager let out a string of curses that made Ava's ears burn. "She's been gone all day. She was here for check-in last night, but took off at daybreak this morning. I'm sorry, Ava. She was doing so well—"

"I know!" Ava exclaimed. "My calls with her—"

"—until yesterday," Charlene finished.

Ava caught her breath. "What happened yesterday?"

"She was in quite a state. Ranting and picking arguments with two of the other girls. Twice I had to fine her for abusive language. I was going to call you if she didn't straighten out. First she was gone all afternoon and then she was on a tear last night."

"She called me yesterday afternoon. She'd gone to our old place and was furious that we'd moved and not told her." Ava closed her eyes.

"Oh, Ava." Charlene's voice lowered. "That must have been a huge shock for her. All she does is talk about you."

Ava's guilt increased tenfold. "I need to go inside. A guy found her in Jefferson Park with bloody wrists."

Charlene was silent for several seconds. "I didn't see anything leading to this," she said slowly. "She seemed so balanced lately."

"I know. I felt the same way."

"Please tell me what you find out," Charlene said. "You realize she can't return here. An incident like this is an automatic dismissal. I'm really sorry."

She could hear the sincerity in Charlene's tone. "I know. I appreciate all you've done for her."

The call ended and Ava sat in the silent car. The pounding of her heart had returned to normal. *I don't want to go inside.* She wanted to turn the car back on and leave. Drive home and read a book. The bottle of wine she'd bought last week dominated her thoughts. *Vodka would be faster.*

She craved blissful nothingness. *Go home and let the doctors deal with Jayne.*

Go inside and deal with the uproar. Stress. Paperwork. Where would Jayne go live now? Who would help her?

Sixty seconds ago her main purpose had been to get to Jayne and find out her condition.

Now she wanted to hide.

Jayne could be dead. She paused, letting the thought sweep through her, analyzing and holding her breath as she waited for her reaction.

Nothing.

I'm numb.

Tears leaked down her cheeks. Had it come to this? Was she so damaged that the death of her twin would mean nothing? She started the car and placed it in reverse. Why had she driven all this way if she didn't care? She looked over her shoulder and wiped her eyes, unable to see. She blinked and wiped again, unable to view any passing cars. She slumped in her seat and reluctantly turned off the car. She couldn't drive—and she couldn't go in.

Indecision froze her. She was powerless.

Mason. More anxiety crippled her. She hadn't called or texted him about Jayne, afraid to face his disappointment. Mason's view on Jayne was clear: she messed with Ava's head and was best avoided.

Call him.

She couldn't do it. She didn't want to hear how wrong she was to have driven to the hospital, to have given Jayne five minutes of her time.

I know he's right. She shouldn't have come.

Ava dug her phone out of her purse and her fingers paused. *He's in Eugene. He can't get here for at least two hours.*

She mashed her lips together—and called Zander.

26

Mason and Ray compared notes in his car. It'd been late by the time they left Tana Britton's home, but they didn't want to head back to Portland until they'd talked with the cousin of shooter Joe Albaugh.

"It looks like he's the spokesperson for Albaugh's family," said Ray as he studied a file. "The parents wanted to stay out of the spotlight after Albaugh was announced as the shooter. Bill Albaugh was at the press conferences and kept reporters away from the immediate family."

Mason understood perfectly. In an emotional time, having someone slightly removed to handle the public was a godsend.

"It's late. Should we call him?" Ray asked.

"I don't want to come back to Eugene. We hit our main goal of finding out about the backpack, which means that last male witness could have left with clothes and might be the real shooter. Now we need to find out who he is. I think finding the connection between the three shooters is the way to pinpoint our suspect."

Ray nodded. "I know Shaver is shifting focus to the young men's backgrounds to look for that connection. I think talking to the cousin would be a good start. Maybe he could pave the way for us to talk to the parents. The parents' interviews from June don't reveal a lot. The investigators thought they had the suspect so they were simply looking for the why. The parents didn't know why he killed those people. Claimed Albaugh gave no sign."

"He was the one with the headaches, right?"

"Yes. That's the only odd thing the parents claimed was going on with their son."

"But he didn't live at home, so they couldn't really know. I wonder how much they saw him."

"This says the parents' phone number has been disconnected," Ray said, flipping file pages. "I bet the publicity was too much for them. Probably got tons of hate calls."

"What's the cousin's number?" Mason asked. "And let's not say a word about the mystery shooter."

"Of course not," said Ray. He read it off and Mason dialed. He connected to his car's Bluetooth so Ray could hear. A male answered and Mason identified the two of them and asked if he was Bill Albaugh.

"Yes. I heard you're taking another look at the shooting because of the recent shootings in Portland, right?" Bill asked.

"That's correct," said Mason. "We're looking to see if there's some sort of commonality between the three young men. We're wondering if they knew each other."

"Makes sense," said Bill. "But that sounds awfully hard to pinpoint."

"I assume you've been following the info on the latest shooting? The shooter was AJ Weiss. Did his name ring any bells for you?"

"Yes, I'm following the news. I've heard the name, and I saw the guy's picture on TV. I didn't recognize him. I asked Joe's parents the same question once the name was made public. They hadn't heard of him, either."

"The number we have for his parents is disconnected," said Ray. "Do you have a new one?"

"I do," said Bill. "But I'm not giving it out until I talk to them about it. You have no idea how this has destroyed my uncle and his wife. There was a backlash from around the world. People are fucking crazy. What makes someone who lives in Tokyo feel they have the right to send them hate mail? It was clear my aunt and uncle had no idea what Joe was going to do. They didn't beat him or emotionally cripple him. This was solely Joe's action, but the public feels the need to berate and hate on the parents."

Mason exchanged a look with Ray. The Internet had opened up instant access to the world, but too many people used it as an instrument of hate. "I'm sorry, Mr. Albaugh. I know exactly the type of people you're talking about."

"I was closer to Joe than anyone—he was only five years younger than me. He lived just a mile away all through his college years. I probably knew him better than his roommate."

"Do you have any ideas about how he might have crossed paths with the two shooters from the Portland area?" Ray asked.

"Believe me, I've been thinking about it ever since the mall shooting. I just can't see it. Joe never went up there. If he had friends in Portland, I didn't know about it. The guy worked like sixty hours a week. He rarely took time off. I have to imagine they're copycats."

Mason bit his tongue, wishing the copycat theory were true. "How come he worked so much?"

Bill gave a harsh laugh. "He always had to have the latest and greatest electronics and toys. There was no filter with Joe when it came to spending; if he wanted it he bought it. He could never seem to catch up, though. He always was moaning about credit card bills. He worked those hours and picked up odd jobs so he could spend. He liked to buy stuff for people, too. Generous guy. Always had happy girlfriends."

"What do you know about Joe's headaches?" asked Ray.

"That they were driving him crazy."

"How'd he manage to work so much if he was in pain?" Mason asked.

"He claimed work distracted him from the pain. Joe claimed it wasn't a debilitating pain but more of a supreme annoyance. He'd learned to live with it."

"He didn't visit any doctors in the Portland area, did he?" Mason asked.

"Not that I'm aware of," answered Bill.

"The list of specialists we got from his parents was all local," Ray pointed out.

Mason nodded. He'd remembered that. But it didn't mean Joe couldn't have visited some off the list. They wouldn't know unless they asked.

"Did he show an interest in gun clubs?" Mason asked. "I'm fishing a bit here, but what about white supremacy or domestic terrorism? We're looking for anything that could shine some light on how these young men could know each other. And we're still looking for a motive in all three shootings. People don't do what these three men did without a motive."

"I understand you have to ask shit like that," Bill replied, his voice growing tight. "But I can tell you in all honesty that I'm not aware of anything like that. The police searched his apartment and took his computer. Wouldn't they have found something there if that was true?"

Ray pointed at the file on his lap and then held up his hands, shaking his head. *All clear.*

Mason wanted to swear. Joe Albaugh's apartment had been cleaned out a few weeks after the shooting. He knew the parents had requested some of the items, while Lane County had kept others. A detailed list was in the file. He asked Ray for the list and looked it over while Ray asked Bill about Joe's hobbies.

There is something here. I feel it.

27

Ava jumped as someone tapped on her window. Zander scowled through the glass.

She'd called him from the hospital parking garage, her voice sounding oddly flat and emotionless in her head as she told him she didn't know what to do. He'd asked a few questions, rapidly understood her situation, and ordered her not to move until he arrived.

It seemed as if she'd hung up five minutes ago. A glance at her clock told her thirty minutes had ticked by.

I've been staring into space for half an hour?

She opened her door. "Where'd you park?"

He took her arm as she stepped out, his mouth in a tight line. "We're going inside the hospital. Did you find out anything about your sister?"

She blinked at him. "No."

"You don't know if your sister is alive or dead?"

"No."

"Did you call Mason yet?"

"No. I don't know what to say to him."

A muscle in his cheek twitched. "As soon as we find out what's happened, you call him."

She nodded and made her feet move toward the hospital doors.

Inside they discovered that Jayne was alive.

Zander asked questions and pressured the clerk at the computer until he found out Jayne's medical status. It took another twenty minutes for a doctor to have the time to talk to them. The ER physician took a hard look at Ava, clearly comparing her face to that of the woman he'd worked on. "She cut her arms deep enough to severely damage a tendon," he said. "I've requested a specialist to take a look. And there's a gash on the left side of her lower chest where it appears she may have stabbed herself. We'll know more after the CT scan. She'll probably need surgery for both injuries."

Ava stared at him, thoughts of insurance, rehab, and costs spinning through her brain.

"At the park, the paramedic administered a medication to offset the respiratory depression she'd caused by taking too many narcotics. We've had to give her a few more doses."

"She anesthetized herself," Ava said. "Nearly to death."

"Exactly," the doctor agreed. "Has she attempted suicide before?"

"She's talked about it several times, but this is the first time she's harmed herself. She has a history of mental illness." Ava's face burned; she felt as if she were betraying her twin. She knew the doctors needed to know; this was not the time for secrets.

The doctor nodded, his gaze never leaving Ava's face. "Physically she's going to be fine; she's stable and out of overdose danger. The next step is to figure out the best treatment for the arms and abdomen. I'll get a psych evaluation and see if we can get her admitted to the psych department—at least while she's recovering from surgery. I want her monitored so she doesn't damage the surgical sites."

Ava couldn't speak. He was absolutely right. Jayne couldn't be trusted about anything—her health or the safety of the people around her. She felt Zander's hand tighten on her shoulder, and she wanted to crawl in a hole. High levels of sympathy rolled off the men, and she ached to run away.

Where is my spine?

She should have been grateful that people were working to help Jayne; instead she was embarrassed, as if she'd been the one to slash her wrists and create havoc. She forced a confidence she didn't feel. "I'm sorry."

"No reason to be sorry," the doctor said. "*You* didn't do this. Clearly your sister needs some help, and I suspect she hasn't accepted the help in the past?"

"You wouldn't believe how much help she's walked away from," stated Zander.

"Can I see her?" Ava asked.

The doctor paused. "Not yet. Let's get her tests and evaluations finished. Perhaps later."

The doctor was called away, and Zander led Ava to an empty waiting room. "You need to call Mason. Now," he told her with a direct look. "I have my own calls to make." He held her gaze until she nodded.

Ava sat in a hard chair and listened to the fluorescent lights buzz overhead.

I don't want to see her.

Shame washed over her, and she slumped in the chair. What good could seeing Jayne do? The doctor said she was out of danger, and she knew Jayne couldn't care less if Ava appeared. She was getting attention from the doctors and nurses. Ava wouldn't enter her thoughts until the fuss settled down. Then she'd reach out, seeking sympathy, satisfying her narcissistic urges.

I won't give in.

In the adjacent hallway, Zander paced as he talked on his cell phone. She tuned out his voice and ignored the pointed looks he continued to give her.

She pulled her cell phone out of her purse and stared at the screen. It felt like a ten-pound weight in her hand. She touched a few buttons and held the phone to her ear, closing her eyes in the bright glare of the overhead lights. Mason answered, and she couldn't speak.

"Ava? You there? Hello?"

"I'm here," she whispered, realizing he was on his car's Bluetooth system.

"What's wrong?" His voice was sharp, instantly aware. "I've got Ray in the car with me."

"Jayne tried to kill herself today." Her tongue felt numb. Everything felt numb.

"Jesus Christ. Where are you? Is she okay?"

"OHSU. She's going to be fine." Her mouth dried up, and she swallowed hard. "She might need some surgery."

Mason swore. "I'll be there as soon as I can, but it's going to be at least an hour. We left Eugene a while ago."

"I'm okay. Zander is here."

"Good. Let me talk to him."

Ava opened her eyes, blinking in the harsh light to find Zander staring at her from the hall. She held the phone out to him, and he swiftly walked over and took it, stepping away to converse with Mason. She closed her eyes and tipped her head against the wall, not wanting to hear their conversation. She didn't care what they said. Her body simply wanted to find a dark room and sleep.

What is wrong with me?

Overload. I'm shutting down instead of dealing with Jayne. Again. I can't think about her. Or anything.

"He wants to talk to you."

She forced her eyes open and took the phone. "Yes?"

"Zander's going to drive you home. I'll meet you there."

A jolt ran through her, and she was instantly alert. "I can't leave. I should stay."

"To do what? Wait around for hours? They're going to do what needs to be done, and I doubt Jayne will be in any condition to hold a conversation with you. Zander says you're practically falling asleep. It's late. I'll meet you at the house, and we'll both go back in the morning."

"I don't think—"

"I'm calling this one, Ava." His fierce tone made her stop, and she waited for her anger to rise at his high-handed attitude.

It didn't come.

He's completely right.

"Okay," she whispered.

"I love you," he stated. "But I'll be damned if I let you sit in a hospital waiting hand and foot on a sister who doesn't give a shit about you or anyone else."

"You're right," she said quietly. "I know. And I love you for it."

"I'll see you at home."

. . .

Ava noticed Zander was taking his time leaving the hospital, and she realized he was stalling to let Mason get home before he dropped her off. She wondered if that had been Mason's idea or his.

Either way, she didn't want to sit alone in an empty house, so someone had made a smart decision.

She stared out the window of Zander's car. Eleven P.M. The bright sign of a bar briefly flashed as they sped by, and she was bowled over with the need for a drink. A big one. One with lots of alcohol and fruity syrup that would drown all thoughts of her twin. One that would put the world on pause and let her take a break before it restarted.

Is that what Jayne wanted? A break? An escape?

Ava understood. Every cell in her body comprehended how Jayne had felt before she swallowed the pills and slashed at her wrists and stomach, and the clarity of the understanding rattled her to the core. Most days Ava had a tight grip on the dark areas of her mind, but tonight they had burst open, and she was fighting to close them back up.

Jayne had lost the fight years ago.

The battle raged in Ava's mind and the air in the car turned oppressive, dense with stress. The holes in her mind were treacherous and icy and deep, and they beckoned her to enter, making promises of ease and relaxation. An escape. Tempting her with a blissful nothingness. *You can go back to reality whenever you want.*

A lie.

Once she stepped over the line, every day of her life would be a fight like Jayne's.

"What's happened with the shootings?" she asked Zander, scrambling for a new chain of thoughts to distract from the beckoning chorus in her brain. It felt as if she were swimming upward through dark waters, holding her breath as she searched for the surface.

"We found Justin Yoder on video as he entered the bathroom before the shooting at Rivertown Mall."

She broke through the water's surface. Her brain snatched his statement and started to analyze, shoving her dark thoughts into a closet. "You could tell it was him? So now we have proof that there were two men that day? What time did he go in? Was he already dressed in black? Why didn't you tell me earlier?" Her mind buzzed with a million questions, and she held tight to the fresh grip on sanity.

Even in the dark car, she could see the wry look Zander gave her. "It didn't seem like the right time to bring it up. He went in about ninety minutes before the shooting started and yes, he was wearing black. No mask. He wasn't carrying anything, so possibly he had the mask tucked inside his jacket."

"I knew our theory was right." Relief rocked through her. "Now we need to figure out how on earth our mystery shooter recruited three young men to go along with his plans."

"And stop the next one."

She took a deep breath. "Absolutely."

"We went back a few days of video to evaluate the camera angles near the bathroom. We figured there had to be some sort of reconnaissance before the shooting."

"And?" His tone told her he had more good news.

"Four days before the shooting we've got Justin Yoder and a tall guy with a cap in the area. Together."

"Together, like . . ."

"Christ, no. I mean they were talking and had purposefully met up. We found them near the bathroom. The second guy was gesturing like he was giving Justin directions. Justin nodded and asked questions. They spent a good five minutes in that area, looking around and pointing at the various shops and even at the roof line."

"Pointing at the cameras?"

"They did, but they were also indicating other spots. It really made my skin crawl to watch it. I felt like the second guy was pointing out places where a sniper would be."

"But there was no one up there the mornings of the shootings," Ava said. "At least not that we noticed. Are you saying there might have been others watching from up there?"

"I don't know. It was really odd. The two of them were laughing and grinning like they were planning a party."

Ava's stomach churned. "You could see the other guy's face?"

"No. Every time he pointed up, he carefully kept his chin down, never lifting his face where the camera could see it. We've got views of the lower part of his face, the back of his head, and some partial side shots, but we can't see the upper half of his face. We need it."

"It's definitely the same guy I talked to that morning?" Ava asked. The memory of his face was a blur to her. The adrenaline from the shooting and worrying about Misty had wiped her mind of his image.

"Yes. And we tracked them on a few other camera views. Near the movie theater and down the main aisle. They were clearly making plans and followed the same path as the gunman that day."

"But they looked like they were planning something fun?" *Who plans a terror act and laughs while doing it?*

"Yes. It makes me wonder if Justin Yoder didn't know what he was getting into. He didn't act like someone who knew he'd be shot in the head in four days."

"We're missing something," Ava said slowly. "Logically, Justin thinks something else is going to happen and is excited for the plan, but how did our mystery man keep Justin from mentioning it to anyone? There were shots and screams and terror for a solid five minutes before Justin was shot in the head. The other men in that bathroom didn't see or hear Justin. What made him cooperate?"

"That's what everyone asked after seeing those clips today. No one has a good theory."

"We need to know more about the three young men."

"We're digging," said Zander. "But nothing has turned up yet. The only thing in common so far is that they're male and they died the same way."

"And they agreed to our mystery shooter's plan."

Zander pulled into the driveway of her house. Mason immediately stepped out of the front door and strode toward her side of the car. His shoulders were stiff and rigid. The outdoor house lights shone on his face, illuminating a clenched jaw. Guilt swamped her for worrying him. She stepped out of the car and was pulled into a tight hug.

"I'm sorry," he whispered. "You okay?"

Her throat closed and tears heated her eyes. "Not yet. I will be."

He kissed her hard and then looked at Zander. "Thanks."

KENDRA ELLIOT   193

Ava glanced at the FBI agent. He'd stepped out of his car but simply stood there with his door open. She couldn't see his eyes.

"Not a problem. See you tomorrow sometime. Night, Ava."

He was back in his car and had closed his door before her reply left her lips. The two of them watched him leave, and then Mason guided her toward the house. "You heard about the videos of Justin Yoder and the shooter at the Rivertown Mall?" she asked.

"Yes. I got an update."

"We were right. Now we just need to figure out—"

He stopped her at the door and faced her, placing his hands on her shoulders. "Not tonight. No more work talk. I need to hear what happened today with your sister."

Her energy dissipated, evaporating at his words. *Hospital.* The image instantly made her limbs and head heavy as if she'd been dipped in thick glue.

Mason's eyes widened and his fingertips dug into her shoulders. "Are you okay?"

She nodded. "I think I need to go to bed." They moved into the house, and Bingo greeted her with his full-body tail wag and sniffing nose. She wondered what scents the hospital visit had left on her clothing. That cloying heavy odor of disinfectant. Did Bingo find it as repulsive as she did? She set her purse on the hall table and kicked off her shoes.

I need to get out of these clothes.

The disinfectant smell overwhelmed her senses, and she lifted the hem of her shirt to pull it over her head as she dashed up the stairs to their bedroom. It gagged her as the soft weave of the shirt brushed over her face. Holding her breath, she moved into the closet and threw the offensive blouse into the laundry basket.

I still smell it.

Her fingers shook as she unbuttoned her capris, and she whipped them off, adding them to the laundry basket. The odor lingered in the still air of the closet.

My clothes are going to stink up everything in here.

She grabbed the basket, whirled around to head to the laundry room, and nearly ran over Mason. He blocked the doorway into the closet, hands resting on the doorjambs, looking at her in her bra and panties as she tried to get past him with the basket.

"What are you doing?"

"I need to wash these. Tonight. They stink like the hospital." Her skin vibrated as if she'd had a huge hit of caffeine.

He didn't move. Leaning over, he sniffed at the basket in her arms. "I don't smell anything."

"Trust me. You don't want these near your clean clothes." She sniffed at her upper arm. "I need to shower. The smell is clinging to me." She tried to push past him again.

"Ava." He stopped her with a hand on the basket. "Nothing smells."

"Yes. Yes it does." She clutched the basket tighter. "I need to do this." Her gaze locked on his, and she silently pleaded with him to let her by. Instead he took hold of the basket.

"Let go."

She paused. And then let go, her hands aching as she straightened her clenched fingers.

He slowly set the basket aside, holding her gaze. The vibrations under her skin grew stronger and a chill took root in her muscles. She wanted the basket back—something to hang on to, something that gave her a purpose.

"I'm cold," she whispered.

"Tell me what happened today." He spoke slowly as if not to spook her, and caution flickered in his eyes.

Am I that obvious?

She was balancing on a high wire, frozen in place, terrified to take a wrong step that would result in a downward spiral to match Jayne's. His gaze held her in place, and she clung to it, seeing him in crystal clarity. The crow's feet at the corners of his eyes. The patches of gray hair at his temples. The pulse at the side of his neck.

"She did it, Mason," she whispered. "She threatened it during our phone call, and I didn't believe her. She reached out, and I slapped her away. I pushed her, and she did it."

His eyes softened a fraction, and he reached for her.

She jerked back, dropping her gaze. "Don't touch me."

The soft catch of his breath broke her heart. Warmth touched her chest, and she lifted a hand to it. Wet. One line of tears had run down her cheek and landed on her chest. Slowly she lifted her gaze back to him, her fingertips touching the side of her face. "I think I'm falling apart."

Before she could blink he had his arms around her, his heat burning her skin.

"I'm so cold."

He held her tighter, running his hands up and down her back, his touch creating trails of heat that immediately vanished, leaving her colder than before. It didn't help. She was ready to shatter into a million pieces, and her mind sought a ledge to grab to keep her whole. The trembling under her skin crescendoed to an unbearable level, numbing all other sensations and stunting her thoughts. "I can't think straight," she whispered.

"Did you take something?" he asked.

His words took time to penetrate the fog around her brain. When they hit home, she froze. "Are you asking if I took something illegal?" Her voice cracked.

"Or legal." His brown gaze looked deep into her soul. *Or is he checking my pupils for dilation?*

"I'm not on anything. As much as I'm craving a miracle drug or drink to make this misery go away, I haven't taken *anything*." She looked away, wanting to sink through the floor. *He believes I'm no better than Jayne.*

Don't I believe the same?

He bent and scooped her into his arms, deftly maneuvering them out of the closet. She wrapped her arms around his neck, wanting to crawl under his clothing. He radiated the heat she so desperately needed. He gently lay her in their bed and tucked the covers tight around her, his face tight with worry.

Is he done with me?

"Mason."

He stopped, still bent over her. "What?"

Words left her. She held his gaze, feeling the two of them drift farther and farther apart. Her hand went to his chest, under his shirt, and she pressed her palm against his heart, and it pounded against her hand. *It's not too late.*

"I need to feel something," she whispered. "I can't feel *anything*. I don't care what it is. Please help me." She moved her hand to tug at the button of his shirt. His chest stopped moving as he held his breath, his eyes narrowed.

"I don't think that's a good idea," he said slowly. He didn't back away.

The button slipped from its hole, and she grabbed the shirt's fabric. "I need you. Please. Make me feel like I'm not about to shatter. I don't know if I'll be able to put it back together." She pleaded with her eyes. She needed to be touched and held, reminded that she hadn't fully turned into a pillar of stone. She'd slowly grown more detached and paralyzed as she lived through the years of Jayne's drawn-out collapse. She'd built too many walls to prop herself up and protect herself from the pain, and now she couldn't find her way out.

His throat moved as he swallowed, the rest of his body immobile.

"It's what I need. Right now. Because I can't see five minutes into the future, and I'm terrified that means I've become her and am powerless over my actions. Show me I'm wrong."

He gave a small shudder, never breaking eye contact. "I love you, Ava." And he bent to kiss her.

. . .

Mason wasn't sure who stared at him out of Ava's eyes.

It didn't sound like her.

But it was her. She was slipping away and begging for help.

He could only imagine what it felt like to lose your shit, and now he had a front-row seat, watching it happen to Ava. His first instinct had been to pull back, give her space, and find her help. But the longer he looked into her eyes and heard her pleas, the more he knew she needed something to hang on to. Right now. She was moving away, and he could feel her disconnecting from him.

Or am I moving away from her?

He'd been low before. He'd seen other people in the depths of despair, but what he saw in Ava's eyes went beyond that. The knowledge of her twin's attempted suicide had ripped open a place in Ava's soul that'd been patched together too many times. He'd known she'd repaired it in the past with tape and thread and tears. But could she pull it back together again?

What can I do?

He kissed her, letting his heart take over for his brain, and it felt right. Rarely did his feelings overrule his logic but this was the time for it to happen. She greedily pressed upward into his kiss, sliding her icy hand under his shirt again and tugging him closer. He pulled back slightly to look in her eyes but they were closed, and her hands frantically worked to open his buttons and push his shirt off his shoulders.

This wasn't going to be leisurely, lazy lovemaking. Or quick and lively lovemaking. Or passionate and heartfelt.

This would be sex.

She'd closed her eyes because she needed to feed from her other senses, seeking something to break through the numbness.

He could give her that.

He kissed her deeply, working off his jeans and underwear with help from her quick hands. She panted under his mouth, her fingers constantly touching him everywhere she could reach. Shifting under the sheet and thin blanket, she pressed her hips up against his, and he understood her need for pressure and weight to make her feel grounded. He slid the covers out of the way, lay on top of her body, and heard the intake of her breath in pleasure. Her hands moved to his back, pressing him harder against her, and he heard her nearly sob.

"Don't be gentle," she begged. "I need to feel everything."

He didn't argue. There was a time and place for gentle. Not right now. He shoved her bra up over her breasts without unhooking the back, and she gasped as it yanked at her nipples. He watched her eyes, but they never opened. She turned her face to the side, breathed hard and nodded. He massaged her breasts, increasing the compression, and she nodded again. Leaning down, he took a nipple between his teeth, and she ground her hipbones into his stomach and exhaled noisily.

Part of him wanted to stop, tuck the covers back around her, and spoon-feed her chicken soup. She was broken and raw. Nurturing wasn't his strong suit, but he could do it for the people he loved. At this moment, nurturing would send her deeper into herself. He moved his hand between the two of them and hooked a finger on her panties, sliding them down her legs. He nipped at her breast again, carefully watching her reactions.

She was in need.

He gently cupped her, slipped a finger between her folds, and discovered she was wet.

All rational thoughts shot from his brain.

His mind no longer cared about giving Ava what she needed. His single thought was about burying himself deep inside her heat.

She turned her head, tipped it back, and breathed heavily through opened lips. He positioned himself and gave a single hard upward thrust as he brought his lips down on hers and felt her shudder in relief. She wrapped her legs around his waist and ground against him.

"Please. Harder."

He traced the inside of her mouth with his tongue as he thrust into her over and over, losing himself in her wonderful tight slickness. Ava begged him not to stop. He barely heard her. He'd let go of any compulsion to hold back and prolong. Right now he simply wanted release and his frantic efforts to achieve it satisfied her need to feel *something*.

It worked for both of them.

• • •

Ava turned her head to nestle her face into his neck, feeling the rasp of his midnight shadow rake her cheek. Mason gave a second shudder as he lay spent on top of her. He'd hurt her. Several times. First with the teeth on her breasts, and then the relentless pounding had left her feeling raw between her legs. She welcomed the tiny pulses of pain flickering in both areas.

She almost felt grounded. He'd started to roll off but she'd held him in place. "Not yet," she'd whispered. She needed his weight pressing her into the mattress. She felt protected, secure. No longer walking a tightrope. But she wasn't ready to let him move away. She was terrified the unstable sensation would return.

Baby steps.

The vibrations under her skin were gone, but something was still off. She felt drugged, still slightly removed from reality. Each time her brain started to wonder about Jayne, she ruthlessly yanked it back. *Think about anything else.* Beaches, warm water, sunshine.

"Better?" Mason asked.

"Yes."

They lay in silence.

"You scared me," he said.

Her heart twinged. "I'm so sorry," she whispered. "I was terrified. I still am." Fresh hot tears streamed down to her pillow.

"You've been through a lot in the last few days. Hell, you've been through a lot this year."

She said nothing.

"I'm not sure where you are," Mason said slowly. "I mean—"

"I know what you mean. I don't know where I am, either." More tears. She angrily brushed her cheeks, frustration welling in her throat.

At least I'm feeling something.

Mason pushed up onto his hands, watching her with cautious eyes, and her skin goosebumped at his close analysis. Or maybe it was the removal of his heat. She tried to meet his gaze and smile; she failed. *I can't pretend everything is back to normal.*

He slowly moved off and turned her onto her side, facing away from him, spooning her close to his chest. His skin felt like fire against her back. His mouth was close to her ear. "I think sleep would be a good thing right now. We can talk all we want tomorrow."

Sleep helped everything. "I love you, Mason. I'm sorry—"

"Stop apologizing for your sister."

She swallowed. *I'm not. It's for me.*

"You're human. And you've experienced more than anyone should today. It'll look different tomorrow." He leaned closer and kissed along her jawline. "I'll hold you tight tonight. And every night after. We don't need to rush through anything right now."

She exhaled and relaxed a degree, letting his heat seep through her skin and into her core.

"I love you, too, Special Agent McLane."

28

He checked the pasta. It needed more time. He kept one eye on the clock as he stirred the sauce and listened for his mother's footsteps on the stairs. She'd come home from work and immediately headed upstairs to change. His job was to have dinner on the table at exactly six P.M.

Dinner would be late.

He prayed she'd take extra time upstairs, but he knew she stuck to a routine. He had exactly two more minutes to get everything on the table. The places were set, the water and her wine were poured, and the bread was covered with a towel in the center of the table. He transferred the sauce to the floral serving dish and placed it on a hot pad near her wineglass.

He checked the pasta again. Still way too chewy.

Sweat broke under his arms. Perhaps he should have chosen the angel hair instead of the regular spaghetti; the cooking time was shorter. No. He knew she hated angel hair. His father had always wanted the angel hair, but once he was taken away, his mother never cooked it again. A lone box still sat in the back of a cupboard. He'd considered throwing it out, but she got angry if food was wasted. So it stayed. A constant reminder of his father's absence.

His father had ended up in prison. He hadn't been allowed to attend the trial, but his mother had gone every day. She'd sworn to her son that his father would be back and railed at the system that was unfairly persecuting her husband. Until the trial was over.

Suddenly his mother became a different woman. She bought new clothing, her hair changed, she wore makeup and got a new job. She went out with people from work and talked about moving to a new state.

He didn't understand.

His father had been unfairly ripped away from their home and sentenced to a decade in prison, but his mother acted as if she had a new life. She ordered him around, assigning him the tasks that had always been her job. Laundry, cleaning, cooking. He was busy from the moment he got home from high school until he went to bed. She simply went to her job and then came home to enjoy the fruits of his labor and point out everything he'd done wrong.

"The plates need to face the same way in the dishwasher or else they won't get clean."

"You put too many items in the washing machine. Run them again."

She yelled. All the time. According to her he did nothing right. What did she expect? He'd never cooked or cleaned. That was women's work.

Dad would have understood. A decade without him was going to last forever. He didn't understand how a man could be locked up for something he'd hardly done. But he'd seen the newspaper article. A female judge had looked at his mother's history of trips to the hospital and blamed his father for every last one. The cops had claimed his father assaulted them twice in jail while awaiting trial. The female judge had strung several sentences together, unfairly locking up his father for a long period.

After that the power in the home had shifted. He no longer had time to listen to music or game. His mother had turned him into the wife, while she went to work, bossing more men around. She'd landed a management position in retail sales. A favor from the husband of one of her girlfriends. He'd even heard her tell someone on the phone that she'd been shocked to receive it with her few years of experience. "But it's like the position was made for me. It feels natural for me and I'm good at it. It's like I never left the industry."

His friends harassed him about his new chores. "He has to wear his apron tonight. He can't make it to the football game."

He'd tried to talk to her about it. She'd sat at the table after dinner one night, a cigarette in her hand and the wine he'd poured her in the other hand. The table messy with the dishes he was expected to clean up. He'd told her he missed his friends and felt it was unfair that he did all the work. She'd blown up.

"You bitch about cleaning some dishes? Do you know how many years I served your father? He had no idea how women were to be treated. Women first, Son. Always. Show your manners and treat them like queens, and you'll never be sorry. Your father was clueless. He saw me as his property and never even gave me a credit card. He counted out money into my hand every Sunday night. That was my money for the week. I was expected to buy groceries, gas, and clothes for you and me out of that. If something went wrong, I was expected to make do with what he gave me. He was a control freak and stuck in a different era."

He'd bitten his lip, thinking of the ten dollars she'd handed him on Sunday for school lunch that week.

She'd continued to rant, sucking on her cigarette and bitching about his father, never addressing his desire to attend a football game. The evening had ended with him picking tiny fragments of broken glass out of the sink. She'd hurled her wineglass at his head when he'd suggested she put away the leftovers. He'd ducked, and the glass had shattered when it hit the window over the sink, spreading sticky red wine drops that he still discovered in odd places three months later.

He learned not to ask for help.

He listened intently for her footsteps as he stared at the boiling water. Hurry!

No woman should make me feel like this. If Dad were here, he'd set her straight.

Steps sounded, and he snatched up a noodle to taste. Not ready. There was no way he could serve it like this. His shoulders tensed as she strode into the kitchen. She sat down in her chair, took a sip of her wine, and closed her eyes, savoring the flavor. Then she looked at him, her eyes ice blue. "Dinner's not ready?"

"The pasta needs another minute or two."

She raised an eyebrow, stood, and then strolled over to look into the pot. She sniffed at the steam and her wineglass clinked as she set it on the counter. "You know dinner is to be on the table when I get home."

"Yes, I know." He didn't offer any excuses. He'd learned she didn't listen to them and didn't care.

He remembered the last time she'd made spaghetti and he and his father had watched from their places at the table as she'd drained the pasta. His father had been livid that it was overcooked.

Now he felt the same anger flooding off of her.

She grabbed the handles of the big pot and flung the contents at his face. "Why isn't it ready?" she screamed at him.

He turned away and the boiling water hit the left side of his neck and scalp. Through his pain he couldn't hear her shrieking at him.

If only Dad were here . . .

29

Ava had lost count of how many times she'd awakened. All night she'd woken, looked at her clock, and fallen back into a hazy sleep. One that never satisfied; she felt as if she were floating with her eyes shut. No rest, no brain break. Each time Jayne tried to enter her thoughts, she immediately shut them down. She'd mastered the light switch to her brain where Jayne was concerned. But then her brain would coast in the off position, unable to focus, unable to follow any other train of thought.

She'd pretended sleep when Mason kissed her cheek and got into the shower. Lying in the dark, listening to the water from the bathroom, she'd struggled to find a mental focus. Her body was physically drained and nothing tempted her to put her feet on the floor.

What am I going to do?

Do in five minutes? Do in five hours? She didn't know the answers.

The shower stopped and a few minutes later she could hear Mason on his cell phone. *The job never ends.*

Work could be the lifesaver for her. Something to keep her distracted and still moving. Her vacation was finished in a few days.

Until then . . .

She had nothing.

Light flashed across her eyes as Mason opened the door connected to the master bathroom. She squeezed them shut and gave up pretending to sleep, shifting her legs so he knew she was awake. He sat on her side of the bed, the bright bathroom light behind him making his eyes and facial expression impossible to see.

"Hey," he said, bending to kiss her forehead. "How're you feeling?"

"Shitty."

He ran his hand down her cheek, pausing to cup her chin, and she felt him study her. She kept her expression as blank as possible; the rawness in her heart was too fresh, and she was still empty from her tears of the night before. His face was a dark silhouette. "I just had a call from Ben Duncan," he said.

Alarm sent sparks through her nerves. *My boss called Mason at the crack of dawn?*

"I'd left him a message last night. He got you an appointment this morning to talk with someone."

"Someone. You mean a psychiatrist?"

"Yes. Don't forget about it this time."

She hated being handled and fought a bitchy compulsion to refuse to go. But the thought of picking up the phone and making her own appointment was currently beyond her energy level. A very small logical part of her brain could see it was in her best interest.

"Do you need someone to take you?" he asked cautiously. "I'm going in to the command center."

Pride forced her reply. "No. I can drive. I'm not helpless."

"I know you're not helpless, and if we weren't so close to an answer on this case, I'd stay home and take—go with you."

His correction made her smile. Mason was well aware that she hated people to do things for her. Her request for Zander to pick her up last night had raised red flags for both men about the precariousness of her emotional state.

"I checked with the hospital about Jayne already," Mason added slowly. "She went through the night fine, has surgery scheduled for this morning, and they have a psych evaluation lined up for later today. They seem to believe they'll have a place for her for a few days while she heals. She's heavily sedated. You wouldn't be able to talk to her if you went there."

"Her injuries are okay?" Ava whispered. It took all her strength to stay emotionally removed from the conversation and not let her brain speed down a Jayne tangent. *Focus on yourself.*

"Yes. No big concerns. They'll know more after the surgery."

Ava nodded and shut the door in her brain that led to her twin. She sat up, attempting to show Mason she was capable of taking care of herself today. "I need a shower."

He pulled her close, his grip tighter than usual. "You scared me last night," he whispered.

Dammit! Tears leaked down her cheeks. "I was scared, too." She rested her head on his shoulder, seeking energy from his heat.

"I need to go. I'll call you later to make certain you're on your way to your appointment," he said firmly.

"You don't need to do that."

"I need to. Let me do it for myself."

A lesson I need to learn . . .

He left and she lay back in the bed, staring at the ceiling and wishing he hadn't left the light on in the bathroom. She craved darkness.

"I will make it to that appointment."

She repeated the line out loud several times for the next half hour, determined not to let her man down.

• • •

Mason started his vehicle and let out a deep breath.

Ava had rattled his core and rocked the foundation they'd carefully constructed.

Is this what I need in my life?

Maybe he didn't need it, but he sure as hell wanted it. He wanted Ava with him every day. No question.

He opened the console under his arm and dug through the papers and crap. His fingers touched a small velvet box and he pulled it out, flipping open the top. The diamond glittered. His heart sank.

Not yet.

The case shut with a loud snap, and he buried it among the debris again.

So when?

30

That morning Mason watched the videos of the two men at Rivertown Mall. Ray and Zander watched over his shoulders. The first clip was a quick one from the day of the shooting, in which Justin Yoder was first spotted, walking outside the parking garage. Another camera caught a brief glimpse of him in the main thoroughfare of the mall, and the third watched him stride straight to the men's room and enter. Mason eyed the time in a lower corner of the screen. Almost exactly ninety minutes before the other man had started shooting. What had Justin done in the bathroom for that amount of time? Read a book?

"I don't understand why he doesn't come from the direction of where we found his car," said Ray. "The parking garage is on the opposite end of the mall."

"Maybe he didn't drive his own car," said Zander. "I'll lay money that our shooter drove Justin's car and left it in that neighborhood. Why else would it be wiped down?"

"That shows a strong level of trust," Ray pointed out. "I don't loan out my vehicle. Not even to Mason."

Mason raised a brow. "I've never asked."

"But if you did, it'd be a no."

"I'd loan you mine if you needed it. Are you saying that if I was in a bind you wouldn't help me out?"

Ray scowled. "What kind of bind?"

"Never mind." Mason lost interest in harassing Ray. "The point is that Justin Yoder was comfortable enough to lend his vehicle to our shooter. It indicates some sort of relationship."

"Or maybe Justin didn't know our shooter took it," said Zander. "I'm playing devil's advocate here, but maybe the shooter helped himself to the vehicle knowing Justin was sitting in a bathroom for the next hour and a half. He could have had Justin's key copied somehow or picked his pocket at some point. We can't make any assumptions."

The other investigators swore at the FBI agent's logic; he was absolutely right.

Mason clicked on the other video. *One step forward, two steps back.* The men watched silently as Justin and their shooter strolled casually through the mall. Justin had a soda in his hand and the two of them frequently stopped to study the buildings, indicating entrances and aisles. They slowly moved into the wide aisle with the men's room and stopped five feet from the kiosk where Ava had hid with Misty. The shooter held his hands up with his thumbs together, looking like a movie director as he studied the area through the space between his hands. He said something to Justin, who bent over in laughter. The shooter's teeth flashed in a wide smile.

Asshole.

The men continued to walk the area and finally vanished into the bathroom.

"Here's a case for cameras in restrooms," muttered Ray.

"No, thank you," replied Mason.

"You can fast-forward five minutes," said Zander.

Mason watched a dozen men go in and out of the restroom, moving in quick jerky motions. The two subjects emerged, and he slowed down the video. The men stood and talked for a few more minutes, shook hands, and parted. The clip stopped as the men moved out of the frame.

"There's nothing else," stated Zander. "All other shots are of them leaving. Justin parked in the parking garage and we show him get in his car. The other guy walks west, and we don't see where he parks."

Mason backed it up again and went frame by frame through one part near the restroom where their shooter nearly exposed his face—but didn't. "Our techs picked it apart," said Zander. "They enlarged and studied every angle we could get of the guy. Nothing worth showing."

"Dammit," Mason muttered. "How can we have all these minutes on camera and no possibilities for identification?"

"Is it time to take it to the press?" asked Zander.

"Hell no," said Ray. "Don't give him a heads-up that we know he exists!"

Mason stayed silent, noticing Zander did the same. He'd weighed the pros and cons of revealing what they knew to the press. He couldn't see much benefit. They could post the best still frame of the shooter and hope someone recognized him, but the clearest image was pretty lousy; it'd trigger hundreds of false identifications. And Mason liked the idea that the shooter didn't know that they were aware of his existence. He wanted the man confident; he'd be more likely to slip up.

"That's Shaver's call," said Zander.

"And speak of the devil," added Ray as Sergeant Shaver joined their group.

Shaver looked as if he'd been running on hits of caffeine for four days and sleeping on a cot in a side room. Mason suspected they all looked about the same. Shaver waved a file at them. "Got something interesting."

"Spill it," said Zander.

"Ballistics on the bullets from the Eugene shooting match a case from a decade ago," Shaver announced.

The group was silent.

"It took *that long* to get results?" asked Ray. "It's been two months since the Eugene incident."

"They didn't assign a priority to getting the bullets through forensics. They had a dead shooter and knew who he was," Shaver pointed out. "Lane County didn't see the point to ask for a rush when they weren't searching for a suspect, and I wouldn't have, either. There're too many cases that need quick answers. This wasn't one of them."

The men slowly nodded in understanding. "And the old case that it matches?" asked Zander.

Shaver looked at his file. "March of ten years ago. Sharon Silva was shot once in the head at her home. She lived alone and wasn't missed until she didn't show up for her shift three days later. This happened in Eugene not too far from the University of Oregon campus and it was never solved." He looked up. "She was a U of O police officer."

His words ricocheted in Mason's head, and he fought down his anger. The senseless deaths of fellow officers who'd put their lives on the line to protect others always pissed him off. And this was a woman. Doubly bad. He saw his feelings reflected in the eyes of the other men. Ray let loose a streak of expletives.

"I remember that. She wasn't very old, was she?" asked Ray. "Every department in the state takes it very personally when one of our own is killed. I can't believe it's still not solved. They threw everything at that case."

"Nothing panned out," said Shaver.

Mason didn't remember the case. "You have her picture?" Shaver held up an image of a woman who appeared to be in her late twenties. She had a warm smile. "Family? Suspects?"

"Some family that lived out of state," answered Shaver. "They questioned the neighbors, but everyone swore they heard nothing. She was shot late at night on a Saturday while the house next door had a live band playing. I imagine it was loud."

Mason groaned. "And multiplied the number of interviews and suspects. She was inside her home?"

"In her backyard. Looks like she was on a bench on her back patio. The report said she had a broken beer bottle near her body and beer in her system. After checking with the party, no one had brought that particular brand, and she had a partial six-pack of it in her fridge. They think she was simply outside listening to the band from her own yard when she was shot."

"Location of shooter?" Ray asked.

"About ten feet away. One shot at the back of her head."

"Jesus Christ," muttered Mason. "An assassination."

Shaver gave him an odd look. "Several of the investigators made a similar observation. Stated it felt cold and calculated. Not an accident."

"It's Eugene again," said Zander. "What made our shooter wait ten years between murders?"

"Maybe we need to check all the cold-case shootings from the last decade in the Eugene area," said Ray. "Maybe it hasn't been ten years. Since the recent ballistics comparison would have hit on any other bullet matches, maybe we need to look at other similar aspects in case he has multiple weapons."

"Other aspects?" asked Shaver.

"Cold cases with multiple gunshot victims? Or women who live alone who've been shot?" said Ray as he stared at the ceiling in deep concentration.

An alarm sounded in Mason's brain.

"Women in law enforcement," said Mason, looking at the other investigators.

"Gabrielle Gower." Zander slapped the table as he caught Mason's train of thought. "The first victim in the Rivertown Mall shooting. She was a former patrol officer from Medford. I think she'd left the force about two years ago."

"Let me see the lists of the other victims in the shootings," said Shaver. "Now!"

"Jennifer Spendlin was the mom who dropped her toddler in Eugene," said Zander. "She wasn't law enforcement, but she was an instructor at a shooting range."

All the men looked at Zander.

He shrugged and met their curious gazes. "I remember stuff. No one had a law enforcement history at that shooting that I recall."

Mason recalled Ava's saying that Zander had a reputation in their office for a nearly photographic memory.

"What about the Troutdale shooting?" Shaver asked.

"Anna Luther," promptly answered Zander. "Retired Yamhill County deputy."

"Bingo," Mason breathed. "We've got a connection."

31

Ten years earlier

He held his breath as Lindy passed by his hiding place. It wasn't exactly a hiding place; he was leaning against a wall and anyone could see him except for the people on the path walking east in front of the campus library. As Lindy had just done. He straightened and casually moved to follow her on the path. The sun had just set and the campus lights illuminated the paths with splotches of brightness that fought to shine through the dense branches of the trees. He started to jog. "Hey, Lindy!"

She whirled around, one hand on her backpack strap, her face instantly wary as she squinted to make him out in the poor light. She registered his identity and her shoulders relaxed a fraction. "Oh, hello."

Her flat tone slowed him to a walk and he clenched his teeth. What would it take to reach this girl? He forced a smile. "Are you heading home? I'll walk you. It's getting late." He knew which dorm she lived in, but he wouldn't reveal that fact. As far as Lindy knew, he was just a nice guy in her chem class who said hello occasionally. He knew his scars were visible down the left side of his neck; it looked as if his skin had melted. But they didn't affect his face—just that little area in front of his ear. A baseball cap made his hair lie correctly on the left instead of slightly askew from the contorted skin.

She took a half step backward. "That's okay. I'm not heading home yet."

He waited for her to say where she was going, but she didn't expand. An uncomfortable silence grew between them. His lips strained to keep his casual smile in place as she started to turn away. "Do you have time to grab a cup of coffee?"

Lindy tucked her dark hair behind her ear as she looked back at him. "I'm sorry. I need to be somewhere." Her gaze skittered away from his.

She's lying. He'd watched her walk the same path three days a week for the past four weeks; she was headed home. She took two steps away from him. "Wait!" He lunged forward and caught her arm, not wanting her to leave just yet. If she'd just give him a chance, she'd discover they'd get along perfectly—but first she needed to listen.

She jerked her arm out of his hand. "Don't grab me!" Her dark eyes flashed.

He held up both his hands. "Sorry about that. I just wasn't done talking to you."

"I was done. I need to go."

"You haven't given me a chance," he blurted.

She stopped and looked back at him, an odd expression on her face. "A chance for what?"

"To talk," he said lamely. *This isn't how this was supposed to go.* "Let's get some coffee," he tried again. He wasn't ready to let her walk away.

"Look," Lindy said firmly. "I need to go home. I'll see you in class tomorrow."

"You just said you weren't going home," he argued. Anger rushed through his brain. *She lied to him and wouldn't listen to what he had to say?*

Fear touched her eyes, and she took another step back, blinking rapidly. "I need to go."

"Everything okay here?" asked a female voice. A woman in a police uniform appeared on his right. *How long was she standing there?*

"Yes, it's fine," he automatically replied, forcing his lips to smile at her. She looked unimpressed. The campus had several police officers, but he'd never seen a female one before. She was tall and thin with her hair pulled back in a tight knot at her neck. She could have been attractive if she'd done something with herself instead of trying to look like a man. *The campus must not pay well if they have to hire women.*

"What do you think?" she asked Lindy. "Do you agree that everything is fine?"

The condescension in her tone made him want to scratch something.

Lindy looked at the cop and didn't answer. The cop wasn't very old, but she acted like a mother who'd caught them misbehaving. She looked him up and down, and her scorn torched him through his clothes. "I think you need to back off a bit. She made it pretty clear that she wanted to leave and you weren't about to let her go."

Blood pounded in his ears.

How long was she listening?

"This was a private conversation," he forced out. "Why were you eavesdropping?"

The cop stepped closer, her brows narrowed, and he read the small gold bar on the left side of her chest. SILVA. A glimmer on her lip told him she wore lip gloss, the sole sign that she utilized feminine beauty products. A hint of fake strawberry odor touched his nose. *Probably from the lip gloss.* "When a woman wants you to leave her alone, you back off," she said, holding his gaze. "She doesn't have to do anything simply because you asked. Give her some space."

His vision tunneled, the trees and paths of the campus disappearing. It was just him and this bitch. "Where do you get off talking to me like that?" he sputtered.

She tapped her badge. "This right here. I asked you nicely to leave the girl alone, and you don't seem to understand that she owes you nothing. Now move along and don't talk to her again."

Shock rocked through him. "You can't tell me what to do."

She smiled sweetly, lips sparkling. "I just did. You can choose to accept my advice or go back to the station with me."

He couldn't move. All he'd done was talk to a girl and this bitch believed she could order him around? Intimidate him? "Are you threatening me?"

She turned her back on him and spoke to Lindy, holding out a business card. "Call the number on this card if he harasses you again. I have no tolerance for that sort of behavior." Lindy took the card and rapidly walked away without a single glance at him.

Rage coated his skin. The cop bitch had completely blown the progress he had made with Lindy. Now she'd never speak to him again. The cop turned around and insolently tilted her head as she studied him.

"Didn't your mother teach you not to pester girls? Maybe you need to take a class on body language. I heard every word the two of you said, and that girl was telling you in spoken words *and* body language that she felt nervous and wanted to leave. Couldn't you see that?"

He couldn't speak through his anger. *She's as bad as my mother.*

"You're in college, so here's your lesson for the day: be nice to women. Don't approach them on dim paths or dark streets. You're bigger and stronger than us, and we automatically see you as a possible rapist and killer. Do you know what it's like to wonder if the man you're talking to is planning to hurt you? I bet it never even crosses your mind."

Rapist. Killer. Her accusations stabbed him.

"Women shouldn't be cops."

She straightened, but still had to look up to him. "And why is that?"

"It's a position of authority. You just told me no one listens to women and that men are bigger and stronger. It makes sense for a man to have your job."

Her expression turned condescending again. "I'm not here to argue with you. I'm here to help college girls make it back to their dorm rooms safely. Now move along before I consider you a threat to myself."

He wanted to punch the smug look off her face. His mother had looked at his father with the exact same expression when she'd thought she knew better than him. Dad had always let her know the reality. And then a female cop—just like this one—had dragged his father away.

"I said *get going.*" She glanced down at his hands.

At his sides his hands were in fists. Her expression narrowed and through his anger-fueled vision, he noticed her hand move to her belt.

He stepped back.

"If I catch you harassing other women, I'll take you in."

He turned and walked away, counting to ten, waiting for his vision to clear. The female cop said something else, but it didn't register in his brain.

Fucking bitch. No one talks to me like that. No one.

• • •

Two days later he followed her home. For a cop, Silva didn't take many precautions. It was easy to scope out the campus police station and wait for her shift to end. She stepped out of a side entrance of the little station in sweats and with her hair down, loose and flowing around her face. She could have been any other college coed, but she was a bit too old. She walked home, blending in with the students. None of them acknowledged her. He'd noticed that when she walked the campus in uniform, students stopped her constantly. They asked for directions and several of them thought it was funny to ask stupid questions. He'd moved closer when groups of college guys stopped her, curious to hear what they said to her. Their questions were lame:

What happens if you caught me with a joint?

Would I go to jail if you found me drunk on campus?

You can't arrest me if I'm drinking in my dorm room, right?

Her answers had been serious and to the point, quickly taking the steam out of what the guys clearly thought was a hilarious topic. He'd watched them ridicule her as soon as her back was turned, and he'd smirked along with them. *See? No one listens to female cops. Doesn't she realize she's the joke?*

But in sweats she was invisible to everyone. Except him.

He'd discovered she lived in a tiny house about a mile from campus. Some snooping assured him she lived alone. The third time he'd followed her home, he'd noticed guys moving amps and speakers and other band equipment into the house next door. He walked closer, trying to see if it was a music group he'd heard of. One guy spotted him and shoved a flyer into his hands. "Only five bucks to get in tonight. And beers are a buck a cup. Gonna be packed."

He took the flyer and walked back toward campus, an idea buzzing around his brain.

He'd show her.

32

Ava woodenly ordered her usual coffee drink. She wasn't thirsty or craving the sugar and caffeine as on some mornings, but the therapist had suggested she continue her usual routine. She'd nearly fallen asleep at the wheel and hoped the caffeine would help, but she suspected her body and psyche were simply trying to shut down and hide from the world. Caffeine might not be enough to fight it.

The only thing that'd resonated with her from her morning session with Dr. Pearl Griffin had been the doctor's suggestion that Ava stick to her usual daily activities. They might feel wrong at the moment, but once her mind caught up with what'd she'd been through, she'd be a few steps ahead by not having let the anxiety change how she functioned.

"If you usually go to church on Sundays, then keep going," the psychiatrist had suggested. "If you see a movie with Mason every Friday, don't stop. Make yourself do those regular things that don't require much thought."

Ava had known the therapy session was hopeless from the moment she'd shaken Dr. Griffin's limp hand. There was no way her boss had ever met Pearl Griffin. She must have been the first doctor who had an opening. Dr. Griffin was from a different generation and her ability to relate to Ava was zero. Dr. Griffin should have been serving tea and crustless sandwiches at a retirement center as she advised lonely women on how to look nice to attract their next husband. *Seriously.* Dr. Griffin was a sweet woman, but Ava needed someone to kick her butt, not compliment her skin. She'd sat down in the freezing office and envied the doctor's thick cardigan as she studied the tiny older woman. "Mousy" had been the primary adjective in her head. She'd reminded Ava of a grandmother on a sitcom, one who baked cookies and whose corny confusion always drew laughter.

But it had felt good to dump her story in the doctor's lap. Ava had been slow to open up, but she'd regurgitated her stress from the shooting and her despair from Jayne's suicide attempt. Once the gate to her memories had lifted, Ava hadn't stopped. She was matter-of-fact about the shooting. It'd happened; she'd handled it. But her stories and complaints about her sister were wide and varied, sometimes making her cry and other times making her angry. The doctor had barely gotten a word in. When ten were minutes left, she'd finally held up a hand for Ava to slow down, and asked a few pointed questions.

She'd suggested Ava request more time off.

Ha! Ava took a long sip of her iced coffee. Sticking her nose into the shootings was currently keeping her sane.

She'd suggested Ava allow her to prescribe some medication. A low dose.

She hated the idea of medication. She'd watched Jayne try too many medications, but she'd promised the doctor she'd think about it. The thought was nearly overwhelming, so she'd tucked it out of sight. *Perhaps that's a sign I need something? That I'm unable to process decisions?*

She leaned against her vehicle outside the coffee shop, letting the sun bake her shoulders and head. Feeling eyes on the back of her neck, she turned around and studied the parking lot. A few people roamed the lot, heading to their cars with their cups of caffeine in hand. Nobody met her gaze.

Am I paranoid now? Flustered, she unlocked her vehicle and worried that her leash on her brain was slipping. Physical movement was what she had used in the past to stay in control. Mason liked to run, but Ava's knees twinged in a bad way when she tried. She'd rather hike and soak in the scenery. Or go to yoga and shift her brain into neutral as she felt her muscles stretch and complain. A little pain sounded good right now; it'd help her stay focused.

Don't give up your usual schedule.

Well, she'd gotten her usual coffee. She was going back to work as soon as her vacation was over. Tonight was her evening yoga class. The one she was always relieved to attend to break up the workweek. Typically she attended twice a week, and she hadn't planned to go tonight. She'd received an email saying that the center had reopened along with the mall and classes were back on schedule. She assumed they'd suffered a drop in attendance from the shooting, but it wouldn't last. People would return after time made their memories fade.

The image of Misty's bleeding leg popped into her brain. That memory would take a while to fade.

Am I ready to return to class?

She liked her instructor and hated to think that he might feel bad that people avoided his class because of the mall shooting.

If she could commit to getting her daily coffee, she could commit to going to yoga. It was a step in the right direction.

33

He watched the young man pace in front of the Starbucks where he'd requested they meet, glancing up at every person who approached the building. Eagerness rolled off of him.

Good. It was easiest when they were anxious to please. He'd found the nature of the event appealed to men in their twenties. The secrecy, the surprise, the reward. He'd created the perfect vehicle for achieving his goals. It'd been simple once he'd thought it through. Finding people eager to help and leaving no record of that search were the keys that made his plan perfect.

"Simon?" he asked the young man as he approached, holding out his hand.

"Yes, Travis? Great to meet you finally." Simon's height and build were perfect. He hadn't fudged his stats.

"Thanks for your interest in helping us out. I know being available on such short notice makes it difficult for some people." He watched Simon's gaze go to the scars on the side of his neck that his hair didn't quite hide. The young man stared for a split second, swallowed, and regained his composure as he went back to direct eye contact.

How many times have I watched people go through the same motions?

Simon grinned, the scars mentally set aside. "But that's the nature of the situation and what gives it the thrill. You guys prepare the absolute best you can, getting ready for every possible outcome, but you rely on the oblivious star of the show to perform as you hope. It's awesome."

Yes, yes it is. "I'm glad you understand." Travis gestured at an outdoor table. "Let's sit for a bit, then we can walk the location."

"So it's definitely happening here?" Simon asked.

"I'm ninety percent certain. Our backup location is the Rivertown Mall. If she doesn't follow her usual routine, I'll call you. You can hustle over there on short notice, right? We won't have the chance to walk through the routine on that site, but I can talk you through it on the phone if it comes to that. Essentially everything will be the same as here."

"You can get all your cameras set up that fast?" Simon asked.

Travis gave a confident grin. "My crew is amazing. They love this work and bust their asses to make every event a success. The excitement of seeing the final payoff is like sex for them."

Simon laughed.

"You watched our YouTube channel, right?"

"Shit yes. Those videos are awesome. I can't wait to be a part of something like that."

He pulled a sheet of paper out of a thick manila envelope. "If you really want to do this, here are the stipulations I mentioned in our phone calls." He lay the sheet in front of Simon, who studied it intently. "First and most important is your silence on the subject until after we finish filming. Once we're done, you can tell everyone you want and even mention it on social media. It's good exposure for us. But until that day, there's no telling your girlfriend, your parents, or your guy friends."

Simon nodded, a serious look in his eyes. "I understand."

"This is one of two stupid things that have blown our cover in the past. One guy couldn't keep a secret and told his girlfriend what he was doing. It leaked and ruined the surprise. I was nice and let him keep the first third of the payment even though he'd signed a contract to agree to pay it back if he talked, but he lost out on the big payoff." Travis lowered his chin and looked hard at Simon. "I know it's hard, but our success is based on surprise. Any leaks ruin it. Not to mention I'm out the cost of setting everything up." He paused. "Did you tell anyone you were meeting me today?"

"Hell no. You made the silence thing clear on the phone. I like your quality of work, and I want to be a part of it. I'm not going to screw that up."

"Fantastic. A lot of blind trust goes into these things. Guys like you make it work."

Simon beamed.

"I have a meeting later today with the client who hired us to create and film this one," Travis lied. "I'm glad I can tell him I found the perfect actor for the part."

"I'm thankful I saw the ad you put on the theater bulletin board at the school. I'm always checking it for extra work."

"Yes, I find most of our actors through postings on online acting forums or an old-fashioned bulletin board. It seems all you guys are constantly looking for work."

"Gotta eat."

"The only other stipulation is your availability. This gig will happen in the next few days. Your schedule is clear, right?"

"Yes, it is. Summer session is over, and I haven't lined up a job yet. Except for this one," he joked. He signed his name to the agreement.

"Maybe we can use you for some other gigs if this one goes well."

The young man's eyes lit up. "That'd be so cool. I've spent hours watching your work. You said a network was interested?"

"I've been contacted by a producer who's made some shows for Spike," he lied, shrugging. "There's always someone showing interest, but no one's made an offer yet. That's okay. We've got people buying ad space, which is how we make our money. I've talked to a few foreign producers, too. We're huge in Germany."

Simon looked ready to kiss his feet.

"Here's one-third of the pay we talked about." He handed Simon an envelope. "The rest on the day of the shooting, okay?"

"Absolutely. Can't wait."

"Let's walk the scene, okay?" He stood and Simon nearly jumped out of his chair to join him.

Perfect. He'll do whatever I ask that day.

They walked around the outside of the building. "The second time we had a production fail, the actor didn't follow instructions and moved too soon. The scene got noisy and he came out of his hiding spot."

"Oh, shit. Did that ruin the surprise?"

"Damn right. All that time and planning flushed down the sewer. The client was pissed and didn't want to try it again on a different day. I didn't blame him. When you're attempting to stage an elaborate practical joke, timing is everything and you'll never catch the subject off guard again. You get one chance. That's it."

"Will I have to improvise anything?"

"Probably not. We'll run over all the possibilities so you're comfortable. But the most important thing is for you not to get surprised and keep your cool. Did you watch the video with the fireworks?"

"Yeah, the one where the guy freaked out because someone was in the backseat of his car?"

"That's the one. We always have fireworks handy in case we need to distract the subject. The target was about to spot the actor before it was time; the fireworks made him look the other way."

"Genius."

"Crap happens sometimes. The worst is when we set everything up, and the target doesn't show. Most people are pretty predictable. They have a routine they like to follow and they stick to it. We do all the research we can so we know their typical movements, but there's been a few times when we've been left hanging."

"You follow them?" Simon asked, wrinkling up his brow.

"A little bit. I like to see how they move and what their habits are, but most of the information comes from the person who hires us to perform the gag," Travis lied smoothly. "They know the target best and give us the background we need."

He pulled a pack of cigarettes out of his pocket and offered one to Simon, who declined. He lit up and relaxed as the nicotine hit his lungs. He was nearly confident that Simon would work perfectly for his next staging, but he still had some questions. He had to be certain he could trust the guy to keep his head down until the right moment. The videos on YouTube were pranks he'd staged with friends during college when they thought they were kings with their cameras and clever ideas. The videos were old, but people still watched them and, according to the comments on the videos, thought they were better than the prank shows on TV. Occasionally he thought about getting the group together and creating more, but right now this was much more satisfying.

"I've got some black athletic gear in my vehicle for you to wear. We'll need you to be as inconspicuous as possible."

"Of course," agreed Simon.

He smiled. The black Nike gear was the uniform he'd chosen for all his soldiers. To him it was anonymous and powerful, and represented stealth.

They stopped at the side of the coffee shop, and he pointed at some bushes lining the adjoining building. "That's a perfect place for a camera. Maybe on the roof, too. I'll have to talk to the owner to see how he feels about us getting on his roof, but either one will give us a good shot of the main entrance and this side door. The parking lot is good, too. We usually have a few cameras in vehicles with privacy glass."

"What about inside?" Simon asked. "Starbucks lets you position and hide cameras?"

"Nah, when it's a big chain like this, I don't ask. I've tried that route with other companies, and our requests have to go up to their corporate office and then it just gets complicated. Instead I'll have my guys inside with discreet cameras, and we'll warn the employees a minute before we start that we're filming a prank or a surprise for someone so they don't interfere. I have one guy whose sole job is to keep the employees and customers from interfering. Usually have to edit him out in production because there's always someone who tries to get involved, and he's caught on camera holding them back and rapidly explaining what's going on."

"That sucks."

"That's his job. Can't blame people who jump into action if they think something bad is going down. Some of our pranks can really freak out bystanders. You need to be prepared if people start screaming or laughing too loud. You can't let it draw you out of hiding."

Simon nodded seriously. "No way."

"One time—"

"Excuse me, sir? You can't smoke out here." A tall female in a green Starbucks apron spoke behind him.

He turned around, the cigarette limp in his mouth. "I'm sorry?"

She smiled. "You can't smoke right outside restaurants."

Rage swamped him and he could barely speak. "I know the law. I'm way more than ten feet from the entrance."

Her gaze did the expected scar bounce, and then she pointed at the side door directly behind him. "But you're not ten feet from that one. And our air system sucks in from over here. We can smell it inside."

He plucked the cigarette from his lips, holding her gaze. *Don't tell me what to do.* Her smile faltered. He dropped the cigarette and ground it against the concrete with his shoe. Her gaze dropped to the movement and she scowled. *That's right, bitch. You can clean it up.*

"Sorry about that. I forgot about the other door," he replied.

She glanced at Simon. "Not a problem." Her ponytail bobbed as she spun around and went back to the front entrance.

He watched her leave, and his empty fingers ached to touch the vulnerable skin of her neck. And squeeze. He'd spin her to face him as he tightened his grip on her neck, as her eyes bulged in fear and her mouth gaped in horror. Make her pay for her arrogance. Make her look into his eyes as he brought her pain. Or see her skull explode in a red mist.

"Hey. You okay?" Simon asked.

He jerked, turning back to Simon, forgetting the man was still there. "Yeah, she was something, huh?"

"Great ass," he replied.

He stared through the glass of the coffee shop, spotting the young woman talking to two other employees and gesturing toward him and Simon in disgust.

I hope you're here on Simon's special day, bitch. You just got your name on a list.

34

"We've got a shooting instructor, a retired deputy, and a former patrol officer. What kind of professions and backgrounds did we get on the other victims?" Mason asked. He, Ray, and Zander were in a small room in the command center where they could hear themselves think. Ray had listed the three women's names and professions on a huge whiteboard. Zander looked at a printout.

"Car sales," he read. "Retired accountant, grocery clerk, two stay-at-home moms, speech therapist, retail sales, and cabdriver."

"Is there more background on the moms?" Ray asked.

"Both attended college and worked in various retail capacities. Neither have worked outside the home in over five years."

"Nothing in that list is grabbing me," said Mason. "Let's move ahead with these three women. We'll keep the moms on the back burner for now. We might need to dig deeper there." But his gut told him they were on the right track with the women's ties to law enforcement. "How long did Jennifer Spendlin instruct at the shooting range?"

"Four years," said Zander. "I talked to one of the other instructors. She taught the women-only classes and some of the advanced classes."

"Any problems with students?"

"Not that he knew of. He said he'd ask around, but the general consensus was that she was well-liked and a top-notch teacher."

Mason eyed her photo. Jennifer was a serious-looking young woman who'd left two children behind. After the shooting her husband had moved in with his parents to get help raising the children. Mason didn't blame him. Raising a two- and a four-year-old had to be a full-time job.

Were you a deliberate target?

"What did we find out on Justin Yoder's shooting range trip?" he asked.

"So far it's been a dry lead. No one there remembered him and none of his friends or coworkers say they ever went shooting with him," said Zander. "All we have is the one time his stepfather took him."

The range Jennifer Spendlin had worked at was nearly two hours from Justin's home. It didn't feel like a solid connection in Mason's brain.

"I think our theory might be a bit of a stretch," Ray said slowly, not taking his gaze from the names on the board. "The two women that were in law enforcement had been out of it for years. Anna Luther retired over a decade ago, and Gabrielle Gower left her job two years before she was shot."

"What's she been doing since?" Mason asked.

"Working on a degree at Portland State. Business," answered Zander. "I think we need to stay on this lead. I like it."

"But how do these women tie to these young guys who died?" asked Ray. "Where do they come in? Hell, what I really want to know is how he gets them to go along with this plan. 'Wait in the bathroom while I kill people until I can shoot you in the face.' It doesn't make sense. We're missing something."

Mason nodded. A clock was ticking down in his head. Every hour and day that passed, he felt them moving closer to another mass of deaths—but he couldn't see the end time on the clock. The air pressure seemed to increase as more time went by.

He dug in a folder and pulled out photos of their shooters—no, they weren't shooters. The young men were victims. He studied each face, wondering what had put the men in the positions that'd caused their deaths. He wished he had video of the first two men. The video at the Rivertown Mall of Justin Yoder a few days before the shooting had brought the young man to life. He'd moved and interacted like a happy man. Not someone who knew he was about to die.

How did the shooter convince them to go along with the shootings?

He closed his eyes, remembering the shooter walking beside Justin, laughing and pointing in the mall. Just another carefree day. And then he'd held his hands up like a movie director. Mason went still. *A movie director?* The shooter had pointed at the mall cameras . . . and then places where there were no cameras, but was he telling Justin there would be cameras? For the performance?

He also studied drama in college and falls back on that when he needs to. Kari Behling's statement about AJ Weiss.

AJ Weiss had had a recent acting gig. And he'd had to buy the clothes for the gig. *Was it possible . . . ?*

"Hey, Ray. Do you have a phone number for Kari Behling handy? You know, AJ Weiss's girlfriend."

Ray pulled a notebook out of his pocket and flipped through it.

Mason looked at Zander. "Do you remember anything in Justin Yoder's background that had to do with acting or drama?"

Zander thought for a moment, then shook his head. "I can look over some of the notes."

"Here you go." Ray handed Mason his notebook, his gaze sharp. "What are you thinking?"

Mason dialed his phone. "I'm thinking that AJ Weiss may have believed he'd signed up for some sort of acting job. Maybe our other guys, too. What other reason would they have to go along with this unless they were killers? Nothing we've found in their backgrounds indicates these are guys that would knowingly stand aside and let someone commit mass murder, right?"

"Hello?" Kari answered her phone. Mason identified himself and plunged right into his questions.

"You told us the other day that AJ had purchased clothing for one of his acting jobs, right?"

"Yes," she answered cautiously.

"What did he buy?"

"I'm not sure. He said he'd been told Dick's Sporting Goods store would have what he needed. I never saw his purchase."

"You didn't ask him about it?"

"I asked him what he'd been told to buy and he'd said exercise pants and jacket."

Yes! "What was the acting job for?" He couldn't help the small quiver in his voice. Ray's eyebrow rose at the sound. Both he and Zander were carefully listening to Mason's side of the conversation.

"Um . . . I'm not sure. He never got to do it."

"You mean it was to happen after he died?"

"I assume so. He never said anything more about it after he'd been given money to go buy the clothes."

Mason suspected AJ had made his last performance.

"Did you find new workout wear in his apartment?"

Kari paused. "I didn't see anything, but I wasn't looking for it. I haven't gone through all his things yet, but I can look if you need me to." Curiosity rang in her tone. Mason didn't press the issue. He knew AJ had been wearing the clothes when he was shot.

"Do you know how he got hired for that particular job?"

"I'm not sure. Probably through one of the websites where they post that sort of thing. He was always scanning for quick jobs. Or one of his acting buddies may have passed it on to him. Often he hears about things through word of mouth."

"What kind of websites?" Mason tucked his cell phone between his jaw and shoulder and flipped to a clean page in Ray's notebook.

"Job posting boards. I don't know what they're called exactly. All the people looking for acting jobs visit them. At least AJ and his friends did."

"Can you give me a name and phone number of his closest friend who does the same sort of thing? Someone who'd know that side of the business?"

"Sure. He has an acting group that meets regularly at Portland Community College. Frankly I think the group did more drinking than working on their craft, but he has a couple of close friends from there. Hold on."

Mason looked at Ray and Zander. "She says AJ went to the sporting goods store to buy exercise pants and jacket for his next job. And there are job boards for actors where she thinks he might have picked up that gig."

"Christ. What'd it say? 'Come star in a mass killing'?" said Ray. "Who'd apply for that?"

Kari came back on the line and recited a name and phone number, which Mason neatly printed in Ray's notebook. Zander held out his hand, and Mason passed him the information.

"Why are you asking about this?" she said slowly. "How can an acting job have anything . . ." She trailed off. "Oh, my God. You think he thought the bullets were fake? That the people he shot were acting? That can't be right."

Mason paused, remembering they hadn't made public the one-shooter theory or shared it with the families. As far as Kari knew, the police still believed AJ had killed several people. "We're exploring several different theories."

"So he didn't know the gun would kill him?" She sounded skeptical. "He's not stupid. He wouldn't pull a trigger on a fake gun in his mouth."

"That's not exactly where we're going with this," said Mason. "Let me pursue it further. If what we're doing amounts to anything, we'll let you know." The evasion felt heavy on his tongue. They were 99 percent certain AJ hadn't shot anyone, but they couldn't risk warning the shooter by having the knowledge go public. Mason ended the call, repeating his promise to update her when they had some facts.

"Okay. We've got a name of an actor friend of AJ's," Mason said. "I'll call him and see if he's familiar with a job AJ may have accepted recently. I bet he can give us more information on those job boards, too."

Zander looked up from his laptop, where he'd done something with the friend's name. "I've got a home address for him if you'd rather go in person. He's not far."

Mason looked at Ray, who shrugged. "Why not?"

. . .

Portland Community College sat on top of a hill on some of the most expensive real estate in Oregon, but Simon's apartment was at the bottom of the same hill and backed up to the interstate. Mason stepped out of the vehicle and slammed his door shut, listening to the roar of the traffic. There wasn't room between the freeway and Simon's apartment for *anything*. A tall concrete wall separated the two, and Mason wondered how unbearable the noise would have been without it.

"I wouldn't be able to live here," Ray stated loudly.

"I don't think it matters much when you're in your twenties," Mason replied. He'd lived wherever he could afford at that age. Especially during college. Sleep in a friend's freezing basement for the winter? Sure. He'd counted himself lucky that it was cheap and had a portable heater. He shuddered, thinking of the ancient heater he'd used. He was lucky he hadn't burned down the house. This squat apartment building had fresh paint and plenty of parking; Simon could have done a lot worse. He and Ray followed Zander up the concrete steps to the second floor and knocked.

"I'll sit back on this one," Zander said quietly. "Unless I'm needed."

Mason nodded, figuring the agent didn't want to intimidate AJ's friend. If Simon appeared to be less than helpful, they had an FBI agent they could dangle in front of him. Footsteps sounded and Mason and Ray pulled out their IDs. The footsteps stopped and Mason held his ID in front of the peephole in the door.

"Can I help you?" came a male voice from inside.

"Simon Goethe?" asked Ray.

A pause. "Yes."

"As you can see, we're with OSP. We'd like to talk to you about AJ Weiss."

The door immediately opened and a tall dark-haired young man studied them. "AJ was a good friend," he said softly. "I can't believe he did it."

Mason nodded. "Well, we're exploring a possibility that he didn't. Can we come in?"

Simon led them into a cramped sitting room with a view of the concrete wall. Mason tipped his head at the window. "I assume your rent's pretty good?"

The young man snorted. "For the area. Anything close to the college costs more than I want to pay. I make do."

"You did acting stuff with AJ," Ray stated. He, Mason, and Simon took seats. Zander leaned against the wall, keeping a close eye on Simon, staying silent. Mason noticed the young man steal a couple of quick looks at the agent. Zander hadn't held up ID the way he and Ray had.

"Yeah, we belong to a group that meets once a month up at the college. We met a few years ago in an acting class downtown."

"I understand there're job boards where actors can find jobs," Mason stated.

Confusion crossed Simon's face. "There are. I assume it's like that for any kind of profession."

Good point. Mason hadn't job-hunted in decades. He wouldn't know where to start.

"AJ's girlfriend, Kari, told us AJ had recently lined up a job, but she didn't know where he'd heard about it."

Simon was instantly wary, and Mason tensed at the sight. "What's that have to do with his shooting?" Simon asked.

"It's a bit hard to explain, but we need to find out where he lined up a job that gave him a clothing allowance and sent him to buy some clothes at Dick's Sporting Goods."

Alarm registered in Simon's eyes. "Why? Why do you need to know where he was going to work?"

"Simon, do you know where he got the job?" Ray asked quietly. Dozens of times over the years, Mason had watched Ray interview witnesses and suspects. Each time someone appeared to hold back, the former college football player would magically shift his shoulders and bulk to increase his size. Like right now. Ray looked like a linebacker sitting in a skeletal chair. Mason had tried the same movement in front of a mirror at home and could never replicate the results. Could have something to do with Ray outweighing him by fifty pounds.

"Why are the police interested in a job he never did?" Simon asked.

"Simon," Mason said slowly. "The world thinks your friend is a killer. What the fuck is making you question *how we do our job?*"

The man looked at the floor and shifted in his chair. "He told me about the job. It was posted near the department up at the school."

"AJ found it?"

"Yeah, someone had made a job flyer looking for guys that were exactly six one, lean build, and stated that it was for a one-time impromptu performance. We both fit the description, so AJ passed the phone number on to me. Usually I ignore job postings like that but when I called and left my number, the guy called me back and the money was decent for a day's work. And he said it could lead to more of the same type of job. Sounded like easy money."

"What type of job was it?" Mason asked. His ears were ringing as his brain realized they were very close to finding their answer, and he leaned forward to hear better. Every receptor in his body waited for Simon's answer.

Simon met his gaze and his mouth turned down, his shoulders drooping. "It was for one of those surprise shows. The ones that pull pranks on your friends. The guy who posted the ad has a whole bunch of them on YouTube that are freaking hilarious. They scare and surprise the crap out of people in their offices or in public places."

"My son loves those things," Ray said.

Mason had caught glimpses of the shows on TV but had never bothered to watch. To him, they were poorly acted and badly produced. Ray's preteen son seemed about the right age to appreciate the humor. Mason found enough surprises in life; he didn't need to watch more.

"AJ was hired to do that?" Mason asked.

"Yeah, but he never got the chance."

Silence filled the room.

"Shit!" Simon made the connection. "Are you saying AJ shot all those people and it was supposed to be a joke? Holy fuck!" Simon stood and paced into his kitchen, pulling at his hair. "That's messed up! There's no way—"

"That's not what we think happened," said Mason. "But the guy who he contacted about the job might be involved."

"Travis?"

The investigators straightened. "That's his name?" Ray asked, pulling out his notebook.

"Yeah, I met with him the other day. He hired me to do a prank at a local Starbucks."

"When?" Mason nearly shouted.

"Dunno. I'm waiting to hear. He's supposed to text me when it's time. But it should be within a day or two."

"Which Starbucks?"

Mason's mind raced as Simon gave the location. "Were you told to hide in the bathroom until the job started?" Mason asked.

Simon nodded, fear crossing his face. "What was going to happen there?"

"What can we do?" Ray said in a low voice as Zander and Mason stepped close to confer, ignoring Simon's question.

"We can close that location. Now. We can't risk another shooting in public," said Zander. "And if the store is closed, he'll have to change his plans, buying us some time." He looked at Simon. "We need the number you have to contact this guy. You know his last name?"

Simon pulled out his phone and started scrolling. "I don't know his last name. One of the conditions of the job was that I couldn't tell anybody about it until we'd completed filming. That's the only reason I held back at first."

Mason gestured for him to hurry up, but figured the guy had probably given Simon a fake name and phone number. "What's he look like?"

"Tall. Slim build. Longish dark hair. Has some creepy burn scars down one part of his neck and on the side of his face. I think he wears his hair long to cover them."

"Did he have any other pranks planned to film?" Zander asked.

"Beats me," said Simon as he handed his phone to Zander with the contact open. "He only talked to me about the one. With all the setup and organizing, I doubt he's got more than one going on at a time."

There're no pranks being filmed! Mason bit his tongue.

Zander snapped an image of Simon's contact page. "We need to know the minute you hear from this guy."

"Maybe we should have a uniform stay close to Simon," Ray suggested.

"A cop? Why? Am I in danger?" Simon's voice cracked. "What the hell is going on?"

Mason put a hand on his shoulder, looking into scared brown eyes. "As long as you don't go near that Starbucks or meet this guy again, I think you'll be fine. We think he's organized these . . . pranks . . . to cover up the shootings that happened this summer."

"He fooled AJ into killing himself?" Simon whispered. "That doesn't make sense."

"We'll let you know when we have all the answers. Did he tell you to buy clothes?"

"Nah, he had the outfit on hand he wanted me to wear."

"Can we see them?" Ray asked. Simon disappeared down a hallway.

"Do we need to close the store?" Mason asked. "Or do we wait until he calls and tells Simon to move into position? And then set up a sting?"

"We have to close it," Ray argued. "We can't risk the chance of a shooting there."

"I'm with Ray," said Zander. "I'm making the call." He stepped out of the apartment. Mason knew it was the right thing to do, but damn he wished they could set it up to catch the guy the minute he set foot near the store.

Simon came from the back of the apartment with two pieces of black clothing. Mason didn't need to see the Nike logo.

Finally. We are on your ass. You'll never see us coming.

Zander reappeared. "I've got them shutting down the Starbucks. They'll make it look like a power or water issue. And that number Simon has is to a burner phone. We'll trace where it was purchased and see if there're any store cameras that recorded the sale. The phone's already been canceled."

"I talked to him on that number yesterday," stated Simon. "There's no way it's not good."

"You said you left a message at the original number on the flyer, right?" asked Mason. "Did he ever call you back on that number?"

Simon shook his head.

"He probably uses a new number every few days. I suspect the next call or text you get from him will be from an unfamiliar number."

"He told me not to screen calls. Said one of the cameramen might call me, so I need to answer every call."

Someone thought ahead.

35

Proud of herself, Ava flipped through a magazine in a waiting area at the hospital. The key to doing something she didn't want to do was to not think about it and simply command her muscles to move. The thought of seeing Jayne made her want to vomit. But she still had an obligation to her sister. She hadn't made up her mind if she wanted to visit Jayne's room, but she'd at least talk to her doctor. She'd never get the questions out of her head if she didn't ask. She'd made a call to Misty when she first arrived at the hospital, reminded that she hadn't heard from the young girl in a day or two. Misty was back home and recovering just fine, but had stated she was done with yoga for a few months. Ava didn't blame her.

Her phone buzzed. Mason.

"I'm waiting to talk to Jayne's doctor," she told him.

"How was *your* appointment?"

She heard the caution in his voice, knowing he wondered if she'd even attended. "It was okay. I don't think she's anyone I want to continue with, but she at least said something that's making my legs move today."

"That's a start," Mason agreed. "You're checking on Jayne?"

"Yes and don't ask me why. I can't just turn it off." She paused. "That makes it worse."

"I know. Let me know when you're done. Say, we got a good lead on our shooter this morning."

She listened as he told her about filmed pranks and young male actors looking to make a quick buck. "You think that's how he's recruiting them? I've watched those shows. They're horrible. Some are funny, but I always feel for the person being pranked."

"It's our best lead. We shut down the Starbucks on Grand Boulevard that we believe was going to be the next location."

She drew in a sharp breath. "That's the one I always go to! I was just there!" She set down the rest of her iced drink, suddenly slightly nauseated. A shudder ran through her as she imagined witnessing a second mass shooting. *I couldn't handle that again.*

"I thought so," Mason said grimly. "What's the word on Jayne?"

Ava took a deep breath. "A nurse told me the wrist injuries weren't as bad as they expected and the wound to her spleen didn't require surgery. They're still watching it. She said Jayne was scheduled for a psych eval earlier today but didn't know more. I'm waiting on the doctor I spoke to last night."

"You sound good."

She couldn't hold back a small laugh. "I didn't think I'd make it out of bed today, but frankly, knowing that I had that damn appointment made me move. I don't like to let people down. Now I'm simply following a checklist of what I need to accomplish today. I feel like a robot."

"Yesterday was draining."

"That's putting it mildly."

"What are you going to say to Jayne?"

"I haven't decided if I'm going to talk to her. I might just listen to the doctor and leave."

Mason was silent for a few moments. "I miss you."

His words touched a tender spot in her heart, and she nearly melted. Neither of them was a sentimental person, but for several days she'd had a huge lonely gap in her gut, making her feel vulnerable and emotional. "I miss you, too," she whispered. The doctor from last night peeked in the waiting room, and she stood up. "I need to go. I love you." Mason said the same and he was gone. She dropped her phone in her purse, and an abrupt loneliness weighed down her shoulders.

She followed the doctor, listening as he repeated what she'd already learned from the nurse. "What about the psych evaluation?"

"We're admitting her for a few days. We're of the opinion that she's still a threat to herself."

Oh, Jayne.

"Then what?"

"We'll find her a facility where she can get back on her feet and receive the mental care she needs."

Ava knew it wasn't that simple. Insurance. Availability. Cost. Jayne's attitude. It all mattered.

I'll cross that bridge when I come to it.

"Are you ready to see her now? I doubt she'll be responsive. She's sedated again."

Ava froze. *Am I ready?*

"I'll just peek real quick."

The doctor gave her an odd look but nodded and opened a door. Ava stepped inside, holding her breath. The shade was pulled and the dim room smelled strongly of antiseptic and something sour. She passed the tiny bathroom and peered around a corner. Jayne slept. Her dark hair spread across the pillow. Relief weakened Ava's knees. *Please stay asleep.*

She stepped closer, moving as silently as possible. Jayne looked like a battered doll. Her weight was still too low and her collarbones protruded, creating shadows below her neck. Ava stopped at her twin's side and firmly kept a lid on her emotions. She noticed Jayne's nails were bitten to the quick and her pink sparkly polish looked as if a five-year-old had applied it. She glanced at her own too-short nails, remembering Mason's comment. *This isn't like you.*

Her sister lay perfectly still, her chest slowly rising and falling. Ava said a quick prayer of gratitude that Jayne hadn't succeeded and tried not to think of what that would mean for the next few months of both of their lives.

There was no easy answer. No quick fix.

Do I want to be dragged along Jayne's path?

She was at a crossroads. Help Jayne or not. Move on with her own life or hold her sister's hand and share the rocky journey.

Mason or Jayne?

Me or Jayne?

Why was there no compromise? Why was her only choice black or white?

She brushed tears off her cheeks. All her life there'd only been stark choices, but lately she'd tried to pretend she could have everything. Her sister, her job, her relationship with Mason. Over and over she'd told Mason she was done with Jayne, but in the back of her mind she had always known she'd jump when Jayne "needed" her.

Was she ready to choose?

Jayne nearly chose for me.

She touched her mother's ring on a chain around her neck. Once Jayne had stolen it out of Mason's home, but Ava had demanded it back. Perhaps Jayne needed it more than she did. She unhooked the clasp and lay the necklace on the bedside table, but stared at it, unable to walk away.

Go!

Her legs followed her command, and she left the room in a daze. Instinct guided her through the maze of hospital corridors until she spotted the sun shining through the big glass doors. She stepped out and welcomed the blinding heat, closing her eyes and putting on her sunglasses. A few deep breaths later, she'd decided she needed someone else to tell her what to do for a while. Suddenly she craved a quiet room where she could stretch and sweat and listen to her yoga instructor's commands. She checked the time on her phone and noted she had plenty of time to run errands first.

. . .

He drove through the strip mall parking lot, doing one of his dozens of drive-bys. He could never overprepare when it came to one of his stagings. This one had the perfect actor and the perfect location. And would eliminate another abomination from his world. The police were confused, trying to figure out why young men were losing their minds and shooting up the public. They sought answers where there weren't any and Sunday-morning psychiatrists made sweeping judgments from their safe distances. *Confused and angry young men.*

It really wasn't that complicated.

Men and women were created differently. There was no equality.

Until society embraced the right roles, there would be chaos. He was an instrument of that change.

He stomped on the brake and his head whipped forward. An electrical company employee had stepped out from between parked vehicles and nearly become roadkill. The employee held up a hand in apology. "Sorry!" he said. A large bundle of orange cord was balanced on the employee's shoulder, blocking his view of oncoming traffic.

Idiot.

He continued across the parking lot toward the Starbucks.

What the fuck?

Electric company employees moved in and out of his Starbucks. Yellow caution ribbon blocked customers from entering the store. Three utility vans filled the front parking spaces. He rolled down his window.

"Hey," he said to a passerby. "What's going on at Starbucks? They open?"

The man stopped. "Nope. Power issue. Can't grind coffee without power. I'm headed over to the one inside the grocery store." He moved on.

He watched the employees unload supplies from the vans and stride in and out of the store. He eyed the mailing store next door to the coffee shop. The store's OPEN sign was lit up. He slowly rolled through the rest of the parking lot, watching the movement of the people. He didn't see a single green apron in front of the store or inside. The bright-red shirts of the electric company moved behind the coffee counter.

He pulled out of the immediate parking area and into a spot at the adjacent grocery store's lot. And watched.

Activity. Lots of it.

The time his old office had lost power they'd sent one guy.

Do they know?

Impossible. He'd been too careful. He'd come back to the store in a few hours and observe again. He was about to start the ignition and pull away when he saw a familiar face drive by.

Her. The federal agent.

He watched her park and get out of her car. Her dark hair was pulled back into a ponytail and sunglasses hid her eyes, but he'd known instantly who she was. He'd spent enough time with her in his sights to know how she moved and how she tilted her head. She didn't walk up to the Starbucks—her Starbucks. Instead she simply stood and observed.

The time of this visit deviated from her routine.

After a minute of watching electrical employees hustle, she turned to survey the lot, slowly scanning each vehicle. He ducked down behind his steering wheel, holding his breath. His skin started to heat and his lungs seized.

She knows.

Fucking bitch federal agent.

Who had told her? Simon? He shook his head. Simon was ecstatic to participate in his game. There was no way he would have gone to the police; he had no cause. The woman couldn't have figured out this was the next location on her own. *Could she?* He stayed low in his car, thoughts ricocheting in his brain, his anger escalating.

She did this. She interfered again. Choosing to make an example out of her was the right thing to do.

"How dare she think she can mess with me!" Fury blurred his vision.

He risked a peek over his dash, spotted the back of her head, and eased back into his seat. His anger stewed in his gut, souring his stomach, but he made himself focus. *I can handle this.* The federal agent watched the activity for another moment, nodded as if satisfied, and got back in her vehicle. He started his car and followed her out of the lot.

Time for the backup plan.

36

Mason picked at his sandwich. The kid behind the counter had put too much mustard on it and now it was inedible—or was he simply not hungry? Across from him Ray worked on a vegetarian sandwich and Zander made silent progress on a Greek salad. He watched guacamole drip onto Ray's plate, decided his problem was lack of appetite, and pushed his sandwich away. After talking with Simon Goethe, who'd decided to spend the evening and night at a friend's apartment, the three investigators had agreed to grab a fast dinner and then head back to the command center.

"Sergeant Shaver says he got some flak from the owner of the strip mall where Starbucks leases their building," said Ray between rapid bites. "The owner says the activity with all the electrical guys is affecting the other businesses and they're complaining."

"Did he tell him to go pound sand?" Mason asked.

"Yep. Pissed the owner off. Shaver wanted to say, 'Do you want to host the next mass shooting?' but he kept his temper. We don't need the word getting out like that."

"No," agreed Mason. He'd had a stern talk with Simon about keeping all information about the Starbucks shutdown from his friends. He crossed his fingers the young man would keep his mouth shut. If the media got wind that a mastermind had orchestrated the shootings . . .

Not yet. They had to keep it quiet for a little while longer. They'd briefed Sergeant Shaver over the phone, stunning him with the stories about the pranks, and Shaver had agreed that it was their best lead. "The phone that belongs to the number Simon had was sold at a local Walmart six months ago," Shaver had said. "They don't keep video that long, and if I was buying the phone, I would have paid cash. There's no way I would have left a credit card trail."

"Shaver's got someone checking out who set up the YouTube channel, right?" asked Ray.

"Yes. The videos appear to be dated, but popular. If our guy is on film in any of them, he's going to be at least five to ten years older now. And they haven't located who created them yet. I suspect all the posting information is false." Mason took a sip of his bottled water and silently watched his dinner companions finish.

I wonder how Ava is doing.

She'd sounded good on an earlier phone call, but admitted she was running on autopilot. She'd said she was going to yoga, and he'd agreed it was a good decision. A big part of him wanted to get her out of town and onto a sunny beach for two weeks. Who cared that her vacation time was nearly done? His phone vibrated loudly on the table, drawing Ray's and Zander's attention.

Simon Goethe.

"Callahan."

"This is Simon—from earlier today." The kid sounded out of breath.

"I know, Simon. What's up?"

"He just texted me. Well, I assume it was him. It came from a different phone number just like you said it would."

"What'd he say?" Mason held very still, willing Simon to get to the point.

"It said to be in place at that Starbucks at seven thirty tonight."

Mason checked the time; it was nearly seven. "Give me the number. Did he say anything else? Did you reply?"

"Not yet. You said to call you immediately. No, he hasn't said anything else." He rattled off the phone number, which Mason copied onto a napkin and handed to Zander.

"Text him back that you'll be on time. Say something like you're really excited."

"I will? You want me to go?" His voice cracked.

"No." *Do I need to use smaller words?* "We'll take it from here. Keep your phone close and call me again if he says anything else. I'm going to send an officer to stay with you until this is over."

"Am I in danger?" Simon asked slowly. "You said he doesn't know where I am, right?"

"I'm just taking precautions. He probably thinks you're on your way to Starbucks, but let's not take any chances, okay? Do you feel like you're in a safe location?"

"I'm still at my friend's apartment in Sandy."

"Good choice. You're miles away from where he thinks this is going down. Give me the address." Mason added it to another napkin. "Keep an eye out for the officer, okay?"

Simon agreed and hung up.

"So Travis—or whatever his name is—hasn't seen that we've shut down the Starbucks," Ray said slowly. "That seems odd."

Mason agreed. "What if the victim wasn't going into the Starbucks? Maybe she works nearby? Somehow closing the store hasn't affected his plan."

"But Simon was told to wait in the bathroom, right?" said Zander. "Travis needs the store to be open for his plan to work. What are we missing here?"

"We need a bigger presence around that store, now!" said Mason. "Get a half dozen cars spread through those parking lots."

Ray grabbed his phone and headed to make a call outside.

Mason looked at Zander, doubt suddenly filling his mind. "Right? A police force needs to be seen to stop whatever he thinks he's planning. Or should we be watching for him, planning to catch him? We sort of know what he looks like. And he should be dressed in black. Shit! What's the best plan?"

"A presence," said Zander. "We'll never spot him in time. He plans too carefully. This guy knows exactly what he's doing."

"Then why did he just activate Simon in a place that's not available?" Questions zinged through his mind like pinballs.

"I wish I knew," admitted Zander. "Let's get over there." He stood and picked up his empty tray. Mason neatly folded the paper around the rest of Ray's veggie sandwich to take to him and then threw the remains of his own in the garbage.

• • •

By seven fifteen the Starbucks parking lot held one electrical van, two police cars, and no customer cars. The mailing shop next door had closed up. With some strong persuading from Zander, the two other stores in the little strip mall closed early and the employees left. The only other businesses still open were the grocery store and big electronics store that sat at the far end of a big shared parking lot. Mason and Zander watched from a corner of the Starbucks parking area as Shaver barked orders at his teams. Three other police cars sat in the larger parking lot in clear view of the Starbucks while another half dozen cars slowly patrolled the lot. Prevention was the primary goal in this operation. Anyone who intended to start shooting would think twice at the sight of the large police presence.

Any sane person would think twice, Mason amended. Chances were that their shooter was quite sane. His planning and success indicated he had a sharp brain and knew exactly what he was doing; but his brain had something very twisted or missing in one corner, which was typical for serial killers and mass shooters. On the drive over he'd wondered where their shooter fell into the killer classification system. He seemed to be a hybrid of mass and serial. He definitely fell into the mass shooter category, but the majority of those killers went into the shooting knowing their chance of survival was very small; they were willing to take that risk. Had their shooter expected to die? Mason didn't think so. He'd created a near-perfect exit strategy and neatly placed the blame on someone who couldn't defend himself each time. This shooter had no intention of dying.

And then he did it again. And again, shortening the window between killings and placing himself firmly under the serial killer classification. Mason knew the FBI profilers would say he was doing it for the sexual-type thrill and power he experienced. The dizzying high from the success—and the belief that he could get away with it over and over.

"This guy is a serial killer," he stated out loud. "We thought we had a rash of brainwashed young men looking to end it all and take people with them. That wasn't right at all."

"Absolutely," agreed Zander. "The mass shootings are his signature, but the murders are his goals. And we know he's not done. He's enjoying this way too much."

"Do you think we're on target believing it's these particular women? Or is it just a coincidence that there's been one female law-enforcement type each time?"

"I think we're following a good lead."

His answer didn't give Mason any satisfaction. "I asked Lane County to follow up with the range where Jennifer Spendlin worked. If we're right that she was the first targeted victim during a shooting, we need to know why he shot her. We've got a killer who's a good shot. Chances are he crossed paths with Spendlin at her place of work."

"Good point," said Zander. "I hadn't put that together. You're right. He clearly sees weapons as a tool of his trade and would have spent some time honing that skill. That's a good place to start."

"Your FBI profilers are going to salivate over his records."

"Hell yes. If we're right about what he's doing, they're gonna love it. A new brain to dissect."

"He's definitely not typical. I think of most serial killers as moving in the shadows, stealthily spying on their prey. This guy makes as big of a scene as possible."

Zander agreed. "But what's his main motivation? What is his primary purpose and final goal?"

"Shit. Now you're sounding like your profiling buddy, Euzent."

"He's the best. I wish he was here right now. He'd have more insight into what makes our killer tick. I emailed him earlier, but it's too late on the East Coast. Maybe we can get him out here."

"I want to catch this guy tonight," said Mason. "I want him to show up here in the next fifteen minutes and have fifty cops take him down."

"You and me both."

Zander wiped the sweat off his forehead and Mason did the same. The temperature had peaked at ninety-five degrees earlier in the day and had barely cooled down. The air was heavy and still. Humidity was rare during the Pacific Northwest summers, but Mason felt it today. "Crime and heat," he muttered. "Hand in hand. Give me some snow or ice that keeps everyone stuck at home."

"Amen," said Zander.

Mason watched the time tick down on his phone. Seven thirty came and passed. They waited, remembering that Justin Yoder had waited nearly ninety minutes before the shooting started at the Rivertown Mall. A text popped up on his phone from Simon. HE WANTS TO KNOW IF I'M IN POSITION. I SAID YES. HE SAID TO SIT TIGHT BECAUSE OUR TARGET IS LATE.

Mason showed Zander, who scowled. "I don't get it. He's acting like things are normal."

"This is the right Starbucks, right?" Mason said.

"Simon said this is where they met. He didn't suggest a different one."

Mason quickly texted Simon, double-checking the address of the location. Simon confirmed. "Is he pulling one over on Simon? Checking to see if he's honest?"

"Don't know." Zander stepped over to confer with Sergeant Shaver.

Mason studied the parking lot. *Were they being watched and played with?* He lifted his gaze and searched for high points where they could be seen from a distance with binoculars. There really wasn't one unless the killer was on the roof of one of the stores.

Zander returned. "Shaver's telling everyone to be alert for single males. And told them again to keep an eye out for scars on the neck. If he's surveying this location we'll find him." His gaze went to the rooftop of the grocery store. "Shaver had the roofs searched already and the access points covered. There's no way anyone is up there."

Sweat dripped down Mason's back as dread crept up and dug at his brain. "Something's wrong."

37

He'd watched her grab her bag and yoga mat out of her trunk and head in the direction of the studio. Now he sat in his car and waited. After she'd gone inside he'd checked the studio's class schedule online. Her class should be finished at eight P.M.

Is this what I want to do?

An odd calm filled his brain. The cops were crawling around that Starbucks like ants on a piece of dropped ham. His perfect plan had been uncovered. And it'd started when that female agent had walked into the men's room and discovered his stash of clothing.

One little mistake had exposed him.

Not even a mistake, he'd simply not had the chance to get to the clothes.

He closed his eyes and recalled her face as she'd huddled beside the bleeding teenager. She'd been inconsequential. A woman on the ground. Someone he'd believed he'd walk by and never see again. Instead she'd ruined him.

He needed to knock her off her pedestal before she destroyed him. No woman had the right to take him down. His destiny was his own. *He* chose what happened to his life. Now she'd forced his hand and he had to take action.

Just like the other bitches before.

That damned instructor at the shooting range in Eugene had been the first in a decade to push him over the edge. She'd disrespected him in front of other men, cheating during a competition and then laughing at him after she'd won. He'd argued that she should only compete against other women, and that she'd distracted the other men, but his complaints had fallen on deaf ears. The other men had gathered around her, congratulating her, their tongues hanging out, turned on by a woman who thought she knew how to use a gun, when all she did was cast illusions. *Women should be separate. Where they're not a distraction to men.*

And they definitely should not hold jobs where they told men what to do. That was asking for trouble.

No wonder men were angry. No wonder their prisons were full of men who'd lashed out in anger. They'd felt the injustice: women taking their jobs, women abandoning their children, women not fulfilling their roles as nurturers.

The world was out of balance.

After he'd taken care of the shooting instructor, the police were so distracted by the number of deaths and so convinced their shooter was dead that they hadn't dug deep enough into the case.

It'd worked. He'd felt validated and empowered.

And he'd known he could easily do it again. He'd ached to do it again.

His plan had worked perfectly the first three times, and what had started as a personal issue for him had evolved into a bigger purpose.

He opened his eyes. This could be his last chance, but his actions would lead others to take a stand. They needed to man up and show who was in charge. Even though the media attention would be negative, his point would be made. If he could fucking do it, other men could, too.

He was a pioneer.

The parking lot at the far end of the Rivertown Mall had thinned considerably. This end was for office space, a day care center, and the yoga studio. At this time of night, the cars primarily belonged to people in class at the studio. The other end of the mall buzzed with late shoppers, people seeking frozen yogurt, and overheated families looking for air-conditioned restaurants. He knew the layout, patterns, and heartbeat of the mall. He'd done considerable reconnaissance with Justin Yoder and on his own. He had time for one last quick look.

He stepped out of his vehicle, knowing his supplies in his trunk were ready to go, but he wouldn't need them for another hour. He'd been prepared, expecting to use the Starbucks to take out the female agent. But this time he'd be on his own. A new experience for him. There wouldn't be a fall guy waiting in the wings to take the blame.

Was it worth the risk?

He could go home and create a plan for another day, but he had the feeling his window of time was shrinking. If the police had found Simon and he'd told them about the Starbucks, his world could already be crumbling. He might not have another chance to make her pay. It had to be tonight.

I am ready.

He headed in the direction of the studio, planning his actions as he walked.

No mask.

Not this time. He didn't care who saw his face this time. Once other men realized what he'd managed to accomplish, they'd recite his name in awe.

Remember the guy who took all those lives and the police had no clue?

They'd study him, stunned at his clever plans. A slow smile crossed his face.

He'd chosen the end to his story; they weren't going to choose it for him.

As they'd imposed on his father, sent to die in prison.

How many people do I want to take down this time?

Indecision crossed his brain. Should he shoot as many as possible or just her?

Just her.

He would miss the rush of power from walking in public and playing God, picking and choosing who'd die. But this was the right way to handle the fed. He'd originally used the mass shootings to help mask his targets, giving the police multiple victims to comb through instead of spotlighting his victim and possibly leading them back to him. And it fell in line with using the young men as the scapegoats. Across the country over the last few decades, young men had taken out groups of people. To the local investigators, it'd appeared to be more of the same.

Time for a small change in the game.

He stopped across the large outdoor aisle and eyed the studio entrance. The door led to a lobby with stairs and an elevator that led to the second floor where the women worked out. Downstairs were empty businesses, their workers safe in their homes.

One shot as she exits the building. The scene unfolded in his brain. A discreet hiding place. Shoot. She goes down. Game over.

It was new and different. A fresh rush of excitement shot through him, giving him a dizzying high. He was stepping forward to take charge this time, not hiding in the wings as he moved his pawns.

It was terrifying and thrilling at the same time.

• • •

She'd pushed too hard. Ava had leaned against the counter in the yoga studio's bathroom for fifteen minutes, searching for a reason to walk into the studio. She couldn't find it. Everything was gone. She'd pushed hard all day long, trying to act normal, and now she had nothing left.

Did I eat today?

She couldn't remember and didn't care.

Go home.

She checked the time and knew she didn't have the guts to walk into yoga class late. She put the strap to her mat over her shoulder, picked up her backpack, and stared in the mirror. The fluorescent lighting made her eyes appear bloodshot and her skin sallow. She'd spent the last quarter hour struggling with indecision and now that she'd made up her mind to go home, relief swamped her and she wanted to go to sleep.

Try again tomorrow.

She strode out of the bathroom, focused on getting out of the building that suddenly felt airless. She pushed through the double front doors, welcoming the slap of heat and fresh oxygen. The building had been freezing. Her stomach growled as she caught a whiff of Thai food, and she considered an order of pho to go. Trapped again in indecision, she glanced toward the parking lot and froze, making eye contact with a man twenty feet away. He'd halted, his surprised gaze locked on her.

It was the shooter. The man who'd offered to help her and Misty. Here. In Rivertown. Again.

Determination crossed his face and he took a step toward her as her gaze caught the scars on his neck, nearly hidden by his hair and cap. *That's why he wears hats.*

His hand went to the large pocket in his cargo shorts.

She followed his hand movement. *Pocket. Gun. Run!* Her indecision evaporated.

Ava dropped everything and ran.

38

A low hum started among the patrol officers. Mason heard radios crackling and watched as their car lights and sirens started. Several of the patrol cars whipped out of the parking lot.

"What's going on?" he shouted at a group of officers.

"Shots fired," answered Sergeant Shaver, his phone to his ear. "Rivertown Mall. That takes precedence over this stakeout!" he yelled at the officers within hearing distance. "I want everyone over there. I'll keep two vehicles here to keep an eye on this building."

Rivertown? Again?

Mason stared at the coffee shop's sign on the building, his brain spinning. Was Rivertown a distraction to get them away from this location? Or . . .

"Any injuries?" he asked Shaver.

"A mall security guard has been shot. Shooter is a tall white male in his late twenties or thirties."

"Masked?"

"No." Shaver got into his vehicle and started the engine.

Related to our shootings? He met the gazes of Ray and Zander. "This isn't right. I've had a bad gut feeling about this location for the last half hour." Both men agreed. "Let's get over there."

Ray drove while Mason monitored the information coming in from the mall. "The security guard is dead and the mall is on lockdown," he told the other two men. "This shooter is using a handgun and started at the other end of the mall."

"Could be a weak copycat," said Ray. "That's not like our guy at all."

In the backseat Zander nodded, his phone at his ear.

"He left the immediate mall grounds before the perimeter was established," added Zander. "They're saying he was running after a woman, headed toward the home improvement store that sits adjacent to the mall."

"A woman?" Mason asked, frowning as he listened to the information from Washington County dispatch. The next report verified what Zander had stated.

"Perhaps it's a domestic dispute," Ray said. "This isn't matching up."

Zander listened intently to his phone as Mason watched him in the rearview mirror. Abruptly his gaze jumped to meet Mason's. "Where's Ava?" Zander blurted.

Mason's heart stopped as he tried to get his thoughts in order. He looked at his watch. "Yoga. Or else home. She was going to try— holy fuck!"

Yoga. Mall.

He spun around in his seat. *"What's going on?"*

"I've got a report that the pursued woman has shouted that she's an FBI agent."

• • •

Her lungs begged for oxygen.

Ava ran. She'd started toward the busier section of the Rivertown Mall, but changed direction when he started to shoot. "Get away," she'd shrieked at casual strolling shoppers. "FBI agent! Get down!" She heard a shot and glanced over as a security guard collapsed. She couldn't lead him into crowds, so she darted down a quieter alley between two stores, knowing it fed into a narrow back road that led to the parking lot of the home improvement store next door. Its parking lot was always less crowded than the mall's, and her immediate goal was to get the shooter away from targets.

He shot at her twice. She zigged and zagged a little, knowing how hard it was to shoot accurately while running. Her best bet was to put as much room as possible between the two of them. A rapid glance back showed her he was in pursuit. She cranked up her speed, thankful she had on good exercise shoes instead of flip-flops.

Get away from people. Hide!

She was unarmed, her weapon locked in her vehicle.

Her legs pumped automatically as she scanned her path for a place to hide. She'd felt his hate and intent the instant they'd locked gazes. The man was a predator and somehow she'd ended up on his list like the other women.

Why me?

She sped behind the buildings of the mall, passing the employee entrances and delivery docks. The sun had gone down behind the trees, and her way was lit by the stark lighting intended to keep trespassers away from the rear of the mall. She didn't try the doors, worried they'd be locked, wasting her time. The slap of his running footsteps sounded in her ears, and she gave another burst of speed. Her path opened up into the parking lot of the home improvement store. A few cars dotted it.

Closed?

The huge sign at the end of the parking lot was off. *I thought these places never closed.*

Confusion jumbled her brain. *Hide.* She scanned the lot as she ran at full speed. Adjacent to the big orange building was the garden supply area with its chain-link fence. *Hide.* She veered toward the fence, his steps still pounding behind her. Planters and sheds and barbecues lined the front of the store.

A shot made her ears ring.

She changed direction toward the front of the store as she spotted a chain and lock wrapped around the gate to the garden center. *Can't get through.*

Behind her she heard him swear and stumble. She stole a backward glance and saw him sprawl face first across the blacktop of the parking lot. She turned up her speed and darted behind the closest shed along the front of the store. He shouted and a shot ricocheted off a riding lawn mower in front of the garden center. She bent over and ran along the front of the big store, hiding behind the lines of barbecues and displays of granite for countertops. Heart pounding, she stopped behind a pallet of fertilizer bags and tried to think coherently.

The store was closed.

To her right, past the garden center, was more parking lot and closed office buildings. To her left was the lumber section and the loading docks of the store, and she didn't know what was beyond that. Roads and businesses? All deserted because of the late hour?

No weapon. No backup.

At least I got him away from the crowds.

Her best bet was to hide. The chain link fence around the garden center rattled as someone shook its gate just yards to her right. She caught her breath and sprinted to pass the front doors of the store and head for the lumber side of the store, hoping to find a hiding place near the loading docks. Shots splintered the glass front doors and an alarm sounded inside the building. She turned and flung herself through the shattered doors. Her feet knocked the safety glass out of the lower third of the door and she tripped. She landed on her hands and knees, the glass chunks digging into her flesh, and fought to catch her breath. From the corner of her eye, she saw a woman in an orange employee apron step out of an aisle. "Get down," she screamed at the woman as she scrambled to her feet, pain forgotten. The alarm resonated through the store, bouncing off the concrete floor and high metal ceiling. Ava dashed straight ahead, down a wide aisle, and took the first right.

She ran, searching for a hiding spot and a weapon. Ahead were automatic glass doors that led out to the fenced garden center. Not wanting to trip the doors and cause them to move, she took a hard left.

Garden tools.

She slammed to a stop and reached for the thickest wooden-handled tool. She hefted the shovel and eyed the other tools. The alarm stopped and instantly a gunshot echoed through the building.

Did he make someone turn off the alarm?

A woman started to scream. Painful, terror-stricken screams. Back in her corner of the store, Ava's breathing was racked and loud, and the woman's shrieks made her want to climb the walls. She tried to breathe more quietly and dark spots formed at the edges of her vision. *Screaming means she's not dead.* She set the shovel back as a wicked long tool with forked spikes and a narrow chiseled blade on one end caught her eye. It looked like a weapon from a zombie-killing flick.

Better.

Now if she could find Captain America's shield, she'd be set.

39

Mason, Zander, and Ray ran across the home improvement store's parking lot to the perimeter that had been set up around the giant store by the Washington County sheriff and Cedar Edge police. Mason had tried to call Ava three times, leaving voice mails demanding she return his calls immediately. He fired off texts, asking for her attention.

He prayed her phone was off because she was attending a calming yoga class. Or she was home and in the shower or fast asleep already.

Another shooting in Cedar Edge. Anger showed on the cops' faces as they paced in front of the home improvement store. Violence had reared its ugly head in their quiet community for the second time within a week. Mason slowed as he saw the broken glass of the front doors. Two cops dragged out a shrieking dark-haired woman as others covered them, their weapons trained on the inside of the big store. They pulled the woman to the side of the entrance, protected from the interior by the heavy walls, and immediately started administering aid. Her screams settled into a low wail.

His gaze locked on her hair, Mason numbly pushed through the line and was grabbed by Ray. "Let go!" He shook off Ray's hand.

"That's not her! Look at the orange apron!"

Mason stopped and squinted. Ray was right. The police were clearly assisting an employee. "What happened?" he asked the closest Cedar Edge cop.

"We got reports of shots fired from the mall, but the shooter ran behind the mall and over here. He was chasing a woman. According to that employee"—he nodded toward a balding man speaking with Washington County deputies—"the store was locked up and someone shot out the front doors. A woman ran in and the shooter came in next. He made the female employee turn off the alarms and then shot her and headed after the first woman toward the back of the store."

"Are there more people in the store?" Mason asked.

"He said there should be two more employees, but we haven't seen or heard from them."

"What's he carrying?" asked Ray.

"All we know is a single handgun. He's wearing cargo shorts, so it's possible he has another weapon stashed, and the witness says he wasn't carrying anything larger." He paused. "The woman he's chasing is unarmed."

"Description of the woman?" Mason's heart pounded in his head.

"Dark hair. Ponytail. Workout clothes."

"Fuck. Was he *sure* she's not armed?" Mason swallowed hard, knowing full well Ava wasn't armed; she would have immediately shot the asshole instead of running away.

• • •

Travis quietly trod down an aisle of cleaning agents. The screaming woman up front had left the building. He'd heard the sirens of the police cars and the shouts outside for him to exit the building. He ignored it all. He had his prey cornered in this building, and he wasn't leaving until he'd finished his mission.

She'd screwed everything up. When she'd stepped out of the yoga studio a solid half hour before he'd expected her, he'd frozen. She'd stared directly into his eyes and her recognition had been immediate. She'd known exactly who he was and what he'd done. Shock and anger had shoved his legs into motion, but she was fast and had reacted a split second before him. She'd sprinted away as if she had the devil on her heels.

If she only knew.

No woman will show me up again.

This agent had gotten lucky when she'd uncovered the clothing that he'd left in the bathroom. And it was probably her smiling face that had convinced Simon Goethe to lie to him about being in position for the Starbucks setup. The police had only temporarily fallen for his ruse at the Starbucks and had responded quickly to the mall, but he wasn't stopped yet. He would see it through. His goal was in this building. All thoughts of stealth and cunning and hiding were gone. His months of elaborate setups to punish the other women suddenly felt cowardly. Intelligent, but spineless. His blood caught fire with excitement as he searched for his target.

He wanted revenge. *Now.*

He didn't care what happened to him next, but he wasn't going to let a woman be his downfall. *She will pay.*

"This is Sergeant Shaver with the Washington County Sheriff's Department. Please put down your weapon and exit the building through the front doors," came from a bullhorn outside the store.

Travis blinked. The sergeant sounded exactly like the guy from the TV truck commercials. He ignored the command and continued his search.

He'd shopped at this store at least a dozen times. He had a general idea of the layout and was pretty certain the only exits were in the west corner of the building, in the front, and through the garden center. He had to track her down before she reached one. He knew the garden center was locked up. He'd shaken the outer gate a few moments before he'd shot out the glass of the front door while aiming at the fed. If he were in her shoes, he'd stick to the outside aisles of the store, circling around until he reached an exit.

The odor of new carpet touched his nose as he padded past the home decor, scanning the nooks and crannies of the shelving for hiding places. He walked quietly but didn't hide. His prey was unarmed, and he was the skilled hunter. He would win.

• • •

Ava slunk along the aisle that ran the length of the back of the store, cautiously glancing down each perpendicular aisle before dashing across. She rapidly peeked around the corner of an aisle of paint supplies, holding her breath. Clear. She darted to the next aisle's endcap and followed the same process. Slowly moving toward the other end of the store. She spotted a sign for bathrooms at the back wall of the store. Would there be an exit, too?

Two more aisles to get across first. The comforting smell of cut wood blended with the acrid odor of fertilizer. Even if she'd been delivered to the store with her eyes covered, she would have known instantly where she was by the smells. She could picture the parking lot full of police and their perimeter forming around the home improvement store. Knowing there were dozens of people who had her back gave her some confidence. But she had to get to them while avoiding the man with the gun. She tightened her fingers around her gardening tool, mentally practicing a strong high swing. If she came face-to-face with the shooter, she'd have to act instantly. Any pause would mean her death.

First rule of gunfights: Avoid gunfights.

Second rule: Bring a gun. Preferably two. And all your friends who have guns.

Her goal was to follow the first rule.

The shooter's actions had triggered the last part of the second rule. Good people were outside.

"Put down your weapon and exit the building backward with your hands on your head."

Ava pictured Sergeant Shaver glaring over his bullhorn, and wondered if Mason and the rest of the task force were close by.

Mason. Does he know I'm the shooter's target? She couldn't dwell on how he must be feeling. He probably wanted to both shake her and kiss her at the same time.

If only she'd been armed. She slapped a hand over her mouth as hysterical laughter bubbled up in her throat. Twice now she'd needed to be armed after a yoga class. A choking garbled sound came from her mouth as she fought to control her reaction to the irony. Maybe she could start a new trend: guns and yoga. She grabbed a chunk of her lip and pinched hard, the pain silencing the need to laugh. Tears threatened, and she sucked in deep breaths.

Focus.

She did her peek-and-dash to cross the next aisle and ended up across from an alcove that housed the doors to the bathrooms. An EMPLOYEES ONLY sign hung on a third door. With a quick glance to the right and left she crossed the rear aisle and grabbed the knob. *Please lead to a break room and rear exit.* The door was locked. Her heart skipped two beats, and she whirled around to dash back to the end of the aisle. She didn't want to be cornered in the alcove.

Keep moving.

A rapid glance down the next aisle revealed her chaser. She yanked her head back and tried to melt into the endcap display of garbage disposals. He was in the center aisle that ran parallel to the aisle she was following along the rear of the store. Tall. Armed. Moving in the same direction as she. She shuddered, thankful he'd been looking in the opposite direction when she'd taken a glimpse. She slid down to a crouch, fighting the desire to crawl between the boxes of garbage disposals and hide. But she wasn't two feet tall. Her vision started to tunnel, and she focused on the deadly head of her weapon, imagining it swinging into his brain.

She could do that.

His steps sounded closer; now he was in the aisle around the corner from her.

. . .

Mason watched the two four-man teams get ready to enter the store.

Here we go again.

It was all too similar. He stood on the outside, powerless, while Ava was inside. No reassuring text messages this time. And there was another big difference. This time they had a good idea of whom the shooter was after. His balls-out chase out of the mall and into the home improvement store was a clear indicator that he was after something he wanted. The shot-out doors and broken glass told Mason volumes. Their killer had it in for Ava.

Why?

When had Ava popped up on their shooter's radar? She'd spoken to him the day of the mall shooting, but he hadn't shown any interest in her at that time. Clearly the shooter had a past history of targeting women who carried weapons, but was that the sole reason? Counting Ava, three of them were in law enforcement. The odd woman out was a shooting instructor—and the first victim. What had happened to make him target these women?

And would they find more women when they dug in his past?

Shaver had told him they were giving the shooter a small window to respond favorably. This man had made his mission clear from the shootings in the past and had lost all benefit of the doubt from law enforcement. They would ask; if he didn't respond correctly, they would act.

"We are sending teams into the store. Put down your weapon and you won't be harmed."

The teams readied their shields and helmets and entered the store.

. . .

Ava backed around the corner and into the aisle behind her, her zombie-killing weapon ready to strike. Beside her in this aisle were the round ends of large rolls of industrial carpet, stacked on top of one another in tall wide slots. She stepped into one of the slots that held a single roll, turned around, and backed up on her knees. She lay her weapon the length of the carpet and scooted back as far as she could into the shadows and out of the reach of the bright overhead lights of the store. He would have to stop and peer directly into the long dark slot to see her.

If he did, she was an easy shot. *A fish in a barrel.*

Her breathing echoed in the tight slot and the heavy grip of claustrophobia squeezed her lungs. *PleaseGodpleaseGodpleaseGod.*

She no longer heard his footsteps, the enclosed place removing her ability to hear quiet sounds, and she abruptly doubted the wisdom of her hiding place.

Female shrieks came from the direction of the bathroom. Ava held her breath. From his cursing and the woman's pleading, Ava gathered he'd found her hiding in the restroom and dragged her out.

"Hey, Ava! Federal agent lady! I've got someone who wants to meet you!"

He knows my name? She couldn't move. *How . . . ?*

More importantly, the shooter now had a hostage. Ava leaned her head against the hard wood of the carpet slot and closed her eyes, the woman's cries echoing in her head.

It was no longer about her.

The bathroom entrances were directly across the back aisle from the next aisle over. She opened her eyes and inched forward in her hiding space, picturing the area in front of the bathrooms. Would he bring his hostage down that aisle or the next one? Would the contact teams spot him first? The situation had suddenly changed with the addition of a hostage. Ava figured Shaver had given orders for the teams to take down the shooter; he was a proven killer. But with a hostage, they would hold back.

A standoff.

Could she get the woman away? Could she get behind him if he was occupied with a hostage? She scooted forward more, picturing the shooter wrestling with his hostage. He'd be intent on the woman, distracted, with at least one hand holding her, lowering his aiming capability.

Was it worth it?

The woman pleaded with the shooter to let her go. Relying on the distance of that female voice, Ava stepped out of her hiding spot and planted her feet, listening carefully. They were over one aisle.

"Aaaaay-vaaaah!" He drew her name out as if singing it. "Come out, come out, wherever you are!" he taunted. "I'm going to blow her brains out if you don't come say hi."

Run. Get out now.

Her feet wouldn't move. She couldn't leave the woman behind with the killer.

She took a deep breath and tightened her hold on the zombie weapon.

40

Travis had found the employee in one of the stalls of the women's bathroom. It was amazing how compliant she became with a gun pointed at her head. She was young, maybe in her early twenties, with long blond hair that gently curled at the bottom. On a regular day she would have caught his eye. Today she was a means to an end. He let her shriek and protest, knowing it would catch the federal agent's attention. The employee didn't matter. He wanted the woman who thought she was smart enough to bring him down.

Women had a role. Just as this blonde currently did. He held her against him like a shield, grinding his barrel into her head occasionally to make her shriek on cue. He guided her to the right, peering down the long aisle toward the front of the store. The paint department in the middle of the store blocked him from seeing to the front.

Where was the agent?

He ignored the police out front. They could squawk and send in as many teams as they wanted. As long as he had a blond human shield, he was safe. He bent his head to her hair, smelling her fear over her floral perfume. Fear had a distinct acrid, bitter scent and it was rolling off her in waves. He inhaled it, feeling his chest swell with excitement and the rush of being in control.

He dragged her over one more aisle and glanced down. Four police in helmets and riot gear halted at the far end as they spotted him, all their weapons pointed his way.

"Don't shoot!" the blonde screamed. "Don't shoot!"

Travis smiled at the cops, knowing they had no shot. He dragged the woman back the way he'd come and paused behind the end-cap. His time was getting shorter. This couldn't end until the female agent was dead.

• • •

"God damn it!" Shaver swore.

"What is it?" Mason asked.

"The contact team says he has a female hostage."

Mason's heart stopped.

"Blond woman, orange apron. Must be an employee." Shaver gestured at one of the patrol officers. "Find that guy who works here. I want to know who he's holding hostage."

Dizziness swamped Mason as his blood started pumping again. "No sign of Ava?"

"Not yet. But now we've got a different situation. Where's the team's hostage negotiator?" he shouted at more of his men.

"Aw, fuck," muttered Mason, turning away. A hostage situation. New rules to play by. He said a silent prayer of thanks that his son, Jake, was back East, working for the summer while he waited for college to start back up. Last Christmas Jake had been held hostage, and it hadn't ended well for the hostage-taker.

"We know where the shooter is," stated Shaver. "I'm creating a perimeter inside the building and want him to know the amount of force we have focused on him."

"Announce it with the bullhorn," suggested Zander. "That will let Ava know what's going on, too."

The balding employee who'd escaped appeared, stress lines crossing his forehead. "Sounds like he's holding Lizzy Marks. Sweet kid. Young," he said to Shaver, shoving his hands in his apron pockets. "That leaves Clyde Simpson inside somewhere."

And Ava.

It felt as if a truck's winch had been steadily pulling Mason's tendons tighter and tighter. Every limb was tense, and he swore his skin would pop if someone physically or emotionally poked him. He noticed the local patrol cops were giving him a wide berth, and both Zander and Ray had been watching him from the corners of their eyes, ready to calm him down if he blew up.

"I'm fine," he said to no one, lifting his hat to wipe the sweat, but he saw Ray and Zander exchange a look.

Shouts came from the front of the store as two of the officers in riot gear escorted out an employee. "That must be Clyde," said Zander.

Sergeant Shaver strode over to the gray-haired man. Mason followed, but didn't hear Shaver's question to the employee. The employee shook his head, holding up his hands. "I didn't see no one. I heard the shots and breaking glass and hid over in the lumber area. These guys spotted me as I was crawling past the check stands. The screaming is coming from back by the bathrooms." He rubbed a hand over his face, looking nauseated. "Sounded like Lizzy."

"I want more teams in there," ordered Shaver, turning to his men. "Right now he's got a hostage near the back of the store." His gaze fell on Mason. "Maybe Ava can get herself out like this guy did."

"I want to go in."

"Hell no."

• • •

Ava knew it was time for action. He would kill that hostage without thinking twice. He'd already murdered over a dozen people; one more didn't matter to him. But for some reason *she* seemed to matter to him.

She could hear the girl begging and the shuffling of their feet. It sounded as if they were at the end of the next aisle over.

Run. Just leave. He's too busy to notice you.

She couldn't leave the girl behind.

"Aaaaaay-vaaaaaah," he called again.

She tiptoed toward the back of the store and peeked around the end of her aisle, expecting to see him huddled near the end of the next aisle over.

He wasn't there. She glanced behind her and to her left. All clear. She tentatively stepped into the aisle that ran along the back of the store, wondering where he'd suddenly hidden. She was just passing the bathrooms when she heard his hostage start to scream again—very close—and she darted into the bathroom alcove. He swore at the girl, calling her filthy names as they came closer. After a few moments, his voice volume stayed constant, and Ava realized he'd stopped at the end of the aisle closest to the bathrooms—directly across from her hiding place. Ava pressed her body against the wall, knowing that if he stood in the right place in the aisle, he'd have a clear view of her. She couldn't dash into the restrooms—the doors were in his clear sights.

She'd trapped herself.

She tried to think. One positive was that he'd already checked the bathrooms, and so he shouldn't do it again.

Shouldn't.

"*Put down your weapon and come out. We are sending more police into the store. There is no exit unless you put down your weapon.*" The bullhorn was louder, sounding as if it was inside the store.

Shaver's good ol' boy voice made Ava's spine relax a degree, and she hoped it did the same for the shooter.

"Fuck you! I've got a hostage, and I'm going to blow her head off unless I can talk to Ava McLane!"

Tension shot up her back. *Why me?*

"Release your hostage and put down your weapon. No harm's been done to the hostage. Let's keep it that way."

Ava bit her lip, wondering when Shaver would hand off the bullhorn to a trained negotiator. Surely one was here by now.

"I don't want to see your teams again! If I see another cop, I'm shooting her in the leg!" the gunman yelled.

"I'll keep them on the perimeter for now, but any sign that you're hurting your hostage and I'll move them closer, agreed?"

"Fuck you! Where's McLane?"

A small part of her brain noticed he never used her title. He knew what she did—he'd called her "federal agent lady" earlier. She was the last person to insist on her title, but she always used it with witnesses, convicts, and arrestees. It was a marker of respect. One this guy seemed determined not to use. She tucked that bit of information away, wondering what it meant about his mind-set.

"Special Agent McLane is not available."

"Ha! Fucking cop bitch. *Hiding in a hole somewhere!*" He lowered his tone, speaking to his hostage. "See? We'll get her to come out. This whole situation is her fault."

What?

"She thinks she can do a man's job. Women weren't meant to carry weapons and lord them over men. There's a natural order."

Ava tipped her head back against the wall, closing her eyes. Zander and Mason had been right. He'd targeted those women in law enforcement and then hidden their executions within the mass shootings. The shootings hadn't been random; he'd had a target. And then managed to add a final victim to each shooting to take the blame.

A risky game.

Which she had figured out.

And now she was his target.

Her hands went numb. She couldn't feel the wooden handle, and cold sweat formed on her stomach. Her rational brain checked off what she knew about the killer twenty feet away. Loaded gun. Hostage. Driven. Suicidal?

That he'd created elaborate hoaxes so victims would take blame for his crimes indicated this man didn't plan on dying. But now he was surrounded by a police presence with no way out. A man who wanted to live would surrender.

Possibly suicidal. A person with nothing to live for but a goal of making one last splash.

A new voice sounded on the bullhorn. *"This is Graham Stevens with the Washington County Sheriff's Department. I'd like to help you get out of here safely. Since you haven't harmed your hostage, you can walk out of here with minimal charges."*

Ava nodded. She knew the game. Remind the hostage taker that things can always be worse and that cooperating makes it better. Make him think he has control over what happens next.

"Christ. Do they think I'm stupid?" she heard him mutter. "Minimal charges? I've probably killed almost half your age in victims, honey."

The hostage gasped. "Don't hurt me," she begged in hoarse tones.

"Not up to me," he said conversationally. "It depends on what happens next."

• • •

Inside the store Mason stood next to the man who'd taken over communications with the shooter. Shaver swore Graham Stevens was a top hostage negotiator, but Mason didn't care. He wanted Ava out of the store. Radio communications with the sixteen officers currently tightening the perimeter inside the store had reported no sign of her. That was good. Maybe she wasn't even in the store?

Of course she is. She'd be standing beside you if she weren't trapped somewhere.

"We've got video of her running down one of the aisles, before she takes a turn toward the rear of the store," Ray stated, appearing beside him. "Clyde let us into the store's security room, and we checked every camera angle. Neither Ava nor the shooter is in a current shot, but we backed up the main entry camera and it showed her heading toward the garden supply side of the store. Somehow she eludes all the cameras after that."

"You can't find either of their present positions?" Mason asked.

"We can tell he's in front of the restrooms. We saw him haul Lizzy out of the women's restroom, but he's holding her out of camera view. The contact team placed him in aisle nineteen, but said he backed out of there when he saw them. He hasn't moved out of the immediate area."

"Ava must be in the same area, otherwise she would have risked coming out."

"Why does he keep asking for her?" asked Ray. "And how the fuck does he know her by name?"

"I'd like to find that out myself. Other than when he stopped to offer help to her at the Rivertown Mall shooting, I'm not aware of any other contact."

"Shit. Think he's purposefully interacted with her, and she didn't realize it was him?"

Acid flowed in Mason's gut. "I hope not."

"At least he didn't shoot at her until tonight."

Sometimes Ray had a way of offering comfort that completely backfired. "We just need to get her out."

"She's smart. She can handle herself," Ray stated, crossing his arms confidently.

Mason knew that. But it didn't settle his stomach.

. . .

"This is taking too fucking long," the shooter swore.

Ava jumped as his gun fired, and his hostage screamed. Her screams subsided into gushing sobs, and Ava clenched her teeth, fighting the urge to step out of her hiding place.

"You're fine," the shooter said. "Your foot will heal. Stand up, God damn it!"

Ava held her breath. *Now. He's distracted with his hostage.*

Ava stepped out from her alcove, holding her weapon like a bat, and saw them. He stood with his back to her, an arm clasping the woman to his chest as he struggled to keep her on her feet. A pool of blood had formed under the woman's left shoe. He pointed his weapon at his hostage's blond head, but Ava focused on her target. His skull.

Brown hair. Tall. One swing would do it.

She silently danced forward, tightening her grip and readying to put all her strength into one swing. *I've got one perfect chance.* She slid to a stop and held her breath as she swung.

He turned.

She met his gaze. In the fraction of a second she saw elation, surprise, and fear. His weapon changed targets, and she saw the end of the gun barrel swing to point at her head. She ducked, affecting her aim, and her swing buried the weapon's pronged head in his left shoulder. He let go of his hostage, who flung herself to the side.

The sound of his gunshot exploded in her ears as she tripped, her weapon's impact sending shock waves into her shoulders. She stutter-stepped trying to keep her balance as his roar of pain filled the aisle. Her fingers froze in their grip on her weapon, and she yanked on it, wanting another swing.

It wouldn't budge out of his flesh. Blood flowed around the prongs.

Her pulls on the weapon made him scream, and he fired wildly. Over and over.

I hear the shots. Therefore I'm not dead. Sirens clamored in her brain from the roar of the close shots and adrenaline exploded through her nerves. *He will kill me.* Ava steered him in a circle, an awkward deadly dance, trying to dislodge her weapon and avoid being shot. His cap fell off and she got a clear look at the melted left side of his neck.

Burn scars.

She ducked and dived as they spun. His dark eyes flashed with anger and pain as he tried to line up his weapon on her.

"You! You bitch!" he screamed. "You did this!"

She frantically wrestled with her weapon, trying to unhook it so she could swing again. This time she wouldn't miss. She wanted to see it sink into his skull.

Out of the corner of her eye, she saw the blond girl dash down the aisle, ducking as she ran.

I'm on my own.

Spit flew from his mouth and she twisted her weapon, wrenching the handle. He shrieked and his eyes seemed to roll back in his head as he fired at the ceiling. She tripped over his foot and clung to the garden tool to keep her body upright, her weight sinking it deeper into his flesh. His scream pierced her ears as his knees buckled, and she knew they were both about to collapse.

I can't last much longer.

His gun swung wildly, giving her a glimpse down its barrel.

She ducked her head out of the way, imagining a bullet speeding from its depths.

"GET DOWN GET DOWN GET DOWN!"

She let go, flung herself to the floor, and covered her ears. Gunfire filled the store. Pairs of thundering boots sprinted toward her, and she pressed her cheek against the cool concrete, suddenly exhausted.

"SHOOTER DOWN! WE NEED A MEDIC!"

Ava closed her eyes in relief, loving the sound of those words. He wouldn't hurt anyone else.

"Agent McLane!" Someone shook her, but she was too tired to open her eyes. "Agent McLane! Can you hear me?" She wanted to tell him she was fine, but she couldn't speak.

"Too tired," she mouthed silently.

Someone rolled her onto her back and pushed a hot hand into her neck at her jaw. "She's got a pulse!"

Pulse? She opened her eyes and met the frantic look of an officer she didn't know. Other officers filled her field of vision, shouting, moving. Their boots causing the concrete to vibrate through her head.

"Her eyes are open! Thank God. You're going to be okay, Agent. We'll get the bleeding stopped."

Abruptly, pain-laced fire raced from a hot spot in her left side and shot into her brain. She tried to touch the spot, but the officer held her arm down. "Am I shot?" she whispered.

"You're going to be okay," he repeated, his eyes rapidly scanning her face. "Stay with me."

Someone applied pressure on her left side, and she nearly screamed as black dots filled her vision. A cowboy hat came into view along with Mason's terrified eyes. "Ava? Holy fuck!"

It must be bad. The black spots expanded, filling her vision, and everything went quiet.

41

One month later

Mason glanced out the window at the darkening sky and then at the clock over the stove. Sure enough, Ava had been gone for over an hour. He put a lid on the panic that rose in the back of his throat and headed out the door in the direction of the park. She'd taken Bingo for a walk. Usually they all took walks together, but tonight he'd begged off, citing a pile of paperwork. She'd smiled, nodded, kissed him good-bye, and put on Bingo's leash. A typical walk lasted thirty minutes.

The days were starting to shorten; the memory of the hot dry summer was slowly fading. He walked faster, shoving his hands in his pockets as a night chill floated by. At the end of their street sat a quiet city park that offered views of Mount Hood. He and Ava had spent hours sitting on a favorite bench over the last few weeks.

Physically she was healed. Travis Meijer's gunshot had ripped through her left side, miraculously avoiding major organs but tearing an intestine that'd required immediate surgery. After the surgery she'd fought a deadly blood infection that had been worse than the injury. It'd been a long slow road for her to recover her strength after her weeklong war with the infection. She hadn't returned to work. Yet.

Meijer had turned out to be an FBI profiler's dream. A quiet man who kept to himself, he was a supervisor at a call center who took orders for several dozen companies. One of those companies sold T-shirts with police department sayings and logos. After a lot of digging, investigators discovered Anna Luther and Gabrielle Gower had both ordered police department fund-raiser T-shirts through the call center.

Records showed they'd both been unhappy with some issue with the shirts and had contacted the call center regarding refunds. Mason had listened to the recordings of both women's complaint calls, feeling slightly spooked as the women seemed to speak from the grave. Both women had spoken with Meijer and the calls hadn't gone smoothly; Mason had been surprised that a supervisor wouldn't follow the "customer is always right" policy. Meijer had sounded extremely agitated during both women's calls, especially when the women mentioned their previous law enforcement service. How Travis Meijer had decided this act made them worthy of murder, Mason couldn't comprehend. Had simply the wrong phrase from each woman sealed her fate?

During their search of Meijer's home, they'd found lists and photos of local female police officers in his computer, making them wonder who else had been targeted. The man clearly had an obsession. Flyers advertising "acting opportunities" for men who were six foot one and of lean build were also found on his computer.

Mason had watched the hours of prank footage on Meijer's YouTube channel and held back his laughter several times. In college the man had known how to stage perfect pranks. He'd used his skills to bury his hit list of women officers, hiding his targets under the blood of innocent victims. How long could his deceptions have continued?

They were unable to connect Meijer to any other unsolved shootings over the past decade. His history revealed his mother had overdosed on alcohol and sleeping pills when he was eighteen. After reading the extensive list of domestic disturbance calls to Meijer's childhood home, Mason and Ava had carefully studied the medical examiner's report, wondering if Travis Meijer could have caused his mother's death. His father had died while in prison, and neighbors claimed the mother had ruled her son with an iron fist after the father was taken away.

The truth would never be known. All parties were dead, and the questions would haunt Mason and Ava for years.

Especially Ava. Mason didn't know if she could heal from her encounters with Travis Meijer.

Through the waning light he saw Ava's silhouette sitting on their bench with Bingo's beside her, his head in her lap. The slant of her neck and the arch of her shoulders told him she'd been crying. He walked faster. Her moods had been across the board for weeks. Effects from her painkillers and the emotional upheaval of being shot. Again.

And Jayne.

They hadn't spoken about Jayne in over a week. Her sister had recovered from her damaged wrists and gash to her spleen. Through some stroke of supreme luck, Jayne had ended up in a facility that treated both her mental and drug issues, but part of the treatment was a long stretch of weeks without contact with her family. One silent week was left. Since the first day Jayne had checked in, Mason had dreaded the moment she could regain contact with Ava.

He knew when Ava had spotted him. Her head lifted and her shoulders straightened, her hand sinking into Bingo's fur after a furtive wipe across her wet cheeks. He stopped in front of her bench. Bingo's tail wagged madly, and Ava smiled at him, patting the space beside her. He gave the dog a head rub and sat on Ava's other side, placing one arm around her shoulders as she leaned against him and looked toward the mountain. During the winter months, the mountaintop was white. Over the summer it faded to shades of gray as the snow melted away. Mason could barely make out its outline at the hazy late-evening hour, but seeing it always made him feel grounded. The mountain was solid. Unchanging.

Silence settled over them.

"Were you coming back home?" he asked, his gaze directed toward Mount Hood.

"Eventually. I had to watch the dark blue of the sky emerge around the mountain. I love that color. It's so deep and rich, I couldn't walk away."

"It'll be back tomorrow. I'd say it's something you can always rely on to be there."

He turned to study her in the dim light, knowing he could stare at her for hours, watching the animation in her face as she thought and talked. The distance that'd settled between them since her injury had grown bigger each day. He'd taken two weeks off work, practically living in the hospital as she battled the deadly sepsis. But when her health returned, her inner self had stayed hidden under layers of self-protection. Layers that had started building up since Jayne's suicide attempt, and he didn't have the nerve to try to break through them, worried it would set Ava back further. He functioned each day the best he knew how. He was attentive, loving, and understanding, but he wanted his Ava back. This shell of a woman seemed to be growing more distant day after day.

He despised himself for standing by and watching it happen.

"You didn't tell me about your call with your boss," Mason said.

Ava shifted against him. "He wanted to know when I was coming back to work."

"And?"

"I told him I didn't know."

The pain in her voice ripped at his heart. "What's keeping you back?"

"I don't know," she whispered. "I know I'm recovered. The surgeon said I'm okay to return to work, but I can't make a decision. I feel like I'm floating around while my anchor searches for something to snag."

"You can't sit around and wait. You have to make it happen."

"It hurts that I see you waiting for me," she said slowly, turning to look at him. "Maybe you shouldn't."

He met her gaze and saw the fear in her eyes. "I'm not going anywhere. I can't. It nearly killed me to watch you waste away with that infection. All I could think about was that I might have to go home to an empty house—our empty house—and I couldn't face it. Now I have you there, but part of you hasn't returned."

Understanding crossed her gaze. "I know. I can't find that piece of me, either. And I feel like the hole is getting bigger every day."

"Is it Jayne?" he forced out. "The disconnection between you two? Is that what's creating the hole?"

She was silent. "I've thought about that for days. I don't know the answer. Her suicide attempt ripped something out of me."

"And I'm powerless to fix it." Mason wanted to hit something. The problem stared him right in the eyes, and he was incapable of finding the answer.

It wasn't like Travis Meijer. The problem of the shooter had been solved with several rounds from the SWAT team through his chest and head as he tried to shoot Ava. Mason had stepped into her aisle and seen her weapon buried in Travis Meijer's shoulder, a look of utter desperation and anger on her face as she spun out of the way while Meijer continuously fired his gun. She'd dropped to the floor as the team shouted and then they'd opened fire.

Meijer had died instantly.

Problem solved, Mason had thought.

He'd been wrong.

Instead Ava's health had been compromised and her emotions severely damaged.

"I don't expect you to fix me." She swallowed hard. "That's up to me."

. . .

The frustrated look on Mason's face broke her heart—what heart she had left. Small chunks had slowly broken away from her heart in a steady pace since the day she heard about Jayne's suicide attempt. She lightly touched the healing wound on her left side where Meijer's bullet had taken a large bite. She'd always carry the scar and reminder of her brief encounters with Travis Meijer. For a man she'd met twice, for less than a minute each time, he'd had a profound impact on her psyche. The police had explained his obsession with women in law enforcement and she'd wondered what she'd done to draw his focus. Had he targeted her simply because she'd seen his face as she sat beside Misty at the Rivertown Mall? How'd he find out she was an agent?

She'd never know.

It shouldn't matter; she'd survived. But the questions still haunted her. She deserved to know what she'd done. Someday she'd stop jumping at loud noises and relax while shopping.

Someday.

A sharp pain shot from the wound to her left armpit, making her catch her breath, and then vanished just as abruptly. The nerves healing, her doctor had said.

Jayne gashed her own abdomen on the left side.

Something always cropped up and created parallels between their lives. Was that what she was waiting for? The arm of the universe to reach down and strike her the way it'd struck Jayne?

Get busy living or get busy dying.

The old movie line echoed in her brain, and she acknowledged that she'd spent too much time waiting for the universe to deal her Jayne's hand. Instead it'd blocked her eyes from seeing the wonderful things she'd received. Like the very patient man sitting next to her. She slid her hand in the pocket of her light coat, and wondered if she'd waited too long. Had she put him through hell to see if he'd stay? To see what he could handle?

Idiot.

She'd known from day one he was the strongest man she'd ever met. He'd told her over and over he loved her despite what her twin managed to do to her emotions. He'd lasted through it all. And wasn't showing any signs of running. What was she waiting for? To test him more? See how much he could take? He'd nursed her through two injuries and several emotional hellholes. How many other men would still be sitting beside her?

"I love you, Mason. You've proved over and over that you're my rock."

"It's not hard," he said sourly.

She laughed. "I'm the hardest person in the world to love. Loving me means you have to put up with my connection to Jayne."

"She doesn't affect how I feel about you. I get that there's"—he paused and searched for words—"a piece of you that will always belong to her and be affected by her. That doesn't scare me. I'd like to think we've made it through the worst it can be."

"God, I hope so."

"She's no good at life," he stated. "But you're wonderful at it. She trips you up, but you always come back swinging. A lot of people would have given up by now."

His words flowed through her heart. He believed in her. *But why?*

She took a deep breath. "I'd like to get married if you feel the same way."

He swung his head toward her. "You don't think I want to?"

She pulled her hand out of her pocket and showed him the small velvet box she'd found four days ago in his vehicle. Her hand shook as he stared at it. "Why haven't you given this to me? I found the receipt. You bought it months ago." Her voice cracked. "Did you change your mind?" Fear washed over her. She'd finally said it, the question that'd been consuming her thoughts for days.

He took the box. "Hell no. The timing was just never right. I've known I wanted you permanently in my life since last January." He flipped open the lid. "I wasn't sure how you felt. I didn't want to rush it if you weren't ready."

The ring gleamed, catching the faint light from the moon. She'd stared at it for hours, loving that he'd understood her simple elegant taste, but worried as all hell that he'd thought he'd made a mistake. "I'm ready," she whispered, and a great pressure lifted off her shoulders. For months she'd felt as if she carried the burdens of a dozen people on her back. Suddenly they were gone, cut loose like balloons, and she could breathe.

He took her hand, and she felt a quiver shake his fingers. He slid the cold metal onto her finger and wrapped his hand around it, clenching it tightly. She looked up, his face close to hers. "Now I'm sorry I waited," he said. "If I'd known how fucking overjoyed I was going to feel at this moment, I would have done it last winter, Special Agent McLane."

"You're so smooth with the sentiments, Detective."

"You bring out the best in me."

"I plan to for a very long time."

ACKNOWLEDGMENTS

My first thank-you is for my readers who email me and reach out on Facebook and Twitter. I appreciate every note and try hard to respond to each one. A simple "I like your books" can turn around a blue day for a writer. The fact that I'm writing acknowledgments for my seventh novel blows my mind; my original writing goal was to see my name on the cover of a book—one book.

I feel as if I thank the same people in my acknowledgments every time, but the list is accurate. I have an incredible network of people who support my writing from the production side, the research side, and the author-mental-health side.

JoVon Sotak, Jessica Poore, and Thom Kephart make certain my books are of the best quality and receive incredible marketing. Charlotte Herscher helps me fine-tune my stories and kindly points out where I might bore my readers. FBI Agent Devinney patiently answers my questions, and former cops Gary Tabke and Lee Lofland share their expertise when I'm smart enough to ask. That's every author's dilemma—we often don't know when we need to ask questions. All errors are my own.

Fellow author Melinda Leigh is always there when I stress over plots or wonder what to feed my kids (they want food EVERY DAY!), or just to share dog pictures. My daughters subtly point out that I'm still in my pajamas when they get home from school and cheer when I finish a book. My husband buys me chocolate and doesn't take it personally when I roll my eyes as he suggests *again* that I solve my plot issues with zombies. Just for him, I worked zombies into this book. Sorta.

ABOUT THE AUTHOR

Born and raised in the Pacific Northwest, Kendra Elliot has always been a voracious reader, cutting her teeth on classic female sleuths and heroines like Nancy Drew, Trixie Belden, and Laura Ingalls before proceeding to devour the works of Stephen King, Diana Gabaldon, and Nora Roberts. She won a 2014 Daphne du Maurier Award for Best Romantic Suspense for *Buried*, which was also an International Thriller Writers' finalist for Best Paperback Original and a *Romantic Times* finalist for Best Romantic Suspense. Elliot shares her love of suspense through seven novels set in the Bone Secrets universe. She lives and writes in the rainy Pacific Northwest with her husband, three daughters, and a Pomeranian, but dreams of living at the beach on Kauai. She loves to hear from readers at www.KendraElliot.com.